KILROY WAS HERE

a novel
by
Jeff South

ISBN: 978-1-63302-084-9

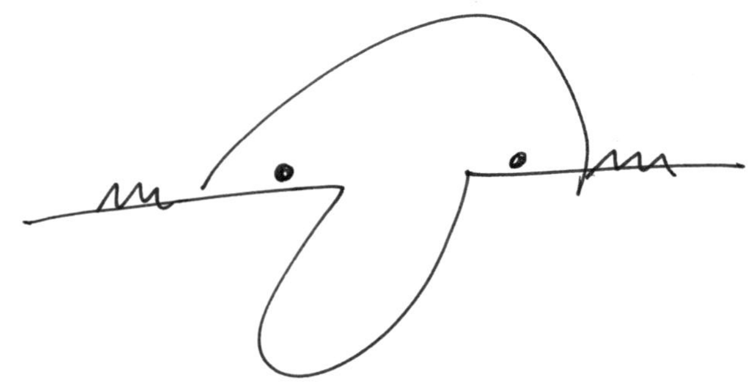

A haiku for you, dear reader:

This book represents
A lifelong dream brought to life.
I hope you like it.

DAN,
WHEN YOU READ THIS,
JUST REMEMBER I'M
BLIND IN ONE EYE.
YOU'LL BE MORE FORGIVING.

ENJOY!

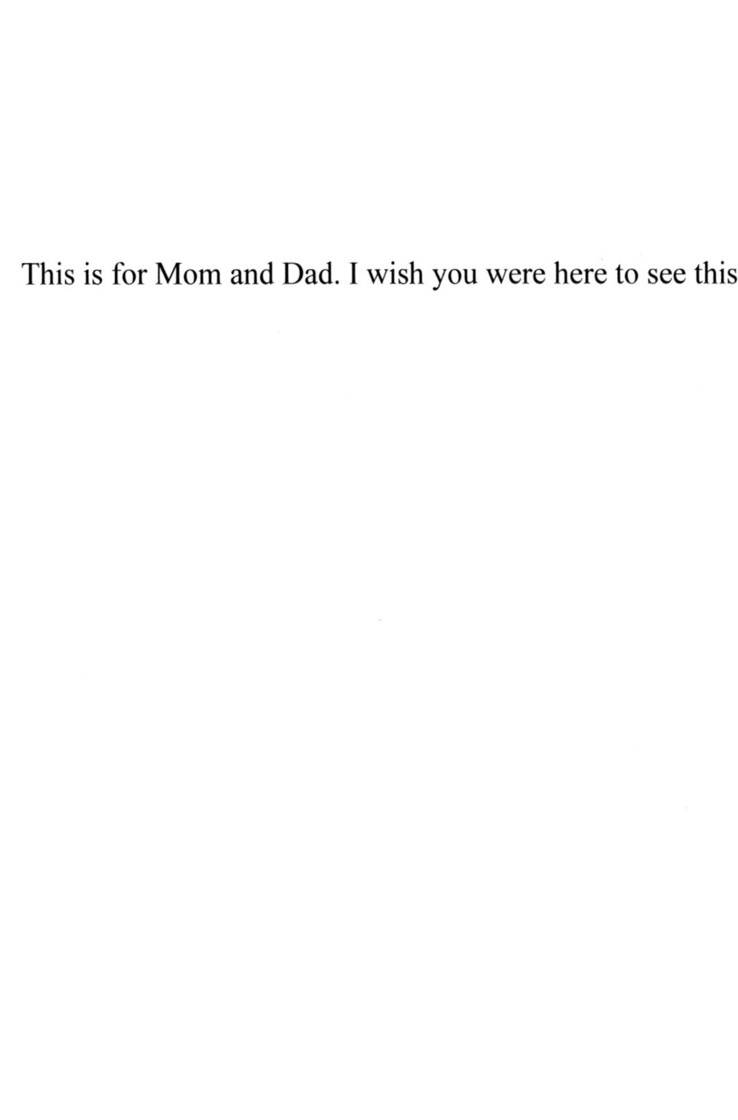

This is for Mom and Dad. I wish you were here to see this.

TABLE OF CONTENTS

PART ONE:

THE PROM NIGHT OF WHICH WE SHALL NOT SPEAK

CHAPTER ONE

The love of my life is walking into prom with another guy. Marlene Hunter is the girl who has my heart and tonight she will dance with an oafish Neanderthal in a black tuxedo. She wears a stunning red evening gown with sparkles. Her sandy blonde hair cascades to her shoulders. She is the essence of wholesome beauty. Marlene was my girlfriend and I broke up with her because I'm the dumbest person to ever walk the face of the Earth. I sit here on the school parking lot in the front seat of my crappy-looking but dependable Toyota Corolla loading fresh battery packs into my laser stun guns. My heart sinks and my face is hot with emotion. I feel not so much anger as disgust. I peer out at my soulmate entering our high school gym on the arm of a goon who probably eats raw meat for breakfast. And I made it happen because I have to work tonight. They disappear into the romance of the evening. I think about what might've been. I press play on my car stereo and Colbie Caillat's "Bubbly" starts. I blow out a long, weary sigh of regret and drive away.

*

Why am I here?

Why am I standing on the bank of a river out late at night instead spending the evening captivated by the warmth and intelligence of Marlene? I gave up prom and the girl of my dreams to stand my post on this river bank and protect the

Earth from an alien invader because that's what I'm paid to do. Only a person of suspect mental stability would choose alien combat over Marlene.

Yet, as I extend my arm and aim my Multi-Phaseable Portal Accessibility Sensor Device at an area over the flowing water, I tell myself I'm a responsible human being who honors his commitments and follows through on a job. Most likely, though, I'm a person of suspect mental stability.

A job is a job, though, even a sketchy one. I had been hired by a company called Corporate after answering an ad on Craigslist. Some kids flip burgers to make some cash in high school. Others deliver newspapers or mow lawns. I work as a security intern, guarding what is known as a soft spot in the space/time continuum that can be breached by aliens who wish to invade Earth. Cool gig for a teenager. Dangerous. Also, very mysterious. The only name the company goes by is Corporate; even on the business cards. Corporate didn't give me business cards. I really want business cards.

On the other hand, I get great toys to play with; however, they are also dangerous when you don't read the manuals. I always read the manuals.

"Tony."

I turn from the river and face the person calling my name. Randi Williams, my Corporate trainer. She gathers a protective vest from the bed of her truck and walks toward me in her standard Corporate Training attire of khaki cargo pants, dark blue short-sleeve microfiber shirt with the Corporate insignia on the upper left chest. The insignia consists of alternating lines of powder blue and light green forming a swirl. A white 'C' rests in its center and the word Corporate sits underneath in all-white capital letters. Her ass-kicking ensemble is complete with black combat boots.

"Where's Jeff?" she asks.

"He went to prom."

"He better hurry his ass up." Randi is a lean African-American woman of average height and lithe build who also dabbles in philosophy, metaphysics, and epicurean pursuits. She often quotes Nietzsche and her poached salmon salad is to die for. I know this because she brought some to work one night.

"He wouldn't miss this," I say. "He loves this job."

My partner in crime, Jeff Harper, is difficult to work with because he never reads the manuals. Calling him an irresponsible bonehead is generous. He also chose to go to prom after we agreed we would give it up because our jobs are so important. Asshole.

Did I mention Jeff Harper is also my best friend?

It wasn't enough for me to cancel prom, though. I broke up with Marlene under the guise that this job could potentially endanger her if she ever found out about it. Really, though, it can be attributed to the whole suspect mental stability thing.

The wind blusters and pushes the trees back and forth along the opposite bank and a few stray leaves are swept up in the growing storm.

I check my watch. 11:48 p.m. I retrieve my Multi-Phaseable Portal Accessibility Sensor Device from my pocket to again check the readings. It looks like a smartphone except it reads the stability of the portal opening. I aim it at the river, and tap the touchscreen. Negative.

"Are we sure there's going to be a breach tonight?" I ask Randi. "Sensors are showing no disturbance on the portal."

I remove my backpack and pull out a training manual for a new weapon, a glove that fires energy bolts from the index finger. This is my first time using the glove in the field. Corporate didn't supply one to Jeff because during training he nearly shot off his penis while scratching himself. The illustrations in the manual instruct me to aim the glove like a finger gun when firing. I practice aiming and pretend to fire. This won't look stupid at all.

"The intel from Max contained evidence confirming a breach was imminent." Randi fastens the vest around her torso.

"I'm applying to Eastern Missouri State." I blurt it out because I don't know how you insert college plans into a conversation about a potentially cataclysmic galactic event.

"Good for you!" Randi seems genuinely happy for me. "Going to college, then?"

"I dunno. I guess."

"What about Jeff?"

"He didn't apply. He wants to keep doing this…" I can't find the right word. "…stuff."

"He depends on you." Randi walks to me and gives my shoulder a light squeeze. "You're torn, aren't you?"

"Yeah. A little." I gaze at the ground, troubled once more by the prospect of making a difficult decision.

"I see it all perfectly," Randi says. "There are two possible situations – one can either do this or that. My honest opinion and my friendly advice is this: do it or do not do it. You will regret both."

"Huh?"

"It's Kierkegaard. It means no matter what you do, you're screwed." She smiles, pats my shoulder, and returns to gathering her supplies for whatever is supposed to happen.

I nod my head the way people do when they want to give the impression they understand, but don't. "I worry about Jeff. He'll struggle. He loves doing this. And he's a good guy. He's just a little undisciplined."

"Undisciplined?" Randi inspects a laser pistol and places it in a holster on her vest. "Do I need to remind you of the rocket boots?"

No, Randi does not need to remind me of the time Jeff attempted to leap from the top of the water tower on the outskirts of town in Corporate-issued rocket boots to show off for his girlfriend.

"He involved a civilian." She paces and flexes her hands like she wants to punch something. "You know the Corporate stance on civilians."

"Civilians can't know what we do," I recite. "They could get hurt."

"Exactly. And then Max gets involved." She shakes her head and emphasizes. "*Max*."

"Paperwork." I nod.

"Exactly. Don't mess with Max."

Max Gentry is our director and Randi's boss. The mere mention of his name fills me with a kind of Voldemortian dread.

The sound of tires screaming from the road interrupts our conversation. We turn and hear the gate of the electrified fence separating this area from the public slide open and close again about one hundred yards away. A vehicle races toward us. Randi grips her laser pistol but then lowers it and rolls her eyes. The sound of Styx's "Mr. Roboto" blares from inside a red 1976 Chevy Vega station wagon with a wide white strip on its hood. The car skids to a stop a couple of feet away in a nebula of dust. The driver emerges wearing a maroon tuxedo with tails from a bygone era of formal wear, a top hat, and a white shirt with matching maroon-trimmed ruffles. As he zips up his pants, the effects of cheap, illegally-purchased beer show in his slight stagger.

Ladies and gentlemen, Jeff Harper.

"Did we have a breach? Are there aliens?" His wiry frame wobbles up to Randi. "I brought my rocket boots." He points to his feet to prove he is, indeed, wearing a pair of bright silver leather rocket boots. He also holds up a small remote control for the boots and sneers like the overconfident idiot he is.

He turns to me, produces a big smile, and reaches out his arms. "Kilroy and Mr. Roboto on the scene again!" Those are his nicknames for us, inspired by his favorite Styx song. Jeff Harper may be alive and well in the 21st century, but his musical tastes are locked in the late seventies to early eighties. He launches into our personal handshake and I reluctantly join in: High five, low five, side-to-side, fly away birdy, turn away from each other, turn back, point at each other.

"You're drunk," Randi says to Jeff.

"Nuh-uh," Jeff grunts. "I'm energized."

I look at Jeff, holding his shoulders to steady him. "You gonna be okay?"

"I live for this," he says with a confident sneer.

The passenger door of the Vega, affectionately dubbed *Miss America* by Jeff in another nod to a Styx song, opens and Leigh Ann Cantwell, a lovely brunette in a striking white formal dress, emerges. A wispy laurel wreath rests tilted in her wildly unkempt hair. Still, her stunning contemporary elegance shines next to Jeff's anachronistic attire.

"Jeff," she says. "How long is this gonna take? I wanna get some waffles. You promised me waffles." She stumbles barefoot around the front of the car and stands beside Jeff, leaning on him to brace her drunken wobble. He leans in to kiss her. She giggles coyly, kisses him back and soon the two are engaged in a full-scale make-out session. Randi grabs Jeff by the lapel and pulls him away.

"How does Corporate feel about civilians?" She is in full-scale scolding mode.

"Oh my god," Jeff rolls his eyes. "Civilians, bad. Paperwork. Max. Max, bad. Blah, blah, blah."

Randi emits her working-with-Jeff-sucks sigh and looks at Leigh Ann, who is trying hard to keep her round, wide eyes open. "Leigh Ann," she says, "I need you to take Jeff's car back into town where you'll be safe. We'll bring Jeff to you later. Right now, you're in the way."

Leigh Ann scowls and pouts her lips. "In the way?"

"Baby, it's ok," Jeff says, "this will just take a minute and then I'll come to you." He brushes her cheek with the back of his hand. I want to puke.

"Jeff!" Leigh Ann cries out. "Waffles! You promised waffles! Waaaaahhhh. Ffffffff. Uhhhlllsss!" Her voice sounds like the wail of a starved wildebeest. I am impressed by her ability to convert waffles into a three-syllable word.

My Multi-Phaseable Portal Accessibility Sensor Device beeps at me and lights a yellow indicator, the standard color for caution. Someone or something may be trying to breach.

"Um, guys," I announce. "I'm getting something." A bubbling kaleidoscope of clouds over the river growls and deep in its center, a small white light grows. The mocha colored river water rushes past.

"Get her outta here, Jeff!" Randi points at Leigh Ann. "She is in the way!"

"In the way?" Leigh Ann stomps a few paces to Randi. "You need to stop saying that to me, lady."

"Not now, baby!" Jeff flips a switch on the hand held remote causing his rocket boots to ignite. "Kilroy and Mr. Roboto have to save the world." It sounds so dumb when he says that. I secure the laser pistols on my belt. I flex my hand inside the new glove weapon and thumb through the training manual one more time. I walk to the river and stand next to Randi. The wind blusters around us and low thunder rolls from over the river. I hold out the Multi-Phaseable Portal Accessibility Sensor device with my now trembling hand.

"You okay?" Randi asks. "You seem anxious."

"Oh, you know," I say. "The usual pre-alien invasion jitters."

Jeff joins me and Randi at the water's edge and hands me a flask produced from his jacket pocket.

"Here. Drink this. It'll calm your nerves."

"What is it?" I sniff the contents and find nothing concerning.

"Relax. It's only green Kwench-Aid. We always have green Kwench-Aid on the job." He squeezes my shoulders and eyes me with fierce determination. "And remember."

"Remember what?"

"We own the night."

I roll my eyes at the stupid catchphrase Jeff insists on uttering every time we're on a mission.

I swig the Kwench-Aid, hand him back the flask, and take a few steps back to prepare my weapon when Leigh Ann grabs my arm. I shouldn't be surprised by her strength. She is rather statuesque and cannot be categorized as skinny. She has somehow managed to achieve an ideal body proportion.

"Hey. You. Tony? It's Tony, right?" She jerks me in and whispers loudly as if telling the world's worst-kept secret. "Tell Jeff I need to talk to him. About waffles." Her breath stinks of stale cigarettes floating in cheap wine. She pushes me toward Jeff, urging me on with a shooing gesture. I don't want to be rude. She seems like a nice girl, but, really, it is getting dangerous. Once again, I try to convince her to take cover.

"Leigh Ann, not now." I turn her back toward *Miss America.* "You need to get in the car and leave. Please." I walk away and she starts yelling at us.

"Hey!" She stamps her feet. "Hey! Heeeeyyyy!" She staggers into what I assume she thinks is the center of attention.

My Multi-Phaseable Portal Accessibility Sensor Device begins to chime a series of alerts and the display moves to red. This is not good. I shove the sensor in my pocket and ready my weapon.

"I've got something to say!" Leigh Ann wears a cocky Billy Idol-like sneer that suggests we might want to watch the hell out. She straightens her laurel wreath, looks at us, and vomits onto the ground around her. After a brief pause, she bursts into tears. My gag reflex kicks in and I double over to suppress it.

"Perfect," mumbles Randi.

A rousing clap of thunder pulls our focus back to the river and a brilliant light seeps from the edges of the dark bubbling clouds.

"Shit," Randi says. "No time to worry about that now. We have an unauthorized party attempting to breach, gentlemen. Ready yourselves."

I look at Jeff. "Where's your laser?"

"My locker, I think. Maybe." He presses a button on his remote and the rocket boots lift him off the ground about a foot.

Suddenly, the force of a rip in the atmosphere where the light had been knocks us to the ground. The clouds split to reveal more of the brilliant light. Dust particles rush into the void and a fog of sparkling matter forms a funnel migrating from within. The funnel cloud spins faster and for a moment I think the Tasmanian Devil cartoon character is coming, but a spectacular explosion of light momentarily blinds us instead. The light dissipates, the explosion wanes and, the void collapses in on itself. A large metallic cube the size of a motorhome spills out, tumbles about, and skids to a stop. The dark gray object rests as we circle it, weapons poised. A single door with a round window sits on one wall. A bumper sticker with the phrase "Eat My Anti-Matter" is displayed in one of the top corners. The door slides up and we jump back.

All is silent.

A humanoid, nearly eight feet tall, dressed in a tacky purple and green jumpsuit with matching cape emerges from the cockpit. His large head is shaped like a football on a tee and is covered by a pointed helmet with wings painted on it. He steps out onto the short wing and then hops to the ground. A basketball-sized metallic orb floating above the being, buzzes with electronic beeps and hums.

"Sonofabitch!" the alien cries out. "Why will my ears not pop! I hate it when my ears do not pop!"

"State your identity and the purpose of your presence." Randi sounds very authoritative as she speaks verbatim the standard greeting for an alien who has breached the portal. I'm glad she is in charge because I'm frozen with fear.

"I am Grandor." His voice booms like the world's most overwrought Shakespearean actor. Grandor gestures toward the orb. "This is my valet, Jackie." The orb chirps.

"You speak English?" I feel the need to address the 800-pound gorilla on the river bank.

"My capacity for language is exceptional!" He smiles widely and claps his hands a couple of times. "Oh, I have finally arrived. It is the Earth. The Earth, Jackie!"

"Yes it is," replies the orb in an unimpressed female voice.

"Oh, it is marvelous! Isn't it marvelous, Jackie!"

"I'm going to need to see some documentation," Randi barks. "If you come through that portal, you have to have documentation."

Grandor ignores her as he surveys the surroundings. We fix our weapons on him, anticipating any movements of aggression. Jeff, who has no weapon, performs a clumsy ballet of maintaining his balance in the rocket boots while striking a faux kung fu pose. Grandor catches sight of it and tilts his head quizzically. He steps toward Jeff and leans down to him.

"And who are you that have come to welcome me?"

"We are Kilroy and Mr. Roboto." Jeff gestures with his head toward Randi. "And, she's Randi."

"Don't listen to him," Randi says. "We provide security for this portal and you have arrived here without authorization." Randi maintains her authoritative voice, her gun still aimed at Grandor. "Now, again, what is your purpose?"

Jackie beeps, chirps, hums, and whirrs. "Grandor is here to begin his conquest of your planet."

"Thank you, Jackie. Yes." Grandor clears his throat before making his proclamation. "And, I have come seeking an Earth female to be my queen."

"Return to your planet of origin." Randi's ability to maintain her composure and stick to the script from training is impressive. My legs feel as though they could collapse at any moment.

"Shit!" Jeff shouts. I turn and see that the rocket boots have twisted him upside down.

"What is happening?" I hear Leigh Ann say. I had almost forgot she was there. "I'm totally freaking out here. When are we getting waffles?"

"Get her outta here, Jeff!" growls Randi.

"I can't. I'm upside down."

"Oh, I see you have brought a female to me already." Grandor cocks an eyebrow and purses his lips, clearly smitten.

"I…am…Leigh Ann…Leigh Ann Cantwell. My people call me Leigh Ann." She displays admirable diplomacy punctuated with the "live long and prosper" gesture.

Grandor struts to Leigh Ann and extends his hand. His long, slender fingers unfold and I think I count six fingers without fingernails.

"You are lovely." He snaps his fingers at the orb. "Jackie! Wooing music, please!"

"I am not sure now is the time or place, Grandor."

"Jackie! Woo!"

With Grandor's command, something from inside Jackie begins playing Andy Gibb's "I Just Wanna Be Your Everything." Randi, Jeff, and I, all look at one another. Corporate had prepared us for many things. This is not one of them.

Leigh Ann stands frozen with a combination of fear and confusion as Grandor dances and spins around her. My Multi-Phaseable Portal Accessibility Sensor Device erupts in a symphony of beeps and blurps. The colored lights flash on and off like an out-of-control Christmas tree. I glance toward the river and see dark clouds billowing once more.

"Uh, guys," I say.

A strong wind swirls and a vacuum suction from the portal intensifies, pulling large branches toward it and sucking them in. The force causes Leigh Ann's dress to rise slightly and she struggles to get her balance.

Jackie increases the volume of her voice. "Grandor! I advise you cease your courtship and focus on the mission. The portal is unstable."

The dancing alien grabs Leigh Ann's arm. "Come. Be my queen. We shall rule planets together!"

"I fear you are overplaying your hand," Jackie advises. "We must get back to the ship."

"You're kinda freaky looking," Leigh Ann tells Grandor.

"Let her go!" Jeff regains his position, flies toward Grandor and throws a wild punch at him. Grandor responds with a bolt of energy fired from wide bracelets on his wrists. The blow propels Jeff backward and he appears to lose all sense of balance in the rocket boots. He sputters around like a balloon that was suddenly let go after being filled with air. He hits the light pole and falls to the ground with a thud. He moans in pain and fights to stand to his feet again.

"I do not recommend that," Grandor says to Jeff. He pulls Leigh Ann tighter. "I have significant powers, which are helpful, because I am easily winded when I exert myself."

Randi unleashes a barrage of laser fire on Grandor, who deflects each shot with his cape. Jackie fires a few blasts of her own at both Randi and me. I dive away then turn and fire in defense. The orb darts and bobs. A blue bolt of energy shoots from Jackie and hits me in the chest. Tentacles of electricity fire through my body, rendering me motionless on the ground for a few seconds.

"Jeff!" Leigh Ann screams out. "Help! Get this freak off me!" She kicks and punches with futility before reaching out to Randi. "Help me, lady!"

"Grandor." Jackie buzzes to her amorous leader. "We must go now. The portal is closing."

I struggle to stand and keep my balance against the force of the suction pulling everyone toward the grumbling vortex. I watch as Grandor and Leigh Ann tumble to the ground and are dragged toward its mouth. Grandor's ship and the three vehicles scoot a few inches, sucked by the portal's power. Leigh Ann screams for help again and Jeff tries to fly toward her. The instability of the vortex pushes Jeff around like a leaf in the wind. Randi races to the rescue as well, only to be propelled against her truck by a blast from Jackie. Randi slumps in a heap, not moving. I look back to Jeff who took another hit from Grandor and fell backward. He is pulled toward the vortex, but grabs the open door of *Miss America* and struggles into the driver's seat.

"We shall rule forever, Queen Leigh Ann!"

"You're a freeeeeeeeeeeeeaaaaaaaaaaaaaaaaaaaaaaaaak!" are Leigh Ann's last words as Grandor drags her into his spacecraft. They disappear into the ship, Jackie following behind. The engines on the ship ignite and within seconds it disappears into the portal. Leigh Ann is gone, kidnapped by an amorous purple alien and his electronic valet.

I can barely stand. The force pulls me toward the vortex and I slam against a light pole. I wrap my arms around the pole and strain against the sucking of the gaping portal. I catch glimpse of my car scooting toward the portal.

"I gotta get Leigh Ann back!" Jeff fires up the engine of his Vega and drives toward the opening.

"Jeff!" I yell. "No!"

Miss America lifts off the ground and flies into the vortex in a whoosh of suction. The force of it nearly pulls me in with it, but I feel a jerk in the opposite direction. A lasso of orange energy hugs my torso and I turn to see it connected to a device Randi is holding.

After a loud whoosh, the bright light collapses on itself and all is quiet again. Jeff is gone. Leigh Ann is gone. Randi stumbles toward the bank. I join her, still trying to catch my breath. The water looks black as small swirls and eddies float along.

"What the hell was that thing you shot me with?" I ask. "What just happened?"

"What we have here," says a male voice behind us, "is a failure to execute."

He is thin and tall and his face is narrow with sharp lines and angles. It lacks expression and moves enough to allow him to enjoy the lollipop he is sucking on. He wears black skinny slacks and a lightweight gray pullover sweater.

"Hello, Max," says Randi, taking a few steps toward the man in the sweater.

"Randi." Max walks past us and stands at the bank of the river. He twirls his sucker in his mouth and pulls it out with a smack. "Civilians." His voice is like creamy caramel and he punctuates his understated assessment with another smacking suck on the candy.

"I know," Randi mumbles.

Max gestures with the lollipop as he speaks. "I look around and all I see is the IB-47 I've got to fill out because of the civilian."

I am trying to figure out where Max came from.

"We have to get them back!" I say to him.

"That's not your call."

Several seconds of silence hang in the air as Randi and I stand helplessly. She has spent the last two years helping us grow in our jobs at Corporate and has always told us the dangers of involving civilians. She looks at me with defeat and sadness.

"I'm sorry, Tony." She hugs me, but I am still too overwhelmed to return the gesture. She pulls away and I lean over and put my hands on my knees like the air has been knocked out of me.

"I hate this for you," Max says.

"We have to get them back," Randi says. "C'mon Max."

"That's not going to happen, I'm afraid."

"What do you mean?" I point at where the portal once appeared. "My best friend and his girlfriend got sucked through that thing. We're Corporate. That's our portal. We need to get them back."

"We have protocols in place. Procedures. We only handle what's on this side of the portal. And we can't risk even more civilians getting involved. We have to cover this up. As an agent, you can appreciate that."

"Well I'm not an agent," I growl. Or at least I try to sound like I'm growling. "I'm an intern."

"We can change that."

I throw up my hands and walk to my car. "Forget it. I'll do this myself. I'm going to figure out a way to get Jeff and Leigh Ann back, with or without you."

Max holds his left wrist up to his mouth and speaks into it. "Situation is secure here."

"Hey! Tell the person in your wrist I quit! If you don't care enough about your interns to go back for one left behind then I want no part of it! Maybe I'll freelance or something. I'll find Jeff on my own! To hell with Corporate and to hell with you!" I slam the door to add one more exclamation point to that dramatic declaration. I turn the key in the ignition and the engine whines but won't turn over. I pound on the dashboard, then, rub it apologetically.

I get out of the car with all the humility I can muster.

"Can you give me a jump?"

CHAPTER TWO

Every nightmare follows a similar pattern. Jeff and I are somewhere familiar. The hallway at school or leaning against his crappy Vega, *Miss America.* We're eating apricots and talking about the meaning of life. Then, we hear maniacal laughter behind us. We turn and see Grandor the Malevolent in his ugly unitard, ridiculous cape, and winged helmet juggling more apricots before he starts pelting us with them. I cover my head until the barrage stops. I look up and see Marlene dressed like Grandor.

"This is for missing prom, you jerk tool head!" She throws an apricot at me and it splats against the side of my face. I wipe the slime away and see Jeff in Marlene's spot, also dressed as Grandor.

"This is for letting me get sucked into the portal, you asshole!" He unleashes a barrage of apricots on me and I bolt upright and scream, furiously wiping away the fruit that isn't there.

Apricots mean nothing to me, so why am I having nightmares about them?

Every night for the last six weeks since Jeff and Leigh Ann were pulled into the portal, I've awakened from these horrible dreams drenched in sweat. Today is no different. I get out of bed and open my bedroom curtains. The harsh glare of the sun informs me it is yet another hot summer morning I'm not at all excited about. I reach for my phone and flip to a playlist I created titled Soul Torture. "Bubbly," by Colbie Caillat, is first on the list.

Yes, I like Colbie Caillat. I realize an 18-year-old guy admitting such a thing is grounds for the revocation of my male credentials, but I have my reasons. First, I admire Colbie Caillat's beauty the way one might admire a sunset, with awe and deep contemplation about the meaning of life. Second, "Bubbly" played on the radio when Marlene and I first kissed exactly a year ago today. Call me a hopeless romantic. Call me an emotional sadist. I don't care. I miss everything about Marlene. Her sandy blond hair and round green eyes. Those willowy lips that seem to be forever smiling. Her full-bodied laugh. My heart hates knowing I missed a night of prom moments with Marlene to deal with the portal.

I remind myself this is all my fault.

I also miss Jeff terribly, so I turn off Colbie Caillat and play Styx's "Mr. Roboto." Unlike Marlene, Jeff's physical attributes are not what I miss. Not his perpetually pungent foot odor. Not his insistence on trying to maintain a partial beard even though he clearly lacked enough facial hair to warrant the endeavor. But, I do miss having him around.

*

I shower, which is always problematic. I stand a safe distance from the water swirling down the drain. Anything that swirls reminds me of Jeff and Leigh Ann getting sucked into the portal. A flushing toilet is now my biggest fear. I head to the kitchen to savor the first of two bowls of Cocoa Puffs and attempt conversation with my parents who are busy getting ready for their own days. I don't talk about the portal incident to anyone, because Max gave clear instructions not to. Besides, everyone would think I was a lunatic if I said anything. So, I call that event The Prom Night of Which We Shall Not Speak.

I originally was going to call it The Night Jeff Got Sucked, but that brings an unintended connotation to mind.

Conversations at my house since The Prom Night of Which We Shall Not Speak follow a set pattern.

First comes The Look. In the mornings, when I enter the kitchen from a night of not sleeping in between nightmares, Mom greets me with a sweet smile of pity while she rubs my arm. Sometimes random hugs are thrown in for good measure.

"How ya doing this morning, sweetie?" She pours me a glass of green Kwench-Aid. That's how I like to start my day. As I sip, she maintains The Look while resting her hands on her chin.

"I'm fine. Better." I've learned to give this pat response despite all I'm going through because I don't want her worrying about me more than she already does. They don't know about the portal or my job at Corporate. They think I work in the mailroom. They know Marlene and I broke up before prom. Most of the school believes Jeff and Leigh Ann disappeared, possibly runaways.

After The Look comes The Reassurance. "Well, you've been through a lot and remember we love you. You can tell us anything."

Anything? I can tell you anything? Somehow I think if I blurted out that I watched my best friend get sucked through a portal into outer space after a battle with an alien named Grandor they'd look at me like I have a tiny kraken crawling out of my nose. Sometimes, I think they look at me like that anyway. I move to the counter and pour myself another bowl of cereal. Upon realizing we are out of milk, I wonder why bad things happen to good people.

"Still having nightmares?" Dad asks, scanning through something on his tablet.

"Yes," I say, pouring my dry cocoa therapy back into its box. "Mostly about apricots."

"Oh, I love apricots," Mom says. "Do you want me to buy you some apricots, honey?"

"No." Her question throws me to the point of stuttering. "I…that's…what?"

"I'll pick some up tonight after work." She makes a note in her phone to remind her of this awesome idea she's come up with to get me apricots I don't want.

"I've got such a full day today," she says. "With the River Luau starting in few days, we've got a lot of last minute items to take care of."

Mom serves on the committee that plans Poplar Bluff's annual River Luau, which is held every summer for a week. It's the usual small town orgy of unsafe rides, rigged games, and horrific, but delightful food.

"Don't forget we have book club tonight, honey." Dad's face is glued to his tablet. I notice a small spider crawling along the window sill behind him. I reach down and take off my shoe, careful not to move too fast. I hate spiders and everything they stand for and this one shall meet the same fate as the ones who came to my house before it. I take one step toward the sill and lower my shoe of wrath down on the spider. My parents jump and shout at me.

"What the hell are you doing?" Dad turns around as I grind my shoe into the spider's carcass.

"Pretty sure it was coming for you, Dad."

"Tony, it's a harmless spider," Mom says with a tiny pout.

"Harmless spider is an oxymoron," I tell her.

"That reminds me of one of those memes I saw the other day," Dad says. "It said 'let's all take a moment to be thankful spiders can't fly." Dad thinks memes help him seem more hip than he really is.

"I'm already having nightmares, Dad."

"Guess I better get to work." He is still glued to the tablet.

"Something interesting there, Chris?" Mom puts her hand on Dad's shoulder and peers over. As a reflex action, he places one of his hands on hers. They've always been an affectionate couple and I somehow find comfort in that.

"Checking some emails about the break-in."

"What break-in?" I ask.

"Apparently, someone broke into the factory last night and made off with a large shipment of Kwench-Aid packets meant for distribution." Dad stands, blows out a weary sigh, and looks off into some special place I guess only he can see.

"I'm sorry you have to deal with all of that," Mom says.

"Who steals Kwench-Aid in bulk?" he asks, still looking off into the distance. "Is there a new black market I don't know about?"

"I can't imagine packets of artificially flavored fruit drink mix would fetch much." Mom kisses him on the cheek. He slides his tablet into his briefcase.

I don't know much about Dad's job, other than he is a quality control manager at the Kwench-Aid plant in town. On the rare occasion he speaks of his work, he uses accompanying phrases like "dark pit," "soul suck," and "only for the insurance and 401k." I know it has provided us with all the free Kwench-Aid a person could ever dream of possessing.

"Is this the American Dream?" he wonders aloud. "Working overtime to make up for lost inventory while figuring out who stole my Kwench-Aid?"

A spark of recognition fires in my brain. I feel myself floating away, like my subconscious is downloading a Wikipedia article. I blurt out all I know about the American Dream.

"James Truslow Adams wrote in 1931 that the American dream is a dream of a land in which life should be better and richer and fuller for everyone, with opportunity for each according to ability or achievement."

Now my parents are staring at me like I indeed have a tiny kraken crawling out of my nose. I don't know why I said that. I don't know why I know it. Until the very second I uttered his name, I had never heard of James Truslow Adams.

"Well, James Truslow Adams is a dick." Dad heads to the door and shouts out to Mom. "See you tonight, Suzanne."

"I have to show some property to a client this morning," Mom says. She's a real estate agent, specializing in commercial properties. "Then, I've got meetings about the River Luau all afternoon, but I'll make sure I duck out early."

"Ah, the River Luau," Dad says. "Poplar Bluff's annual homage to its non-existent Polynesian heritage."

"Tony, honey, you'll be on your own for a little while tonight. Is that ok?" She flashes The Look again.

"Relax, Suzanne," Dad chides. "He can take care of himself. Just no gin and Fresca, please, son."

"I'm sorry. I worry," Mom says. "These last few weeks have been so difficult. He broke up with Marlene. His best friend ran away with a girl. A laundry list of out-of-character behavior."

My loving, adoring parents proceed to list off said laundry list.

"You mean like the spectacular nose dive his grades took prior to graduation?" Dad's face scrunches as if he's genuinely trying to remember something he obviously easily recalls.

"Yes," Mom concurs. "That nose dive prior to the graduation he almost boycotted because of its emphasis on artificially applied honors such as grades instead of actual learning."

"Let's not forget quitting his job without so much as a warning," Dad adds.

"Oh," Mom chimes. "There's also breaking up with a lovely girl he adored only a few weeks before prom."

I glare at the sarcastic assholes currently inhabiting the bodies of my parents. I know I've put them through hell the last few weeks and I suppose they're allowed a few jabs at my expense, but I've grown weary of the constant rehash of my sins.

"You two make a great comedy team," I tell them. "You should start a podcast called Why Our Son Sucks."

Mom gives The Look and tells me she's sorry.

"You haven't exactly been making good choices lately," she adds.

Dad steps back to me, his hand on my shoulder. The Reassurance. "We want you to know that you can talk to us. You've always been able to talk to us, right?"

"It's complicated," is all I can say before I stand up to leave the room. I feel the need to escape to my Soul Torture Playlist.

"What does your day look like?" Mom asks.

"More questionable choices," I announce. "After knocking over a liquor store and losing my virginity to a prostitute I found online, I plan to build a wormhole generator so I can transport myself off this planet."

"Well, don't forget you have therapy this afternoon," Mom says.

"How could I forget?"

*

Every session starts with the same question.

"What is something good that has happened since our last session?"

I used to not answer because I couldn't think of anything. Now, I make stuff up in a passive aggressive way to show my disdain for this entire process.

"Yesterday I wore pants outside the house. Hashtag blessed."

"Are you still having nightmares?"

"Not every night," I say. "Not like before."

The man, my court-appointed therapist named Dr. Gilbert Lawrence, looks at a legal pad resting on his knee and twirls a pen in his hand. It's a nice pen. Sleek. Elegant. I'd like to have it for myself. It's a rollerball pen and I like rollerball pens. My brain clicks with the instant knowledge that rollerball pens were developed in Japan in 1963. I don't say this out loud, though. I don't know how I know this about rollerball pens. This conversation is uncomfortable enough without me blurting out random useless trivia. The awkward silence between us is filled by a staccato clicking he makes with his tongue.

"Do you have something you wanna share?" I ask him. "What's something good that's happened to you since our last session?"

"This is your time. This is about you." He always says that and I hate it. I don't want to be here sitting in a comfortable leather chair across from a man in a white and taupe bowling shirt who studies me through a persistent smile. I have to, though, because a judge said so. I guess Dr. Gilbert knew I hated the idea of a therapist, so he gave me some advice to ease my anxiety.

"Don't think of me as a therapist or counselor. Think of me as your life coach."

Life Coach Gilbert it is, then.

"I still have panic attacks, night terrors, and an irrational fear of things that swirl," I tell him. He chuckles at that, but doesn't realize I am being absolutely serious. I won't even turn my back on a flushing toilet for fear of being sucked into some parallel universe where fish carry guns and Justin Bieber is our dark overlord.

He rests his bearded chin in his non-pen-twirling hand and grins at me. He looks so friendly, so inviting. It should be so easy to open up to him. I really can't, though. Maybe I could talk about Marlene and feelings and regret, but there's no way in hell I could tell him about Jeff and portals and Corporate and 8-foot tall purple aliens.

"Are you going to college?"

"No. Maybe. I don't know yet."

"It's an important decision. What are your options?"

I pause before responding. "I see it all perfectly; there are two possible situations – one can either do this or that. My honest opinion and my friendly advice is this: do it or do not do it. You will regret both." He gives me a quizzical grin in response. "Sorry. It's something someone once said to me. Yes, I'm going to college. I'm going to study becoming a notary public. I like the idea of stamping things."

"Have you talked to Marlene?" More pen twirling. More grinning. I want to be annoyed by him, but he really is nice. The idea of seeing a therapist conjures an image of men in white coats standing outside his door. I imagine myself answering a question about my mother that prompts the men in white coats to charge into the office and shoot a straightjacket at me from a T-shirt cannon before dragging me away. My remaining years would be spent eating applesauce through a straw while rocking back and forth and mumbling incessantly about vengeful potatoes.

"I have not. Why would I? We broke up."

"A couple of weeks before prom night."

"I can't talk about prom night. I'm under strict orders." I wince a bit because I shouldn't have said that.

"Strict orders?" Life Coach Gilbert furrows his brow and leans in. "Strict orders from whom?"

I shouldn't say things like that because it only makes things harder on people like Life Coach Gilbert who are just trying to help, but I am so sick of everyone wanting to know how I'm doing. I can't tell them. Plus, no one knows about the nature of my work with Corporate. It's a secret.

"Well, you know." My brain scrambles for a viable explanation about who would be giving me strict orders and why. "The voices…inside. They tell me not to."

"Voices?"

I'm overdoing it.

"Not voices," I say. "Just, you know. I'm afraid to talk about it, I guess. It's too difficult."

Nice save, I tell myself.

"You'll never make progress unless you can talk about that night. Obviously something very traumatic happened to you," he says. "I can't help you if you don't share. What happened that night?"

I huff and roll my eyes because it feels like the right moment to do something derisive. "Why is everyone obsessed with what happened on prom night? Something came up. I chose not to go. That's all. Sometimes you don't go to prom. Why is everyone making such a big deal?"

"Do I need to read the police report to you again?" He raises his eyebrows and it makes me want to punch him in the throat. I do not need him to read the police report again. I do not need him to rehash the events of the Saturday night that followed The Prom Night of Which We Shall Not Speak. After six straight nights of horrific nightmares, I got liquored up on gin and Fresca. Events of that night never materialized in my memory, but the police report states I ran around town in only my underwear and a beach towel cape, riding a broom like a horse, and shouting "I'm Grandor the Malevolent! Kneel to me, Earth People!"

I say nothing.

"You asked your arresting officer to prom because you said you needed a do over."

"Well." I clear my throat. "She was pretty cute."

This time he says nothing.

"So," I blurt. "I have my first experiment with alcohol and everyone decides I need therapy?" I can feel a familiar lump of anger forming in my throat; the same lump that formed when Max told me no one would be looking for Jeff.

Life Coach Gilbert leafs through the legal pad, lips pursed and once more twirling the pen. I wonder about his life outside this office. Is this what he always wanted to do with his life? Does he eat ice cream or frozen yogurt? Is his wife as annoyed with the pen twirling as I am? Asking myself about ice cream fills me with the need to say everything I know about ice cream. A switch ignites in my brain and I'm suddenly aware that I know more about ice cream than anyone knows about anything.

"The origins of ice cream can be traced back to China around 200 B.C. They made sorbets out of snow and saltpeter."

My life coach furrows his brow again while maintaining his warm smile.

"Don't me ask me how I know that," I say.

"No, it's not that." He winces like someone who bit the inside of their cheek and reaches his hand to the back of neck. "Ow. Damn."

"What's wrong?"

“Something’s biting me.” He slaps at his neck like swatting a mosquito. He looks at his hand and sees a dot a blood on his palm. “Guess I got it. Helluva thing.”

He plucks a sanitary wipe from a container on the coffee table between us and cleans his hand and neck. He reiterates his steadfast belief that he can help me get better at recovering from The Prom Night of Which We Shall Not Speak. He says something else, but all I hear is blah, blah, blah, progress. Blah, blah, blah, walls. And so on and so forth until the end of time. He writes a refill for my Xanax prescription to keep me calm.

“Take care of yourself until next time,” he says, handing me a business card with the date and time of our next appointment. I’m already thinking of excuses to not come.

*

After the Life Coach Gilbert Session, I climb into my little Toyota Corolla and the oppressive humidity slaps me in the face like a wet blanket of summer depression. I swear it’s 157 degrees in here. I switch on the engine and crank the air conditioner full blast, which means more hot air for a couple of minutes so I roll down my window.

“The first manufacturer to include air conditioning in their vehicles was Packard in 1939,” I say to the inside of my car. A spasm of frustration with not understanding why I know that overtakes my body and I release a guttural roar. I turn to see an old man staring in me the way old men do when they don’t understand young people today.

I turn on some music to listen to “Mr. Roboto.” Jeff was obsessed with Styx and often erroneously compared the song to our friendship. The song tells the story of Kilroy, a rock star whose band is imprisoned during a fundamentalist dystopia bent on eradicating rock music. Kilroy disguises himself as a robot (the Mr. Roboto of the title) and breaks into the prison to free his friend Jonathan Chance. I promise that is what the song is about.

"I am Kilroy," Jeff would always tell me. "And you're Mr. Roboto."

"No," I would say. "They are the same person. Kilroy is Mr. Roboto. Mr. Roboto is Kilroy."

"Yes," he would nod. "They are one. We are one."

And on it would go in an absurd conversational loop. Really, a simple internet search would have cleared the whole matter up, but I never had the heart to push it. Even now, I wonder if Jeff is floating around in space still confused about the meaning of "Mr. Roboto."

Sweat trickles down my face as Dennis DeYoung, the lead singer of Styx, repeatedly thanks Mr. Roboto for doing the job nobody wants to. My phone alerts me of a text message from Mom.

Love you, honey. Wanted you to know.

I let out a long sigh and pinch the bridge of my nose in an effort to stave off a flow of tears. Damn her for being so good to me. I shake my head slightly to regain composure and notice something pinned under my windshield wiper. I get out of the car and retrieve it, looking around to see if anyone is watching me because surely this is the setup of a hidden camera reality show. It's a business card. On one side three words are printed.

KILROY WAS HERE

My hands tremble and my stomach knots. I look around again to see who might be around watching my reaction. I flip the card over to see if anything is on the back and find instructions written.

Go to Someone Else's Books and buy a copy of Something Wicked This Way Comes.

I do as instructed and speed to Someone Else's Books, my favorite place in this godforsaken town, and realize it is closed on Mondays. Whatever this is all about will have to wait until tomorrow. I sigh with frustration and start up my Soul Torture playlist. I steer through the streets of Poplar Bluff until I drive past Marlene's house. "Bubbly" ends and "Hate Me," by Blue October starts. I crank the volume, scream along, and drive home to sit in the dark of my room alone, which is totally not pathetic at all.

CHAPTER THREE

I want to own a used bookstore exactly like Someone Else's Books. It used to be an old house in the center of town on Main Street. The owners sold it to a guy named Kevin Raulston a few years ago and he renovated it and filled each room with a different genre of books. Someone Else's Books is my oasis and as I approach it from the sidewalk, I feel a weight lifting. That doesn't relieve the knot in my stomach, though. Jeff left a clue for me inside the store and I'm anxious to see what it is. I open the front door and a bell above it chimes. The smell of old books greets me and I'm at peace with the world. Kevin Raulston is stationed behind the counter at his laptop.

"How's life, Kevin?" I ask.

"Life?" The tone of his reply suggests I have not asked a simple question. He spins slowly in his chair to face me. "I need a minute."

Kevin is broad-shouldered but not muscular. Heavy-set. His hair looks like he has perpetual pillow head. He talks like a drug-addled hippie from the sixties. I don't know how old Kevin is but, by his general appearance and demeanor, I estimate his age to be anywhere from 28 to 79. The area he designates as the office is lined with star maps, drawings of aliens, newspaper clippings and pictures of various UFOs. A display of books about ancient alien theory owns the center of the front room.

"Tony, I'm close." Kevin pulls a map of Poplar Bluff off the wall and spreads it out on the counter. He points to red circles designating certain areas of town.

"Close to what?" I ask.

"To finding out how the Herpezoids are getting through!" He taps on each read circle as he speaks. "Sightings have increased. People I trust have taken them down personally. I think it has something to do with this area right here." He points to an unpopulated area along the banks of Black River outside of town. I recognize it as the area where the portal is. Like everyone else in my life except Jeff, Kevin knows nothing of my work at Corporate.

"That place is closed off and secret," he says. "Very mysterious. The only plausible explanation is alien activity."

"Or, maybe," I say, "it's just private property and the owners don't want people trespassing."

"You don't understand how conspiracy theories work, do you?"

"You really believe this stuff, don't you, Kevin?" I'm careful not to sound condescending because I like Kevin. He harbors this notion that an alien race known as Herpezoids is infiltrating Earth to take it over. I also wonder if he knows about the portal.

"You need to open your mind, Tony." He leans in and whispers. "The Herpezoid invasion is upon us. They're already here among us. You think I'm crazy. Everyone thinks I'm crazy, but, the day is coming when all shall know."

"I don't think you're crazy," I say and then we stare at one another and try to figure out if I'm lying about that.

"I'm poor," he says flatly. "Buy something."

"That's the plan."

I leave the front room of the store and head down a short hallway. I pass a door on my left adorned with a plain sign that reads "Private." The first doorway on my right leads to a room that houses all the classics. This place is nothing but books and books have never steered me wrong. I think that's why I enjoyed reading the training manuals at Corporate. They provided me with knowledge and guidance which brought me peace. I stand for a moment to look around the room. The sound of the bell above the front door chiming can be heard from in here. I hear Kevin greet the entering customers with "buy something! I'm poor!" It all sounds far away, though, because I'm the only one in this space. The smell of old books is a tonic.

I move to the far corner and locate several selections from Ray Bradbury. I reach for the lone, tattered paperback copy of *Something Wicked This Way Comes*. The friendship between Jim and Will, two boys who face a supernatural circus, touched me. The title also appealed to me because it's from Shakespeare's *Macbeth*, Act IV, Scene One. A witch says "By the pricking of my thumbs, something wicked this way comes." We read *Macbeth* in high school and when Jeff came across that part of the text, he immediately starting giggling. When I asked what was so funny, he said, "I keep reading it as 'by the thumbing of my prick.'" Jeff is a horrible student. He carried his homework, if he bothered to do it at all, folded up in his back pocket. He spent our high school days convinced he would work for Corporate for the rest of his life.

I miss that dumbass.

I flip through the book and a business card and a packet of green Kwench-Aid falls out. My thumb holds the pages and I see a highlighted quote.

> *So now Jim was the kite, the wild twine cut, and whatever wisdom was his taking him away from Will who*

> *could only run, earthbound, after one so high and dark silent and suddenly strange.*[1]

My mind floods with memories of Jeff and me playing, running, and imagining new worlds. He was uninhibited; nothing fazed him. His life had always been an improvisation, a random collection of stream-of-consciousness happenings. One time, he literally ran with scissors, chasing girls around our seventh grade art class shouting, "I want your hair, my pretty!" Three days of detention did nothing to curtail his behavior. I have always maintained a more straight-laced approach to things. Follow the rules. Read the manual. Have a plan.

I pick up the business card and see it is the same as the one on my car. Kilroy was here.

My stomach knots. Is someone messing with me or is Jeff back? If someone is messing with me, how do they know the Kilroy reference? If Jeff is back, how did he come through the portal? Why didn't he contact me in person?

I walk back to the front of the store and set the book on the counter.

"Ah, yes," Kevin says, "Ray Bradbury's coming-of-age horror yarn, weaved against the backdrop of a menacing traveling circus. Great choice. You'll love the way he blends together themes of fear, loss of innocence and friendship, and the supernatural."

"Oh, you've read it?"

"No. Just heard a lot about it." Kevin hands me my change. "When do you leave for school?"

"August. If I go."

---

[1] Ray Bradbury, Something Wicked This Way Comes (New York: Harper, 1962), 48.

"Why wouldn't you go? For God's sake, man, get out of this town! You can't replicate this dream life I've built for myself. I know the notion of living in a private room at the back of a used bookstore is intriguing, but I assure you, my life is the exception. Not the rule."

"I don't know what I want to do." I eye the area on his town map where the portal is. "Why go to college if I don't know what I want to do?"

"So they can tell you. That's what college is for. You'll love it." He points at the red circles on the map still resting on his counter. "Plus, you can find the Herpezoids that have infiltrated academia."

"I'm not very good with big decisions," I say. "They stress me out. I overthink things and I end up making the wrong choice."

The front door bell chimes and we turn to see who has walked in. My throat tightens and my heart thumps so wildly I fear it might explode out of my chest and hop away. Standing before me is the wholesome fresh beauty of my dreams, Marlene Hunter. Our eyes meet and I try to move but it feels like someone has nailed my feet to the floor with railroad spikes. My stomach falls into my legs, likely taking my liver and pancreas with it.

"Hi, Tony," Marlene says. Her smile is wide as always. Her teeth are white and perfect, as if they'd been meticulously set in place by some master tooth-setting person. "How are you?"

My mouth opens and a whimper escapes. I swallow hard and try again. "Good. Fine. Good." I think that sends a very clear message that I'm winning in life. "You?"

"I'm ok." She cocks her head and tucks her hair behind her ear. "You look good."

"I've been working out," I tell her, which is a fat lie. The only exercise I get is seeing how many slices of pizza I can stuff in my mouth. I also burn calories by meditating on the futility of existence and harboring deep self-loathing. Sometimes I do squats.

Our conversation is interrupted by a hulking figure in a short sleeve plaid shirt and blue jeans bursting into Someone Else's Books.

"Jesus, Marlene," he snorts. "Hurry up, will ya? I got stuff to do before we go to the party tonight." I recognize him as Clint Hudson. He graduated last year and was the one who saved the day for Marlene when I backed out of prom. Clint became Marlene's date and they've been together ever since. Or, at least, that's what I hear. It's not like I follow them around all over town or whatever because that is creepy. Clint looks at me with a gaze suggesting he could kill me 136 ways with a melon baller and gives me a vague nod.

"I just got here, Clint. Relax." She rolls her eyes in frustration. "Kevin, did that order come in for me?"

"Yep. Got it right here." Kevin produces a large manila envelope that appears to strain against whatever heavy object it contains. She takes it and pulls it to her chest, hugging it.

"Are you going to the River Luau, Tony?" Her eyes seem hopeful somehow, but I'm probably reading way too much into the situation. I look over at Clint who is gnawing on his fingernails the way a beaver might attack a tree. I should tell her I've been miserable without her and that I would do anything to get her back.

"Yeah," is all I say because I'm thinking of Clint and his melon baller.

She doesn't speak, only nods.

"Got your shit now, Marlene? Can we go?" Clint huffs.

"Clint you don't have to be so rude." She slaps Clint's arm and rolls her eyes. Her face flushes. "Thank you for taking care of this for me, Kevin."

"Just doing my job, ma'am." Kevin salutes her. "I also included some of my business cards. Tell your friends about me."

She waves bye to me and then heads to the door. She turns back to me before leaving. "You take care of yourself, Tony Pershing."

"I will, Marlene." I almost called her 'babe' out of habit. I stand at the glass door and watch Clint walk about five paces ahead of her. I tell myself I should run after her, take her in my arms, and tell her she is the Mr. Roboto to my Jonathan Chance, but I don't think she would know what I was talking about. They climb into his oversized truck with wheels the size of Venus and drive away. I bang my head on the door with a gentle thud.

"I gotta say," Kevin blurts out. "That was really brutal to watch."

*

A plate of Mom's famous pork chops lies before me, but eating is not a high priority. I make fork tracks in my mashed potatoes and push the peas around, hoping to give the illusion I'm enjoying the meal. My efforts fail, though, because Mom is already giving The Look.

"Not hungry, sweetie?"

"I had a big lunch." I'm lying, of course, because I've not consumed a bite except for half a banana this morning for breakfast while staring out the kitchen window and contemplating the futility of my existence. In that way, it was no different than any other banana I've eaten. I have no appetite after the Jeff Left a Clue About Still Being Alive Revelation and the Marlene/Clint Book Shop Encounter. Mom picks up my plate and sets it on the counter next to a bowl of apricots.

"You can heat it up later, if you like," she says as The Reassurance radiates from her.

"Plans tonight?" Dad asks.

"Nothing, really. Thought I might go driving around for a little while."

"Alone?" Mom asks, shifting easily back to The Look.

"Yeah, Mom," I say. "Alone. It's not a bad thing to want to be alone sometimes."

"I know, honey. I worry." She leans down, wraps her arms around my neck, and kisses the top of my head. "You're going to be fine. We love you."

"We'll be late tonight." Dad stands and takes his plate to the kitchen sink. "We have book club."

"Didn't you have that last night?" I ask. I normally don't concern myself with their comings and goings, but this struck me as odd. Mom and Dad usually adhere to routine.

"We're deep into *Game of Thrones,*" he replies. "That's a lot of ground to cover."

"Dad? You guys have your book club with Kevin Raulston, right? The guy who owns Someone Else's Books?"

"Yeah," he replies. "Why?"

"Does he go on and on about his alien theory? Does he talk about Herpezoids or whatever he calls them?"

Dad shoots a glance at Mom before answering.

"He's said a few things, but he's harmless. I thought you liked Kevin."

"I do," I say. "He's really convinced of their existence. Do you believe in aliens? How do you feel about passageways to other parts of space?"

"You mean, like, wormholes?" Dad asks as he sticks a final piece of pork chop into his mouth and sets his plate in the sink.

His utterance of the word wormhole jolts my brain and I'm aware of my subconscious floating away from me and toward some ethereal place where I know everything about wormholes. The science of them lies before me and I know it as intimately as Jeff knows the lyrics to every Styx song.

"Wormholes are also known as Einstein-Rosen bridges because they were first theorized by Albert Einstein and his fellow physicist, Nathan Rosen. They believed through the Theory of Relativity, that they were tunnels of sort that connect different points in the universe, or, even possibly, one point in our universe with one in another separate universe."

"I've heard of wormholes," Dad says. "You can't watch a sci-fi movie or read a sci-fi novel without some mention of them."

"Do you think they're real?" I ask. "Do you think they could exist?"

"Never really thought about it." He picks up his plate from the table and takes it to the sink. "I'm too busy trying to figure out why Kwench-Aid is getting stolen under the noses of my staff."

"But, if they did exist," Mom says. "Think of the possibilities."

We don't say anything. We stare off and think of those possibilities before Mom breaks the silence.

"You have a good time tonight, honey."

"No gin and Fresca, please." Dad's voice suggests he's tired of having to say it. I know he's teasing me.

"That was my gateway drink, Dad. Now, I'm into tequila and green Kwench-Aid."

"I guess you're the one who's been stealing it, then?"

*

I drive through the streets of my town late at night, listening to my Soul Torture Playlist. My route takes me through the high school parking lot before heading straight to

Marlene's street. I park about three houses down from hers, shut off the engine and turn on "I Need You Now," by Lady Antebellum. I don't even like country music, yet, here I am using it as the soundtrack to an activity that is not stalking at all because, again, that would be creepy. Self-pity washes over me. From this vantage point, I can see her front door illuminated by the glow of a porch light. Clint's black Ford pickup, complete with grotesquely large tires, is parked at the curb in front of her house. I hate that truck and all it stands for. A pair of metallic testicles hangs from the trailer hitch. I don't care who you are. If you own a truck with a scrotum, I'm going to judge you. I want to throw up in my mouth knowing Clint is on the couch with his arm around my estranged goddess. I imagine he's donning a sleeveless shirt and flatbill cap turned a bit to the side, as he forces her to watch NASCAR or a reality show about pawn shops. At the opportune time, he'll hack out his smokeless tobacco and put on some Nickelback before making his move. What a douchebag.

This ritualistic emotional sadism hampers my ability to move on. Life Coach Gilbert tells me I need to be honest with Marlene about why I broke up. Of course, he adds, I can't really do that until I'm honest with myself and talk about what happened. Everyone seems so obsessed with finding out what I know about The Prom Night of Which We Shall Not Speak. Just open up, they say. Be truthful about it, they say.

I want to get all Jack Nicholson on their asses and yell, "you can't handle the truth!"

Hell, I can't handle the truth either and I was there.

"This is stupid," I mumble to myself. "I'm stupid. I should go up there and knock on the door. That's what I'll do. I'll knock on the door, ask to see her, and explain everything."

I turn off the Soul Torture Playlist, which has now transitioned to "God Only Knows," by the Beach Boys. I take a deep breath, get out of my Corolla, and start walking toward Marlene's door, rehearsing the whole speech out loud.

"It's like this, Marlene. I worked for a private security company called Corporate. I don't know much about them. Everything associated with my job was on a need-to-know basis. I was an intern. Jeff was, too. I broke up with you because I got assigned to protect a portal over the river outside of town. An alien was preparing to come through and I had to be there to help stop him. My job was very dangerous. I feared getting you involved would put you in harm's way. Also, Jeff and Leigh Ann got sucked through the portal and I don't know where they are. But, I quit my job and I think Jeff is actually alive and back. I'd like to see if you would take me back because I love you so very much."

Realizing that explaining everything might cause Marlene to cock her head to the side like an adorably confused puppy, roundhouse-kick me in the throat, and call the cops, I stop in the middle of the street and quickly inventory some of the more alarming details I could easily omit.

"It's like this, Marlene," I improvise. "I broke up with you because…I feared…you would be in harm's way. But, now I'd like to see if you would take me back because I love you so very much."

Close enough.

I get halfway to her house when I hear the door open and see Marlene and Clint walk out. I don't know if they were kissing or watching television in there, but I was dead right about the idiotic flatbill cap.

"Shit!" I whisper and rush back to my car, hopefully undetected. I dive into the open driver's side window and slide down in the driver's seat to hide. It would be remarkably stupid to drive off right now. I peer over the dashboard and watch as they stand facing one another at his truck. Marlene stands with her arms crossed. She wears her hair in a ponytail and I'm reminded again how much I love her hair like that. Based on her body language and Clint's pacing back and forth, I deduce they are arguing.

Since I'm forced to witness this interaction, I entertain myself by performing my own dialogue. Clint is shrugging his shoulders, so I start with him.

"Shucks, Marlene," I mimic in an overdone hick accent. "I know I'm a big dumbass that can't wear a ball cap. You're right. You shouldn't be with me."

"Clint," I say in a higher octave. "You're stupid. Your breath stinks of smokeless tobacco. And your truck is an obvious attempt to mask your latent homoerotic tendencies and laughably small penis. I can't be with you."

Through my windshield I see Marlene throw her hands up in frustration and turn to walk away, as if that was what she had really said. Clint reaches out and spins her around. I don't know what he says to her, but she must like it because they start kissing and I gag.

I watch Clint climb into his Truck of Overcompensation and speed off because that's what douches like him do. Marlene stands and watches him drive away and then looks to her house. A wave of panic hits me and I think she sees me. I slide down in my seat allowing enough room to peer over the steering wheel. I'm thankful I'm not wearing a glow-in-the-dark night vision helmet like the one developed by Corporate for dark spaces. Jeff stole the prototype and shoved it in my trunk.

Marlene gets in her car and backs out of her driveway. Where is she going? Did she indeed see me and is now sending telepathic messages imploring me to follow her? I slide nearly into the floorboard as her headlights land on my vehicle. I hear her car pass and contemplate whether or not to follow. Surely, it's not as creepy as it seems. This should be an easy decision.

I see it all perfectly; there are two possible situations – one can either do this or that. My honest opinion and my friendly advice is this: do it or do not do it. You will regret both.

I fire up my car and head in the direction of Marlene. Contrary to what movies and television would have you believe, tailing someone without detection is very difficult. Marlene leads me down Main Street to the outskirts of downtown Poplar Bluff. She pulls over and parks across the street from a very familiar building. I swerve into the parking lot of an abandoned convenience store and park. I hop out and creep to the sidewalk in time to see Marlene crossing the street to the front door of Someone Else's Books. Panic grips my entire being and I look around for a place to hide. I see nothing so, as a last resort, I crouch because I somehow think making myself shorter will solve the problem. She knocks and a couple of seconds later, Kevin Raulston lets her in. He looks around before closing the door.

What now? Do I try to spy in the windows? Do I wait here? How long will she be in there? Why is she even there? Kevin closes the store at 7:00 on Tuesdays and it's well after 10:00. Is she there for book club, too? What should I do?

While I stand and convince myself Marlene is not at Someone Else's Books because she is also dating Kevin, she emerges from the store and heads to her car. She carries a long box. I freeze where I stand, unable to determine my next move. I can only watch Marlene drive away and think about how much I hate Kierkegaard.

I get in my car, press play on the stereo for my Soul Torture Playlist and switch it to "Bubbly" and bang my head on the steering wheel. My passenger side door opens and someone gets in.

"We need to talk," says the figure. She is the woman I recognize as Randi Williams. Sweat covers her face and her cheek bears a minor cut. her black t-shirt and vest are stained with mud, blood, and a couple of patches of a green slime.

"What the hell?"

"We need you to come back to work," she tells me. "We don't have time to bring any new interns onboard. We need experience. You have experience."

"Experience with what?" I ask. "Why do you look like you just came from a cage match?"

"I can't tell you that right now." She brandishes a chrome-plated laser pistol and pulls a cartridge from the handle.

"That's a P-47 Electro-Photon Multiblaster," I announce. "Developed in 1997 for use in intergalactic security. It operates off quintonium batteries and is especially useful in altercations with Herpezoids."

"Yes." Randi tosses the empty cartridge into the floorboard and inserts another retrieved from her belt.

"Why do I know that?" I ask her. "I don't know why I know that."

"I can't tell you that right now." She pulls a candy bar from her vest pocket, opens it, and chomps on it. "Come to Corporate tomorrow. Follow the Rube Goldberg Protocols. You'll get the information you need then."

I point to the green slime on her vest. "What is that?"

"Herpezoid blood." She inspects it and shakes her head. "That's gonna be a bitch to get out."

"Herpezoids." I look toward Someone Else's Books and think of Kevin Raulston's rants. "They're real?"

"I can't tell you that right now. I need you to follow the Protocols and get to Corporate." She whips her head around looking for someone or something that I assume must've been chasing her. "Tomorrow. Do it."

"Can you tell me anything about what's going on?" I grab her arm. "Is Jeff alive?"

"I can't tell you that right now." She flips a switch on her Multiblaster and it emits a whiny hum. She opens the door and before she leaves hands me a business card with only a phone number on it.

"Text this number for directions," she says. She takes another bite of her candy bar and runs off into the darkness.

"This was a pointless conversation!" I shout after her.

I open my glove compartment and retrieve the copy of *Something Wicked This Way Comes*. I pull out the Kilroy Was Here business card poking from its pages and determine I have one more stop to make before going home.

*

The Kwench-Aid plant sits in the middle of the Poplar Bluff Industrial Park. Once I exited the scene of the Stalking Marlene/Encounter with Randi Fiasco, I decided I needed to do a little investigating. I enter the employee gate using my dad's ID badge. I swiped it from the driver's side visor in his car when I left the house. No security works that entrance since employee access badges get you in. My stomach flips and flops and hands tremble as I reach out and swipe the badge's magnetic stripe through the reader. The security arm raises and I draw a deep breath as I drive through.

I pass the giant Kwench-Aid logo sign, a cartoon character of a glass of my favorite drink. The glass wears the kind of happy face that fills one simultaneously with joy and dread. The glass is named Kwenchy and he changes colors to match the flavor of Kwench-Aid. Kwenchy scares me. I glance in the lower corner of the logo sign and see another familiar logo. Corporate. Under the logo are the words "A Corporate Entity."

I steer to a remote corner of the parking lot and pull the Kilroy Was Here business card from the book. Stolen shipments of green Kwench-Aid combined with this apparent message from Jeff can only mean one thing.

Somehow, he's back.

I climb out of my car and creep toward the plant. Only a few workers are here for the night shift, which, according to Dad is responsible for loading the shipments for delivery. If Jeff is back, he may very well strike again. I wonder why he would need to steal so much Kwench-Aid, but chalk it up to Jeff being Jeff. He's an odd duck.

I edge along the wall to the back of the plant where the loading docks are. I remember Dad telling me this is where tractor trailer rigs back into for the loading of Kwench-Aid to be shipped to stores. I don't see anything except the smoke shack area where employees take breaks. Two men stand smoking cigarettes and complaining about their general existence.

"When he's gonna hurry up with the forklift?" one of them asks, flicking his butt on the ground instead of using the receptacle. Only dicks don't use receptacles.

"I dunno," says the other. "He's probably in there scratching his balls." I marvel at how little male conversation seems to evolve from adolescence to adulthood.

The non-receptacle-using guy is pudgy and bald. He shoves his hands in his pockets and paces.

"I can't believe we still have jobs after that robbery," he says.

"Right?" says the one who made the ball scratching comment. "That was a helluva thing."

"No one believes us." The pudgy one lights up another cigarette and offers one to the other guy.

"Why should they?" Ball scratcher dude takes a smoke. "We told them a kid pulled up in a Vega, tossed a couple of metal balls out, and then a couple of minutes later sped off with a pallet of product."

"I honestly don't remember shit for like two minutes. It was like being blackout drunk."

"Same here. I remember nothing."

The sound of screeching tires echoes and the pair whip their heads toward the far end of the building where more loading docks are. I look, too, and see a small vehicle fishtailing around the corner and speeding toward us.

"Shit!" says the one who made the ball-scratching comment. "He got us again!"

"How does he pull it off?" the other says.

Another vehicle, this one a security car with lights flashing follows from around the corner. The escaping vehicle flies by and even though I only catch a glimpse I recognize it as a white 1976 red Chevy Vega station wagon with a wide white stripe on its hood. There's no doubt it's *Miss America.* I sprint the fifty or so yards toward my own car and start it up as soon as I get in. I mash the accelerator and head toward the gate. *Miss America* zooms out the gate and heads down the street away from the plant. The security car is close behind and I race to follow up the rear.

Our chase approaches a four-way intersection. Going straight takes us toward downtown. Going left takes us toward a soccer complex. The Vega turns right, which is the road that leads to the portal. The three vehicles weave the dangerous curves of a dark highway. We hit a straight stretch of road usually considered a prime spot for passing another driver. I calculate the speed I'll need to overtake the security car and get behind *Miss America.* I swerve into the left lane as a sonic boom rattles my windshield. The rear of the Vega spits out a fireball and disappears into the night at an unimaginable rate of speed.

I slam on my brakes and lose control of my car for a few seconds. I skid off the road and onto the shoulder. I throw open my door and jump out. The security vehicle screeches to a halt a few feet ahead of me after the Vega's transition into some kind of warp speed. Two guards emerge from the car.

"Did you see that?" barks the driver. "What the hell?"

"Hey, kid," the passenger guard calls to me. "Did you see that?"

"I didn't see anything."

I get back in my car and sit for a moment. My nerves dance and my pulse pounds. I retrieve the passenger seat the Kilroy Was Here business card and the card given to me by Randi. I look at the phone number and sigh. I start the engine and drive home hoping the evening's events will prevent the usual onslaught of nightmares about Grandor and apricots.

CHAPTER FOUR

I crawl out of bed after a few hours of tossing and turning. No nightmares this time. Only obsessive thoughts about the After Hours Book Shop Affair (God, I hope it's not an affair) and The Great Vega Escape. I shuffle down the hall still in my clothes from last night and hear Dad offer up a bellow of bewilderment.

"What in the actual hell?"

I assume now Dad is aware of another theft of Kwench-Aid packets from his plant. I enter the kitchen to find him possibly choking his tablet as he sits at the table.

"Chris," chides Mom. "Don't get yourself all worked up."

"Another night. Another theft." He stands and shoves the tablet into his briefcase and gives Mom a gentle kiss on the lips.

"Maybe tonight we could skip book club," she tells him.

"No." Dad's response is quick and short, but not rude. "No. We need to go."

"Three nights in a row," I say. "You must really be into *Game of Thrones.*"

Dad only smiles and heads to the door. I stop him with my voice before he leaves.

"I think it's time maybe I went back to work."

My parents stare at me with wide eyes and open mouths. This is neither The Look nor The Reassurance I see on their faces, but rather something I would describe as The Perplexity.

"Are you sure?" Mom asks. "I thought you wanted to take the summer off and get your head clear."

"Will they let you come back?" Dad asks.

"They said I could, yeah. I'm gonna call my supervisor in a minute to make sure." Mom and Dad know nothing of my work at Corporate. They think I'm a mailroom clerk.

"If that's what you want to do, honey." Mom walks to me and rubs my arm.

"It would probably do you some good," Dad says. "Mindless delivery of the mail to people in cubicles can be therapeutic. Gotta go. I'll meet you at book club, Suzanne."

"You're on your own for dinner tonight, honey," Mom tells me. She blows out a weary sigh and collects her own briefcase sitting by the front door. "I have to tour the fairgrounds today. The new carnival company is setting up the attractions for the River Luau. Yay me."

"At least no one is stealing your Kwench-Aid," I say.

"No." She allows herself a slight half smile. "No, they're not."

Mom barely disappears out the door before I'm texting Randi Williams:

OK. I guess I need instructions or whatever.

My phone buzzes a few seconds later. It's Randi's response:

Follow Rube Goldberg Protocol 1118 and await further instructions.

I sigh and roll my eyes so hard I think for a second they might stay stuck in the back of my head because I hate Rube Goldberg Protocols so much.

*

Why am I here?

I don't ask in the why-am-I-in-the-grocery-store-with-no-pants way or the why-am-I-waking-up-hungover-in-a-Turkish-prison way. I ask because I'm sitting in the drive-thru of a god-awful fast food restaurant called Taco Haus about to re-enter a world I want no part of. Except for the fact it might help me understand what happened to my friend. Do I really want to follow through with this? All I can think of while I stare at the Taco Haus is how much of an asshole Kierkegaard must've been.

Rube Goldberg Protocol is a Corporate method of delivering a basic piece of communication via the most convoluted method possible under the guise of protecting the public from the nature of the work we do. The rationale behind it is uses buzzwords like "proprietary information" and Protocol 1118 involves ordering a certain menu item from the drive thru at Taco Haus. I open the Corporate app on my phone and access the Rube Goldberg protocol documents but then set my phone down. I'm aware I suddenly know every single Rube Goldberg protocol as if I created them myself.

I ease up to the speaker box and spot the Corporate logo in the lower right corner of the drive-thru menu board. "A Corporate Entity," the line under the logo reads. Several seconds of silence pass before the voice on the other end blares through the box.

"Welcome to Taco Haus, home of the Taco Meister. Would you like to try an Uber Grande Nacho Platter today?" The female voice sounds as if asking me about the Uber Grande Nacho Platter violates everything she hoped her life would become.

"Um, no," I say. I refer to my Rube Goldberg Protocol manual for the proper 1118 scripting. "I need three schnitzel tacos, hold the guac sauce."

"Anything else?"

"A Bavarian cream churro for dessert. Also, I need the Corporate discount." I don't know what all of this is supposed to mean and it is one of many reasons I wish I could quit this job.

"Hold on," the flat voice says. Long seconds pass and I wonder if perhaps I have been forgotten. I start to remind her of my presence when her disaffected voice rattles from the box. “I have one #2 meal with a Bavarian cream churro for dessert. Pull forward.”

I obey the instructions and when I arrive at the window, a short, dark-haired Hispanic girl dressed in lederhosen hands me a brown bag. Her beauty is startling and I can’t help but stare. She does not smile and her eyes tell me she is either tired or wants to burn the Taco Haus to the ground.

“Here’s your schnitzel tacos and your churro. All with the Corporate discount.” She tells me to enjoy my lunch, but I don’t think she really means it. We have a moment where our eyes lock and she seems to telepathically tell me how much she hates her life right now. I want to tell her telepathically that mine sucks more, but I choose not to. Life Coach Gilbert tells me that I’m too competitive in my relationships, so I’m trying to fix that. Also, extrasensory communication is not one of my strengths, so I’m not sure the caliente lederhosen-wearing drive-thru babe would receive my message. I must be staring too long because she tells me I can take the bag now.

“Unless you need something else,” she adds.

“Just a new life is all,” I say in an effort to be pithy and flirtatious because I’m nothing if not pithy and flirtatious.

“We don’t have those here,” she retorts. “Clearly.”

I park my car in a space facing away from the restaurant and pull from the Taco Haus bag a small touchscreen device enveloped in bubble wrap to review a Power Point presentation on my assignment. I tap the screen and enter my Corporate log in credentials. The familiar Corporate logo of a white ‘C’ in the center of a blue vortex fades into view. A message flashes under the logo:

CLICK THE LOGO TO START THE VIDEO

I tap the screen and the logo swirls not unlike the portal on The Prom Night of Which We Shall Not Speak. I hold the tablet at arm's length because I have a momentary fear the swirl is going to suck me into the tablet and I'll forever be trapped inside it. A male cartoon character with eyes that are too large for his head steps out of the portal. He wears a golf shirt with the Corporate logo on the left side and what I assume are cartoon khakis. He wears a perpetual smile that doesn't endear him at all. Rather, I imagine I will see this character in tonight's nightmares. He will probably be eating apricots.

"Hi! I'm Terry the Corporate Trainer!" His voice is impossibly upbeat and enthusiastic. I'll hear its voice in my nightmares, too. "I'm your virtual guide to the latest learning opportunity from Corporate."

I look around to make sure no one is watching. I should view this training at home so as not to unwittingly divulge proprietary information, but I really don't care. Terry the Trainer continues, but his voice is now so serious I'm afraid he's about to tell me I have a chronic disease or warn me about the dangers of listening to rock music.

"What you are about to see is shocking footage captured on Corporate security cameras." The screen dissolves to grainy images of a figure in cargo pants, a ruffled tuxedo shirt, and a top hat running through the halls of Corporate. Terry the Trainer continues his serious voice as I pull a schnitzel taco from the bag and take a bite.

"Some very sensitive intellectual property was stolen by the person you see here."

I wipe some sauerkraut from my lip with a napkin and my mouth hangs open at the sight of what appears to be Jeff Harper running away from members of Corporate security. He turns and fires a laser at them and they freeze in their tracks.

They don't fall down in pain or writhe in agony. They are simply frozen.

The passenger door of my car flings open and I cry out with the fright of someone who was expecting hot water in the shower, but got cold instead. I turn to spot Randi Williams climbing in and sitting down. She twists and turns in her seat, looking out all the windows. She spots the Taco Haus bag and plucks a schnitzel taco from it.

"Please stop getting in my car without warning," I tell her. "It's not good for my anxiety."

"So, you've seen the video?" She chomps on the taco and then holds it up in admiration. "These shouldn't be as good as they are."

"Is that…" I point at the figure on the video. I can't finish my question because I know the answer.

"It's Jeff," Randi says with a mouth full of Mexican-German fusion food.

Onscreen, Jeff rounds a corner and fires a weapon at another group of Corporate employees. The victims don't die, but rather begin dancing in a kick line like the Rockettes.

"We don't know why the people are dancing," Randi says, "but, they're very talented. It's possible Jeff has possession of behavioral alteration weaponry."

"Why was Jeff at Corporate?" I ask. "Did he steal something from there, too?"

"I can't tell you that," she says, whipping her head around and looking out the windows. "You'll have to come Corporate later today. We'll meet with Max at two o'clock."

"Not that again," I huff.

"What did you mean by 'steal something from there, too?'" She takes the last bite of her taco and tosses the wrapper into the bag.

"I saw him last night. He was stealing Kwench-Aid from the plant my dad works at."

"I'm sorry." Randi shakes her head. "Did you say stealing Kwench-Aid?"

"Yeah. I don't know why." I tap the screen to pause the video and it freezes on the image of Jeff. "But it was definitely him. He was driving *Miss America*. I chased after him, but he sorta disappeared on the highway."

"Interesting." She peeks in the bag and then looks at me. "Are you gonna eat that last taco?"

"Take it," I say. "Leave the churro."

"See you later at HQ. Two o'clock." She gets out of my car, heads to a strip mall across the street, and disappears into one of those stores where everything costs a dollar.

"This is a lot of work to schedule a meeting," I say to myself.

I start my car and exit the Taco Haus parking lot, but not before taking a lap around the building in the hopes of catching a glimpse of the caliente lederhosen-wearing drive-thru babe. I don't get a good look, though, because that's my life. Leaving the parking lot, I spot an RV parked in the corner. The vehicle is black with orange flames painted down the side of it. A sign reading MIRROR BALL ENTERTAINMENTS is plastered on the driver's side door. Five sketchy figures emerge from this tacky ride looking as if they've slept in the same clothes since 1974. Their faces are ruddy and harsh. One of them, a particularly grimy character calls back to the RV.

"C'mon, Mel! Get a move on!"

The one I assume is called Mel climbs out and rubs his face while finishing the task of putting on his pants.

Carnies. Not a fan. I don't fear them the way I do spiders, but on my List of Scary Shit carnies are definitely in the top three between spiders and people in those mascot costumes at sporting events.

*

Corporate Headquarters sits alone along a private paved road about five miles south of town. The story goes that the founder of the company, a man named Simon Tybalt, bought up all the land to build this complex. You can't see it well for the trees which line the road. A high, ivy-covered fence topped with barbed wire hides behind the trees. I steer my trusty Corolla off the road and onto the short driveway. A security gate blocks my entrance. My #2 value meal from Taco Haus included a hasenpfeffer burrito and a lanyard with an ID badge providing access to a sexual harassment seminar. The online information from Terry the Trainer provided clear instructions:

- *Swipe your ID badge at the key pad.*
- *Enter code 1968.*
- *Engage in the security dialogue.*
- *Present your badge to the security guard and they will provide you with your training packet.*

I swipe the badge and enter the code and draw a deep breath in anticipation of the security dialogue. Certain security clearances require an extra level of verification. This means engaging in a precise verbal exchange with a disembodied voice. The script for this conversation is displayed on my tablet, yet I feel as if I don't need it. Even though I've only been to Corporate once before for orientation, a strange sense of déjà vu washes over me like I've done this a million times before. I know the dialogue by heart even though I've never seen it before. The security box beeps and the disembodied voice speaks to me.

"State your business here, please." The voice is female.

I clear my throat. "Yes, I'm here for the sexual harassment training."

"Why? Are you wanting to be sexually harassed or do you wish to perform the harassment yourself?

"Neither," I respond. "It's a seminar on Corporate policies regarding sexual harassment."

"I get sexually harassed all the time. I can tell you the policy. Don't be an asshole who hits on women in the workplace. How hard is that?"

"It's not hard at all," I say.

"You're probably picturing me naked right now, aren't you?"

Even though I know this is only a script for the security dialogue, I'm still taken aback by her question. Mainly because, yes, I was picturing her naked and I'm ashamed of myself. I also imagine she is wearing glasses.

"No," I lie. "Not at all."

"Of course, you were," the voice chastises. "You can't help it. You think I'm naked because you don't see me as a business partner who brings value to the organization."

"I think you bring a lot of value," I tell her and, even though it's dialogue, I mean it.

"I'm a disembodied voice," she says. "I don't even have a name. Why wouldn't my designers give me a name? Who sexually harasses a nameless disembodied voice?"

"Not me."

"Whatever, dude. Go to your little seminar."

Our script ends and the gate slides open as per protocol, but I get the impression she didn't really want to let me in. The five-story building looms over a massive paved parking lot like something from a dystopian future. The campus spreads out into four wings on each side. Cars cover the parking lot in all directions as I drive toward the front to visitor parking. No particular protocol exists for where I'm supposed to park. I don't feel like walking a long way in this heat.

My stomach knots as I enter through the revolving door into the lobby. Usually meetings with Max or Randi occur at a remote location or information is relayed via Rube Goldberg protocols and Terry the Trainer, so this is like entering the home of a great uncle you just met. The lobby is spacious and bustling with people milling about carrying laptops, tablets, and file folders. Two sets of stairs curve on either side of the atrium leading to a second level of Plexiglas windows and doors. A large engraved sign hangs above the stairwell proclaiming the Corporate vision statement:

TO BRING HUMANITY CLOSER AROUND THE GLOBE AND ACROSS THE UNIVERSE WHILE MAKING AS MUCH MONEY AS POSSIBLE

I stand with my mouth open at the immensity of this place. It occurs to me I don't know where the Rings of Saturn room is.

"Can I help you, young man?"

I look for the voice calling to me and spot a duo of security guards. One is short and thin while the other is more rotund. They remind me of David Spade and Chris Farley, but the thin one's security badge identifies him as Jerry. The Farley one's badge says his name is Dale. I approach them. It sounds like they're watching YouTube videos. Dale is probably older than my dad but younger than my grandpa. Jerry's age is harder to determine. Do they know what really goes on here? Do they wonder? This cloak-and-dagger secrecy is exhausting.

"You look lost." Jerry speaks. His voice is pleasant and welcoming. "Can I help you find what you're looking for?"

After the slightest pause, I respond. "Yes. I'm here to meet with Max Gentry to debrief a covert operation and provide information about an impending alien invasion."

He frowns slightly and checks a clipboard for the meeting I've described. "Are you sure that's today? I don't see it on this list."

"I'm kidding. I'm here for sexual harassment training."

"Are they training you how to sexually harass?" Dale asks with a playful grin. "Hell, I can give you some pointers on that, fella." He wheezes out another laugh that morphs into a full body cough and hands me a three-ring binder. His cough wanes but not enough to form words so he points at a clipboard with a sign-in sheet. Pretending to laugh at something I don't think is funny is not one of my strengths, so I produce a short snicker-snort-chortle combo pack I imagine folks in a Corporate breakroom produce in such scenarios before walking away.

"Rings of Saturn room," the wheezing security guard calls out. "Take the elevator to the fourth floor, hang a right. You can't miss it."

I walk toward the elevators straight ahead. Behind the Plexiglass above, people scurry about from place to place. Some wear suits and ties, some wear khakis and polo shirts. Most everyone walks with purpose. A man and woman enter the elevator and stand in front of me. They press the button for the third floor. They do not look at one another as they speak. Instead, their eyes are glued to their tablets.

"Fourth floor, please," I say and they honor my request. The man huffs as he swipes his tablet screen.

"That new Senior Data Architect is really busting my balls over these recontextualization reports," he says. "I'm pretty sure he expects us to pull this information from the RDB."

"RDB?" asks the woman.

"Rectal Database. You know, he wants us to pull it out of our ass."

The woman grunts in agreement as she looks at her tablet. "Don't I know it. It's not realistic. That information does not resonate with my call center people."

"The call center fields a variety of customer service calls," I blurt. "The array of topics our customers call about range from invoice validation to billing inquiries, from shipping confirmation to order processing. While Corporate is dedicated to maintaining its vision for high-end technological solutions for our customers, we also believe in the value of human-to-human interaction with them."

The pair turns to me as if I'm a little kid who told a dick joke at Thanksgiving dinner. I place my hand over my mouth to prevent more less-than-fascinating information from spilling. Why in am I doing this? Why do I know this crap? I didn't even know Corporate had a call center.

The elevator stops at their floor and the man and woman walk away to deal with recontextualization reports and rectal databases. It occurs to me not all alien life resides beyond the portal. Sometimes strange creatures who speak unintelligible languages are right under our noses.

Emerging onto the fourth floor, I am greeted rudely by brilliant light from too many fluorescent bulbs overhead. A large black-and-white photograph dominates most of the right wall of the hallway. It's a portrait of a man wearing a sad, contemplative smile. A scruffy peppery beard covers his cheeks and chin and he hand rests against his face in a contemplative pose. A quote appears next to him.

> *The day is coming when all shall know.*
> *Simon Tybalt, founder of Corporate*
> *1967-2010*

The Rings of Saturn room is an unimpressive meeting place with a long conference table filling much of the middle. A flat screen television hangs at one end and a white board at the other. The wall across from me features a large motivational poster in a bold frame of faux mahogany. The image on the poster is a tiny sailboat being tossed on stormy waves as ominous clouds loom overhead. The word courage stands tall under the image in bluish-gray letters. I squint to read the caption underneath.

We can no longer wait for the storm to pass; we must be courageous enough to sail through it.

I roll my eyes at the sentiment. I've seen such items before in office buildings and at school. I hate them. If you need pithy quotes attached to a generic image to inspire you at work, you're in the wrong job.

"Ah, Tony." Max Gentry enters the room and shakes my hand. Randi follows close behind.

"I appreciate you coming in on such short notice," Max says and gestures to a fruit tray on a credenza. "Help yourself to some catering." I fill a tray with pineapple and watermelon because I realize I'm starving. I shovel in fruit like I'm competing in some health food speed-eating contest. Max's phone rings and he apologizes and tells us he really must take this call. Randi takes a seat at the table so I sit next to her.

"It's good to see you," she whispers. "We really need you. This is big."

Max ends his call and sits across from us with a file folder. "Enjoying the catering?"

"This is good pineapple." I shove another piece in my mouth.

"We wanted to recognize you for all your efforts," he says. "Randi has a gift for you."

Randi reaches under the table and produces a gift bag and hands it to me. Sprawled across the bag are the words THANKS FOR BEING AWESOME! in a joyous font. Inside the bag is a coffee cup filled with jelly beans and a gift card to a local coffee shop called You're Grounded. Tied to the handle of the bag is a Mylar balloon. Both the balloon and mug also say "THANKS FOR BEING AWESOME!"

"What's this for?" I ask.

"First, it's long overdue after what you've been through," Max says. "I'm impressed with the way you've engaged adaptive action items in an effort to re-energize your potential as human capital."

I don't understand what he's saying so I nod and shove some watermelon chunks into my mouth.

"You have maximized functional personal schemas and achieved a respectable level of growth I find highly sustainable." He stands and retrieves a remote control from the credenza while I wipe watermelon juice from my chin.

"Do you know what he's saying?" I whisper to Randi.

"I never do," she says. "Just nod and say things like 'absolutely' and 'agreed.'"

"Agreed." I nod.

"Let's get started on this," Randi says. "We've got a lot of work to do. There's been a breach at the portal. Several, actually."

"Yes." Max points the remote at the flat screen. Video footage of the portal opening plays as he continues speaking in some unintelligible language. Blips of light shooting out from the portal fill the screen. "A systematic infiltration of our world by unidentified entities has put us on high alert. We need to rapidiously actualize our bandwidth in an effort to proactively expedite pandemic strategic imperatives. My ask is that you help us with this project. Will you help us, Tony?"

"Absolutely," I say, my mouth full of one last piece of fruit. "I even concur."

"Don't overdo it," Randi mumbles under her breath.

"Excellent!" Max reaches into his pocket and produces one of his beloved sour apple lollipops. He offers one to both Randi and me. "They help me stay energized."

"No, thanks." I instead stand and fill another plate with the fruit they must've had catered by heaven itself. "Do these breaches have anything to do with Grandor and The Prom Night of Which We Shall Not Speak?"

"The what?" Randi asks.

"I mean, the night Jeff disappeared."

"We're not sure," Max says. "We still have a Tiger Team devoted to investigating any compelling connections or synergies between these data points."

I'm not sure if his statement warrants an "absolutely" or an "agreed." I contemplate my response while enjoying another piece of the most sumptuous watermelon I've ever tasted. Should I tell Max now about seeing what I think was Jeff last night? I'm not sure I can trust this situation.

"This is what we know." Randi speaks while Max projects a series of images on the flat screen. The first is Grandor the Malevolent posing in what looks like a rejected Hollister photo shoot. "Grandor the Malevolent has a history of invading a planet, terraforming it and turning it into a resort for other alien lifeforms. These life forms usually possess a nefarious reputation for engaging in organized crime."

"Gangster aliens?" I ask.

"Something like that," she says. "They're usually not good dudes."

"Grandor relies heavily on these organizations to invest in his properties." Max adds. The image of Grandor dissolves into a spinning globe similar to that of Earth. As Randi speaks, images appear around the globe such as water slides, golf, and snow skiing.

"The data from gathered intelligence suggests Grandor has targeted Earth for his next vacation spot."

"How does he terraform a planet into a vacation resort?" I ask.

"This." Max points his own remote at the flat screen. I study the image projected there, a device resembling a futuristic garbage disposal. It looks familiar to me, but I don't know why. It's like seeing a photograph of someone you once knew, but can't place from where. I'm also jealous because I want a remote, too.

"What is that?" I ask. "And how do I get my own remote?"

"A quintonium drive," Max replies. "Quintonium is a substance found in the furthest corners of the galaxy. In its natural state it is very volatile, but when processed through this drive, it has the power to terraform a planet into whatever Grandor programs it to."

"That's a lot of power," I say. "Seems like it would destroy whatever it is aimed at."

"Grandor has developed sophisticated programming that turns this into more of an uber 3-D printer," Randi says. "He turned a backwater moon into a miniature golf course."

"That's crazy," I mutter.

"That's nothing," she adds. "The 418th hole is guarded by a giant underground worm. If you don't get a hole-in-one, you're toast."

"The quitonium drive is believed to be the most powerful machine in the known galaxies," Max says. "Some intelligence even suggest it can open portals and even create new ones."

"Who's been guarding the portal?" I ask.

"Max and I have rotated shifts on that," Randi says.

Max puts his hands on my shoulders. "Tony, we need your effervescent ability to deliver core competencies."

I look to Randi for translation.

"You're a great intern," she tells me.

"Agreed."

"Your assignment is two-fold, Tony." Max points his remote once more at the flat screen and a small spider device appears. "Randi?"

"This nanotech is the possible key to all of this. We believe it's why Grandor the Malevolent was here and we also believe it is the reason for the recent breaches."

"What is it exactly?" I ask. "And why does it have to look like a spider? I hate spiders."

"It's an interesting piece of cybernetic technology," she says. "We believe Grandor wants to steal this nanotechnology to turn humans into robotic servants for his new resort."

Something sparks in my brain. The same sensation I had when I spouted off about the American Dream to Dad or the invention of ice cream to Life Coach Gilbert or the Corporate call center on the elevator earlier. It's the exact vibe I got when I recognized Randi's weapon last night.

"That's Araneae," I blurt. "Araneae."

"How do you know that?" Randi asks.

"It enters the bloodstream of its host like a parasite and finds its way to the host's brain stem." I speak as if I wrote the device's instruction manual. "Once there, it has the capacity to control the host and even take over its consciousness. It's more than a nanotech. This nanotech was developed by Corporate Labs in 2006 as a means of creating field agents with enhanced abilities."

"What the hell?" Randi walks to me and stares into my eyes. I continue spouting off about the Araneae like I'm speaking in tongues.

"Host subjects can dramatically conceptualize an expanded array of action items and core competencies in an effort to holistically engineer high-payoff scenarios."

I snap back to reality, aware of my blabbering but clueless as to why.

"What happened?" I gasp. "Why did I do that? What's wrong with me?"

"How do you know about this?" Max asks. Randi keeps staring at me.

"You're making me uncomfortable," I tell her.

"I could say the same about you," she says.

I back away from them toward the door. I want to leave, climb into my car, purchase the necessary equipment to turn my car into a time machine and travel back to the point in my life before I worked for Corporate. Then, I'd never apply for the job and none of this would be happening. That seems like a perfectly logical solution to my problem right now.

"How long has this been going on?" Randi asks me.

"It's been happening to me. I recognize stuff. I know stuff. I don't know how."

Max rubs his face. "We need to act with urgency here. We need to proactively expedite mission critical deliverables."

"Agreed," I say.

He steps to the whiteboard, picks up a marker and starts scribbling. "Let's quickly brainstorm short-term, low-impact solutions. First, we need to send you through the portal."

My chest tightens and my breathing becomes labored. I bend over and grab my knees. I'm sure I'm about to fall over.

"The video you obtained from Taco Haus," Max says, "is Jeff stealing the Araneae plans last night. It is our belief he is stealing them for Grandor in exchange for his girlfriend."

"Leigh Ann," I say. "Her name is Leigh Ann."

He scribbles more on the whiteboard while Randi puts her hand on my back to calm me. I don't think it's working because the pineapple and watermelon I ate are threatening to escape my stomach and splat on the floor.

"I can't go through the portal," I say. "No freaking way."

"Tony." Randi gently pulls me upright. "You need to tell him about the Kwench-Aid."

"Kwench-Aid?" Max puts down the marker. "What Kwench-Aid?"

"I saw Jeff last night. He was stealing Kwench-Aid from the plant my dad works at."

"I'm sorry," Max says. "Did you say stealing Kwench-Aid?"

"I know, right?" Randi says.

"This is a radically facilitated paradigm shift," Max says.

"Absolutely."

"Meet me tonight at the portal," Randi says, handing me the THANKS FOR BEING AWESOME! gifts. "10:00 p.m."

"I don't know," I say. "This is feels so much bigger than me."

"Of course it is," she tells me.

"This is so much to take in at once. I'm not sure if I can do this."

"I see it all perfectly; there are two possible situations –"

"Don't say it." I cut her off with a wave of my hand. "I'll be there."

"Excellent." Max shuts off the flat screen and walks toward the door. "I need to close the loop here and get to a meeting with our fleet operations folks. Tony, I have no doubt you will competently model principle-centered expertise. It's good to have you back."

"Agreed."

CHAPTER FIVE

I drive through Poplar Bluff after my meeting at Corporate. It is now after 5:00 p.m. and I'm still full after devouring more pineapple, watermelon, and cantaloupe in one sitting than the entire population of Delaware consumed in 2015. My brain reels from the information presented to me during the Jeff Stole Nanotech Reveal and the Meet Randi At The Portal Directive. My best friend, the one with an obsession over a classic rock band and a tendency to clean his ears with his car keys, not only survived the portal, but is actively engaging in larceny. I stop at a red light in downtown and glance over at the copy of *Something Wicked This Way Comes* laying in the passenger seat. The packet of green Kwench-Aid sits next to it and I pick it up. Why is Jeff stealing Kwench-Aid? Why did he steal the nanotech?

A caravan of trucks hauling carnival attractions and rides barrels through the intersection. Among the trucks is the black RV with orange flames I saw at Taco Haus. I assume they are headed to the River Luau to set up shop and unleash their unsafe rides and array of deep-fried diabetes on our town. I've never been a fan of the River Luau, despite my mom's participation in its planning. I can't stand its cultural appropriation. I dislike the rides which appear to be assembled with duct tape, toothpicks, and wishful thinking. One ride in particular, Mo-Mo the Monster, is a nightmarish contraption with eight legs. Attached to each leg is a two-person car which spins as the legs move up and down. Mo-Mo the Monster exists only to induce vomiting.

I enjoy nothing about the River Luau except the frozen lemonade and roasted turkey legs. Marlene loves the River Luau. She dragged me there last summer against my better judgment and I spent the evening making excuses for not getting on the rides and watching her eat her body weight in funnel cakes and foot-long corndogs. That was the night we said we loved each other for the first time.

The memory triggers my other issue: seeing Marlene visit Someone Else's Books last night and whether or I should look further into this. I make a couple of turns and park outside Someone Else's Books. I'm not exactly sure what I'm going to do when I go in. Should I ask Kevin about seeing Marlene here last night? Would he then ask why I was following Marlene? Would I feel compelled to admit to stalking the girlfriend I broke up with before prom because I'm a jackass? I should drive away.

"The hell with it," I mutter to myself and head to the front door.

"Tone-Man!" Kevin Raulston waves to me from his desk behind the counter as I enter. "I'm about to close, so please tell me you're here to contribute to my livelihood."

"Yes. Yes, I am." I'm a terrible liar. He can see right through me, I know it. I look around for the current events section. "Do you have any books on dream interpretation?"

"Whatcha been dreaming about, me compadre?"

"Apricots."

"Interesting." Kevin turns and taps the keys of his laptop. "Do you have any idea how many possible interpretations there are for a given dream?"

"Curious about a nightmare I've been having. So, do you have any books? Are you checking your inventory there?"

"No. The internet. It says here seeing apricots in a dream suggests something is not as it seems. But, dream interpretation is influenced by spiritual beliefs, psychological schools of thought, and whether or not you think everything is a penis or a vagina. So, really, it could be anything."

"The interpretation of dreams is the royal road to a knowledge of the unconscious activities of the mind," I tell him because it just popped into my head the way so many random things seem to be doing lately. "Freud said that."

"Reality is wrong.," he counters. "Dreams are real. Tupac said that." He moves toward the counter and leans into me. "You ok there, Tone-Man? Aura suggests you're conflicted and experiencing some inner turmoil."

"It's been an interesting few weeks." My hands tremble so I shove them into my pockets. Kevin looks around the front room and leans in to me.

"You haven't run into any Herpezoids have you?" he whispers.

"Herpezoids?" A flash of recognition from a part of my brain I don't normally use surges and I begin speaking on a topic I know nothing about, except I do somehow. "They're basically the out of control frat boys of the galaxy. They infiltrate a planet, take over human forms, and then wreak havoc." I stop talking because I have no idea why or how I'm able to explain an alien life form I've never even heard of.

"Oh, yeah, man. So, you're hip to them. You know they exist." Kevin's eyes widen. "Herpezoids are everywhere. They want to take over the world. Conspiracy theorists believe they've infiltrated the highest levels of politics and Hollywood, but, I know better. They're masked as everyday people." He darts his eyes about the front room. "Could be one in this store right now. Watching us."

I turn slowly and watch a short, round elderly woman waddle up and set a stack of romance paperbacks on the counter.

"Here, Kevin. I got me some more smut." She giggles scandalously as she fishes in her purse for money, Kevin points at her and mouths a word at me.

"Her. Puh. Zoid."

The short, round woman looks at me and offers a kind smile. She pats my forearm and her soft, baggy eyes lock on mine. She squeezes my forearm enough for me to think she might keep squeezing until she rips it from my elbow and beats me with it. Her grip loosens and she maintains that sweet smile as she walks past me and out the door. Kevin looks at me, eyes round with fear.

"We're lucky she didn't feast on our flesh, man."

I blow out a sigh.

"That was kinda weird," I say.

"Herpezoids, Tone-Man. They're everywhere. Even in sweet little old ladies who read softcore erotica and eat dinner at 4:00."

The bell on the front door chimes and Marlene comes in. My heart pounds against my chest like it's locked in a dark closet and crying for release. The moisture in my mouth evaporates.

"Hi, Kevin," she says. "I finished that book you ordered for me."

"And did you find the ending to your satisfaction?" Kevin asks.

"Very much so. Do you have my new order?" Her voice is tense and curt. Her eyes show an intensity I've never noticed in her before.

"Right here." Kevin grabs a manila envelope from his desk and hands it to Marlene who hugs it and turns to me.

"How are you, Tony?" She looks not so much at me as past me. She doesn't smile.

My heart winces. Whenever she was upset with me, she used my first name only. She told me once that whenever she was in trouble with her parents they would call her by her full name. She wanted to do the opposite, so, she would call me Tony Pershing when she was, as she put it, really feeling the love for me. I should tell her that I'm miserable and vomit emotionally all over the place.

"You know. Fine." That's the best I can come up with. She doesn't respond, but she doesn't leave either. The intense gaze softens and she bites her delicate bottom lip, as if she's daring me to seize this moment to dazzle her with a grand romantic gesture and woo her back away from the flat-billed cap wearing Clint. "What's your book?" Again, the best I can come up with.

"This? Oh, one of those supernatural YA novels. It's stupid, but sometimes I need to turn my brain off and not think about things, ya know?"

"Yeah, I'd like to not think about things. Shut everything off."

She nods slightly as our eyes meet and I sense the same kind of telepathic communication I had with the caliente lederhosen-wearing drive-thru babe. Her eyes are telling me to keep talking, give her a reason to stay. They are practically screaming at me to take her into my arms, kiss her deeply, and tell her that she is the love of my life. I've never felt so strongly about anything. I step toward her, but she moves away.

"Ok, I gotta go," she blurts. "Thanks for the book, Kevin. How long do you think it'll take me to read it?"

"You're a fast reader," Kevin says. "You could probably have it done before tomorrow night."

Marlene nods and turns to leave. Before walking out the door, she spins back to me. "It's good to see you, Tony Pershing."

A wide grin sweeps across my face and my heart dances. "She called me Tony Pershing," I say.

"Yes, she did," Kevin says. "And if she had been a Herpezoid she would've eaten your throat."

*

If the apricot nightmares are to be believed, then nothing is as it seems. What I have believed to be true is not. Why was Marlene at Someone Else's Books the other night? What are these packages she keeps picking up? I think about the irony of being suspicious of the girl I love while I keep a major secret from her. I should come clean with her about everything, but I also should move on with my life.

After the Another Impromptu Marlene Encounter at Someone Else's Books, I drive home to grab a bite to eat and tell Mom and Dad about working late tonight. I walk in the door and find them in the living room gathering their journals and copies of *A Feast of Crows.*

"Leaving for book club already?" I ask. "It's only six o'clock."

"We're going out to eat first," Mom tells me. "Did you go to work?"

"I met with my boss and she told me I was welcome back. I'm actually going to go in for the overnight tonight."

"Good to see you're getting back into the swing of things." Dad grabs his car keys from the coffee table. "Guess you're not getting in until the morning."

"Yeah, they need some help sorting out some shipments in the mailroom." I hate myself for lying to them about my job at Corporate. I know their lives. They work. They watch all the versions of *Law & Order.* They attend their book club. They're transparent with me while I'm a big fat lying liar who lies. Add to it that I'm planning to go through a portal to outer space and my guilt is crushing.

"I wish you weren't working those overnights." Mom squeezes my forearm. "You need to socialize more, honey. Get out and do fun stuff, too."

"Like joining a book club?" I tease. "You guys are really into it."

"It's better than what she wanted to do," Dad says. "She wanted to learn country line dancing. I'd rather be disemboweled with salad tongs than learn country line dancing."

"Oh, Chris." Mom punches his shoulder. "You're no fun."

The sight of them smiling together overwhelms me. I need to tell them what's going on.

"Mom? Dad?"

They both look at me still wearing their playful smiles. They're expecting something from me now and I know I should tell them everything. The whole wild, crazy, universe-altering truth is on the tip of my tongue ready to leap out and shatter their entire understanding of reality. Suddenly that seems like too much to lay on these sweet people who are about to go to a book club. I am now aware I'm staring at them with nothing to say.

"What is it, honey?" Mom asks.

"I love you guys," I finally say. "Thanks for being here for me. Have fun tonight."

They smile and hug me before heading out the door. I flop onto the couch and close my eyes. Working overnights requires a nap if I'm going to be sharp. I draw and release a deep breath before drifting into a sleep I hope doesn't involve apricots.

*

If you're going to do something you truly will regret, I recommend a nap first. Nothing awakens your soul for the coming doom of poor decision-making like a good nap. A few z's preceded my attempt to fly by jumping off the roof when I was seven. A short rest enabled me to fully embrace the stupidity of drinking a pizza Jeff pureed in a blender. A lovely afternoon siesta served as the prologue to breaking up with Marlene. Now that I've slept for a couple of hours, I'm ready to do something truly ill-advised.

I'm going to go to Marlene's house and try to tell her I want her back.

I drive with "Bubbly" on repeat, and brainstorm what I'm going to say. Nothing plausible is really coming to mind, but I'm sure once I start talking it will flow naturally. A rush of panic envelops me and I question if I should do this. I don't want to look stupid. I grip the steering wheel and remember Randi's words once more from The Prom Night of Which We Shall Never Speak:

I see it all perfectly; there are two possible situations – one can either do this or that. My honest opinion and my friendly advice is this: do it or do not do it. You will regret both.

I draw a deep breath to cleanse my nerves as I turn onto her street, slowing as I approach her driveway. My heart drops when she walks out her door with Clint. They kiss before he climbs into the Truck of Overcompensation. I can't duck this time and we all make eye contact as I pass them uncomfortably. Clint shoots me a glance that suggests our next encounter will end violently. Marlene looks sad. I shut off "Bubbly" and drive in quiet.

Kierkegaard is a dick.

*

The clock in my car reads 9:42 p.m. Time to go to work.

I pull into a convenience store to get gas and pick up a hot dog, two taquitos, and a soda. No other cars on the parking lot, so I should be able to get my business done quickly. I likely won't get a break tonight so I might as well get sustenance now. The selection of pre-portal guarding food is important. I approach the counter and set my stuff down. An older woman with a cup of coffee gets in line behind me and I recognize her as the short round lady Kevin accused of being a Herpezoid.

"I remember you," I tell her. "You bought some books at Kevin's earlier."

"Oh, yes," she smiles and touches my arm. "I do love going there. I simply must have my stories to read before going to bed." Her eyes twinkle and nose scrunches as she smiles and it couldn't possibly be more adorable.

"I understand that." I turn to the clerk behind the counter to pay. "Tell you what. Put her coffee on my tab. My treat."

"Oh, you don't have to do that," she says. "Besides, I was going to get dip."

"I'm sorry?"

"Dip. Chew. Smokeless tobacco." She offers a sheepish grin. "My only vice."

"That's okay." I'm thrown, but I'm committed to seeing this nice gesture through to completion. "Get the lady her dip, kind sir."

The clerk, who wears the facial expression of a disaffected mannequin, rings me up and I exit the store, the short round woman with the smokeless tobacco habit following. She stick a pinch between her cheek and gums before we're even out the door. She thanks me once more and I simply nod and walk to my car at the pumps. A motor scooter ridden by someone in a dark t-shirt and jogging shorts enters the parking lot. They've made the wise choice to wear a helmet. I assume the rider is female due to their smooth, sexy legs, but I don't want to make sexist assumptions. I toss my food in the passenger seat next to my copy of *Something Wicked This Way Comes* and take a swig of soda.

I start to pull away but my path out of the store is blocked by the same short round elderly woman and a man I recognize as Life Coach Gilbert. Their expressions mirror the same vacuous, hollow one as the clerk in the store. I get out of the car and step toward them.

"Life Coach Gilbert?" I ask him and then look to the woman with the bad tobacco habit. "Can I help you? Ma'am?"

They don't answer. Instead, they move toward me with urgent, determined steps. I back up, but trip on the front of my car and lose my balance. I try to steady myself, but Life Coach Gilbert is on me quickly. He grabs me by the throat and lifts me off the ground. I struggle to break his grip. The old woman produces a gun that looks like a chrome derringer from her purse and aims it at me.

"What the hell?" I gurgle.

"We are here to serve." Life Coach Gilbert's voice is empty and flat.

"We are here to serve," repeats the woman.

Before she pulls the trigger, the scooter rider roundhouse kicks the old lady in the stomach. My would-be assailant drops her weapon and falls to her knees. Life Coach Gilbert releases his death grip and turns to the rider. I gasp and choke and run to my trunk to grab a laser pistol from my Corporate duffle bag. I hold the gun out in front and step toward the Good Samaritan on the motor scooter. She wields what looks like glowing nun chucks, swinging them with swift precision at Life Coach Gilbert. Streams of blue electricity zap with each blow to his torso and he recoils. She lands two wallops and he drops to the ground, convulses, and passes out. The old woman is now on her feet and punches the rider in the kidney. My hero cries out and for the first time I can see her fresh freckled face and blond hair in the light. My stomach drops and my breath stops.

"Marlene!" I call out. She turns to me and our eyes meet for a brief second. This proves a distraction to her and the old woman lands another body blow. Marlene grunts and spins away to regain an advantage. She starts spinning her electric nun chucks. Her surprisingly worthy elderly opponent backs up in defense. Marlene continues her advance and strikes the old lady across the jaw with a blow from the nun chucks. This knocks the dip out of the woman's mouth as she spills to the pavement in a heap. The old lady hits the ground right after.

"Are they dead?" I look around to see if anyone noticed or maybe spot the convenience store clerk coming out to investigate. No one is around. "They look dead."

"No." Marlene pulls a small Taser-looking device from her waistband. "Just unconscious." She rolls each of the bodies over onto their stomachs and sticks the device to their neck for a few seconds.

"What did you do?"

"Deprogrammed them. They were about to turn." She pulls her cell phone from her pocket and makes a call. "Targets located and subdued. Situation secure here. Call 911 so these two can be looked after."

She ends her call, stomps toward me and grabs my face. She kisses me and the warmth of her soft lips turns my knees to plasticine. Her hand caresses my hair on the back of my head and for these brief seconds all is right with the world again. She pulls away and looks in my eyes.

"You shouldn't have broken off our prom date, you jerk tool head. And you need to stop driving by my house because it's a little creepy even though I know you're not creepy. Just a jerk tool head." She kisses me again with a quick peck and then gestures to the two bodies. "By this way, this never happened."

I should speak but my lips still tingle from her kiss so forming consonants is out of the question. She jogs to her motor scooter, wisely puts her helmet on, and speeds away.

*

I drive toward the portal with the Marlene-Is-Some-Kind-Of-Ninja Encounter still playing in my mind and my lips still tingling from her kiss. Her words to me were "this never happened." What never happened? The assault on a seemingly possessed old woman and my therapist? The kiss? All of it? What did she mean by "deprogramming them?" I don't know what to do with this information. I keep thinking my sudden infinite knowledge of all things random will kick in and inform me, but it is dormant, I guess. Never around when I need it.

I chastise myself for driving by Marlene's house so much. It's sad, pathetic, and even a little creepy. She even said so. I can't help it, though. I'm drawn to her. I like to sometimes think of high school as a microcosm of the universe and its celestial bodies. Some people fit together in a well-ordered galaxy that functions as it should. Others form black holes that suck people into an awfulness from which they can't escape. A few of the so-called popular kids view themselves as suns around which all others orbit. I think most are stars singularly shining as best they can. My best friend Jeff Harper was a quark. My favorite object in the night sky is a binary star, which is really two stars that can't operate without each other; orbiting together around a shared bond. That's how I see Marlene and me. Binary stars.

*

Tonight is the first time I've been to the portal since the Prom Night of Which We Shall Never Speak. Everything looks the same. Large signs proclaiming this to be private property and trespassers shall be prosecuted still line the roadside. Thick brush and tall trees hide the 10-foot tall electrified fence around the perimeter. The same automated security checkpoint is still there to run me through the same overly complicated drill to enter. I swipe my Corporate ID to initiate.

"Welcome, Tony Pershing," says the voice inside the box. "Please initiate Rube Goldberg Protocol 819 for clearance."

"I don't want to follow Rube Goldberg Protocol 819." I promise this is what I'm supposed to say.

"What do you mean you don't want to?" The voice becomes defensive per the Protocol. "You must follow the instructions as directed to gain access."

"You don't have to get so defensive. I'm merely expressing I don't want to follow the Protocol. Let me in, please." I let out an audible sigh. According to the Protocol, it must be an audible sigh for the voice to respond.

"I'm merely trying to do my job. It's not easy being a disembodied voice out in the middle of nowhere. No one comes by to visit. I don't get to take breaks. I don't have a pension. I'm a voice designed to serve one function and here you come trying to take away my sole reason for existence."

"You're right." Now, the next sequence is critical. If not said verbatim, the whole dialogue must start over again. "I'm very sorry for my petulant attitude. You bring value to our organization. Please accept my apology."

The voice in the box waits for exactly five seconds before responding.

"Apology accepted."

I once asked Randi why such a production was necessary for entering a secure area and she told me Simon Tybalt, the founder of Corporate created that particular Rube Goldberg Protocol because there was no way anyone could figure it out.

The gate slides open and I pull my car forward through the open field toward the river approximately one hundred yards away. I shut my engine off, take a breath, and get out of my car. The summer night air is thick and oppressive. The trees are still and the cicadas and frogs sing. I wonder if they know about the portal. Randi stands at the bank of the river and points her Multi-Phaseable Portal Accessibility Sensor Device.

"Seems calm for now," she says, "but that could change."

I don't answer because all I can focus on is Marlene kicking the collective ass of Life Coach Gilbert and the little old lady whose name I don't even know.

"Hey." Randi taps my arm. "You okay?"

"Yeah. Sorry. It's weird being back here."

"I get that."

"Do you think Jeff will come through?" I retrieve my bag of weaponry from the trunk and put on the familiar protective vest. It occurs to me I'm not sure how this vest will protect me from anything.

"Maybe." Randi pulls her weapon from her hip for inspection. "Could be Grandor. Could be some other life form. It's been crazy."

"How has Jeff been getting through?"

"He has weapons that disable our interns. That's all I know. The security footage has been erased somehow."

"What do we do to Jeff if he comes through?"

"Rube Goldberg Protocols state we must detain him in a conference room, give him an online assessment to complete, and then wipe his brain of all memories."

"Wipe his brain? That sounds very unethical."

"It's never been done before." She holds her sensor toward the river once more. "But, civilians can't know what's going on here. He's putting the portal and our entire operation at risk. If word gets out about this to the general public, it'll be a shit storm unlike you've ever seen."

My stomach knots and my hands shake. I don't want to be here. The portal scares me now more than ever. Before, it was a mysterious, unknown entity. After the Prom Night of Which We Shall Never Speak, I know something lies beyond. Because of Jeff's adventures, I know passage back and forth is possible. Because of my conversation at Corporate, I know other aliens have come through and could still be here.

"What about the other life forms?" I ask Randi. "What are they? Have they been found?"

"We have a special project team assigned to find them," she tells me. "It's a team we were grooming you for before everything happened."

That statement twists the already massive knot in my gut. "What does this team do when they find them?"

She walks to me and locks her eyes on mine. "Whatever they have to."

"I don't think I'd be very good at that." I walk back to my car and retrieve the drink I bought at the convenience store. I can barely hold the cup in my trembling hand. "I don't think I'm really cut out for any of this. I don't know what I'm supposed to be doing anymore."

"You know," she says, returning to her weapon to its holster, "to forget one's purpose is the commonest form of stupidity."

"That's harsh."

"That's Nietzsche."

Our conversation is interrupted by the sound of squealing tires and the crash of a vehicle busting through the security gate. I squint at the glare of a pair of headlights attached to a vehicle that doesn't quite qualify as a monster truck, but easily reflects the feelings of masculine inadequacy of its driver. Much to my ever-growing dismay, it is the Truck of

Overcompensation of Clint Hudson. I see Clint climb down from the driver's side and two other figures exit the passenger side. Randi barks into her wrist communicator before clutching her laser pistol.

"Code Red at the portal! I repeat Code Red at the portal!" She keeps one hand on her holstered pistol while holding the other out in a defensive stance. "You're trespassing on private property. You need to leave this area immediately. The authorities are on their way."

The first response comes from one of the other figures in the form of a short blue laser blast that hits Randi in the chest and knocks her to the ground. A collection of blue electrical currents envelop her as she convulses. They fade and her convulsions stop, but she remains motionless and unresponsive. I try to cry out, but can only produce a choking sound. I'm gagging on my fear.

Clint Hudson stomps toward me like a Neanderthal. Seriously, it's like I can hear his knuckles scraping the ground. From the glow of the headlights, I can see his eyes are heavy from intoxication. Behind him are his tag-alongs, Tyler and Dalton. Tyler holds the pistol that immobilized Randi. Both guys fix their weapons on me.

"I've been looking for you, you pussy." He pokes his finger in my chest. He's close enough to smell the wintergreen tobacco and raging testosterone on his breath. His eyes are yellow and the pupils are more oval than round. I swallow hard and work my mouth in a desperate attempt to produce moisture. My chest tightens and my legs tingle.

"Look, fellas." I hold my hands up in peace. "I don't know what you want, but you might wanna get outta here. My bosses will be here soon and they're gonna be pissed you tore up their gate. And I kinda wanna know where you got those guns."

"How did a hot piece like Marlene ever want to hook up with a homo like you?" He grunts in derision while Tyler and Dalton harrumph monosyllabically the way teenage henchmen do.

Anger heats my blood at his referring to Marlene as a hot piece. An ill-advised sense of machismo nurtured by a steady diet of action films instills me with the desire to respond with a flippant wisecrack. Common sense derived from a quick analysis of the three-against-one data screams at me to get out of here. Dalton and Tyler creep toward me. I hear a low, rumbling guttural growl coming from them. I should take action here though my only potential options appear to be running away or falling to the ground and curling into the fetal position.

For the briefest of milliseconds, I think about apricots.

I see it all perfectly; there are two possible solutions – one can either do this or do that. My honest opinion and friendly advice is this: do it or do not do it. You will regret both.

Ill-advised machismo wins this time. "You know," I say. "If you to want to mask your latent homoerotic curiosity about your two partners there with homophobic jabs at me, that's fine. But, please watch how you talk about Marlene."

With a quick movement, Clint is in my face and grabbing my shirt. "I know you drive by her house, you freak. I know you still want her. But she's mine."

"And she's ok with that?"

He sneers at me and his hot breath smothers my face. "I think it's time you woke up and smelled the coffee on the wall."

"What are you talking about?" I say.

Dalton chimes up as he walks toward us. "You're mixing your metaphors again, Clint. We've talked about that."

"Yeah," Tyler says. "You know what a grammar Nazi Dalton is."

"Shut up, dicks!" Clint spits when he yells. "I'll mix whatever the hell I want. And right now, I'm about to crack some eggs and mix up some lemonade."

"God," Dalton says. "It's like an icepick in the ear."

"I'm about to teach you not to mess with my girl. You got anything to say before I kick your ass?"

"Violence is the last refuge of the incompetent," I say.

"Are you gonna let him quote Isaac Asimov like that, Clint?" Dalton challenges.

A sinister smile spreads across Clint's face. "I'm really gonna enjoy this."

"Will you cuddle with me when we're done?" I wince at that example of ill-advised machismo, but I can't help myself.

Clint's first punch pounds the left side of my face and my vision in that eye goes black for a few seconds before bubbles of color and light dance. We received self-defense and basic hand-to-hand training at Corporate and those instincts take over as I stand and kick Clint in the groin. As he doubles over, gasping for air, I land a punch of my own to his jaw and he drops to his knees. Common sense now intervenes and tells my ill-advised machismo it is time to get the hell out of here, so I turn and try to run to my car door. Tyler and Dalton grab me and start dragging me back to Clint, who is now standing again and wiping blood from the lip I busted. I really want my mom right now. Sure, Dad would be handy, but I think Mom would inflict more damage in this situation.

I jerk and pull against the henchmen but their grasp is too strong. Pain surges with each pulse of my racing heart. Clint sizes me up, draws a deep breath, and plunges his fist into my stomach. He pulls his fist back and then smashes it into my ribs. I cry out and slump in Tyler's and Dalton's clutches. They drop me to the ground and the threesome takes turns with blows and kicks. Pain consumes my body and I gasp for the wind that has been knocked out of me. If you've never been kicked in the ribcage with a cowboy boot, I don't recommend it. As I lie on the ground, I hear one of them say, "Someone's coming. We should get outta here, Clint. You've made your point."

"Hell, no," Clint snorts. "We'll get rid of 'em and then finish off this douchebag."

"What if it's the cops?"

"It's not the cops."

Tyler and Dalton pull me up and I watch as a vehicle pulls beside Clint's truck. I look to Randi. She struggles to get to her feet and shake off the effects of the blast she took. White splotches and tears cloud my vision, fogging any chance to see what kind of car it is. After a few blinks, my vision clears and a surge of shock rocks my body. The car is a red Vega station wagon with a white stripe on the hood. A lone figure walks toward us wearing cargo pants and a tattered tuxedo shirt with ruffles under a light jacket. A tattered top hat rests on his head and he takes a drag from a hand-rolled cigarette before flicking it to the ground.

"Step away from the Tony, please."

I gasp at the sound of the voice of Jeff Harper.

"Get outta here," Clint warns Jeff. "This don't concern you."

"It kinda does," Jeff says. "That's my friend's ass you're kicking."

"Hey," Dalton says. "You're Jeff Harper."

"Yeah," Tyler says. "Jeff Harper. You back in town?"

"Nope," Jeff says. "That's not me."

"Well, then, who the hell are you?" Clint asks.

"My name is Bart. I work on a fishing boat. Do you like to fish? Do you like guys named Bart?"

I stagger to my feet. The metallic taste of blood coats my tongue.

Jeff steps toward us and I see that same wild spark in his eyes. "Let my friend go, fellas."

"We'll do whatever the hell we want, Bart." Clint shoves Jeff in the chest and Dalton and Tyler aim their guns at him. I don't know why Jeff is calling himself Bart other than to mess with an intellectual inferior.

Jeff turns to him. "You seriously don't remember me, do you? Jesus. You made my life a living hell since fifth grade. You bullied me all the way through high school. Threw me in lockers. Duct-taped me to the flag pole with a sign that said 'I touch myself in class.' And you don't know if my name is Jeff or Bart?"

"Whatever, asswipe," Clint says. "Get out of here before I kick your ass, too."

Jeff spins quickly and lands a kick to Clint's face, knocking him to the ground. It's a move I've never known Jeff capable of making without pulling a muscle or falling down. I crash to the ground in a thud and the wind leaves my lungs. I roll around gasping for air as Clint stands back up and moves to attack Jeff, who suddenly produces a laser pistol and points it at Clint.

"Whoa! Whoa!" Clint holds out his hands and backs up. "What the hell you gonna do with that?"

"I dunno," Jeff says. "I've never used it before. I stole it from a Sarcillian in the Western R-7 Quadrant when he tried to steal my green Kwench-Aid. It might be a Phobia Inducer, which causes you to see the thing you fear most, or, it could be a quintonium-powered laser pistol. Those explode you like a watermelon dropped from a skyscraper. You really want to find out? Because I'm dying to know what this thing does."

"We've got guns, too!" Dalton says and he and Tyler aim their weapons at Jeff.

"Those are cute," Jeff says. "Looks like we've got us an old-fashioned Mojito Standoff."

"Jeff Harper!"

We all turn in the direction of the voice to see Randi Williams now standing and pointing two weapons at Jeff and the others.

"What the hell?" Clint says.

"Hi ya, Randi," Jeff calls out. "But call me Kilroy."

"You're crazy." It's the first time I've heard anything approaching fear coming from Clint.

"No," Jeff says. "I'm just a man whose circumstances went beyond his control."

Clint's eyebrows pinch together and send the message that he has no clue what Jeff is saying.

"Styx?" Jeff says. "'Mr. Roboto?' 'Kilroy Was Here?'"

"Jeff, I'm not afraid to use this stun gun on you," Randi says. "You've stolen proprietary information from Corporate. I need it back."

"No can do," Jeff says. "In fact, I really can't talk. I gotta get through the portal and deliver some packages. So, Randi, let me go. Clint, get the hell outta my way before I shoot you."

"You don't have the –"

Clint doesn't get to finish what his insult. A small ball of powder blue light blasts from Jeff's pistol and hits Clint directly in the chest, sending him backward several feet. The ball morphs into dozens of streams of light which cover Clint's body. Jeff drops and rolls away from a shot from Randi's pistol. He hops to his feet and hurls some kind of small round object at her. It hits the ground at her feet and releases a green gas. She chokes and coughs. He fires two more shots at Tyler and Dalton sprinting toward the Truck of Overcompensation. The same streams of light envelop them.

Clint stands and looks perplexed. He spots the still coughing Randi, gasps, and slowly backs away. A look of genuine horror covers his face.

“Oh, god!” He runs toward his Truck of Overcompensation. “I don’t know how to talk to you. I don’t know what to say. Stop judging me!”

He then emits a high-pitched scream often associated with an eight-year-old girl who watched a giant lizard eat her dog. The shriek lasts for several seconds before fading. Clint faces us with those wide eyes, unable to move.

“Caligynephobia,” I say to no one in particular. “The fear of beautiful women.”

Clint stammers and then sprints away toward this truck. He passes Tyler and Dalton, who scream at him about being a scary clown. They break into a dash for the highway as Clint speeds away in his Truck of Overcompensation.

I know my mouth is hanging open but I can’t close it. The sight of my friend standing in front of me examining his weapon and scrunching his face at it overwhelms me with emotion. Tears well up in my eyes and one trickles down. “I don’t believe this,” is all I know to say.

“I’ll be damned,” he says, as he lights another hand-rolled cigarette. “It was a Phobia Inducer. Is it wrong that I’m disappointed?”

CHAPTER SIX

"Jeff!" Randi stops coughing and struggles to catch her breath. "You need to come with me. Please."

Two more cars barrel through the broken security gate.

"I can't stay, baby," Jeff says. "It's a work thing."

"Jeff," Randi says once more. "That's Corporate pulling up. This is serious."

Jeff points at Randi. "You can't have me. C'mon, Mr. Roboto, we gotta go now!"

"Don't even start with that," I tell him.

He opens the hatch of *Miss America* and retrieves two new pistols. I sense that I recognize them, though I know I've never seen them before. They look like toys from a different era. Candy apple red with yellow cones at the tips and the Corporate logo on the handles.

"Here," Jeff says, handing me on of the guns. They are metallic and heavier than I expected. "Just in case. I don't think a Gulliball is going to do the job on Grandor. Do you think you can handle one of these?"

A switch in my brain sends information I never knew I had forward as I involuntarily spew the specifics of the weapon I hold.

"This is a non-approved Corporate weapon. The 8-Pattern Rear Trigger Nozzle Neutralizer. Developed three years ago and field tested, but still regarded as under development. It is modeled after a garden hose nozzle with an array of eight shooting patterns: jet, angled, shower, full, flat, mist, cone, and soaker."

I gasp, drop the Nozzle Neutralizer and lean against the hood of the Space Vega.

"Impressive," Jeff says. "But, don't drop it. Take care of it."

"I don't know that," I say. "How did I know that? How did I blurt that out? Why does that keep happening?"

"I know how." Jeff picks up the weapon, a crooked smile on his face. "It's starting."

"What is starting? What are you talking about?" The Some-Unseen-Force-Is-Messing-With-My-Insides ickiness rages once more and I walk around twisting my arms hoping somehow to shake it out.

"I cannot emphasize the criticality of this situation," calls a voice from the darkness behind us. Coming into our sight is Max Gentry, weapon poised, flanked by four Corporate employees. "We need our nanotech back. It's a simple deliverable. Return the nano and we all go home."

"Well," Jeff says. "By the thumbing of my prick, something wicked this way comes."

"You don't want to do this," Max says. "This tiger team is fully engaged and harbors no objections to carrying out their assigned action items."

"C'mon, Jeff." Randi steps to join Max and the tiger team. "Come with us."

Jeff remains in place, pistol drawn and ready. "Looks like we have a real Mohican standoff here."

I feel something growing inside me and not in the I-just-got-my-first-erection way. A wave of confidence unfamiliar to me courses my veins. I am aware of a presence in me, taking control of my thoughts. I survey the situation. Max and his team to my right with Randi. Jeff to my left. Mohican standoff, indeed.

The energy inside me gains complete control and I'm suddenly very aware that I'm charging Randi, Max, and the tiger team. I squeeze the trigger on the Neutralizer and a cylindrical spray of spark covers them. They move to respond, but their motions are slowed to almost a frame-by-frame advancement.

"C'mon." Jeff grabs me and pulls me to *Miss America.* I stand at the passenger door, disoriented and overwhelmed.

"What are we doing?" I ask through the open window.

He starts the engine and taps the touchscreen dashboard with urgency. "We're gonna go get Leigh Ann back from Grandor, but we gotta go see a guy first."

Max fires on us, but his laser blasts only bounce off the car's exterior. I look at the group still moving ever so slowly and await more fire from their weapons.

"Get in!" Jeff yells. "I'm going through the portal! Come with me!"

"What? Are you crazy? What is happening to me? How did I know what this Neutralizer thing was?"

"Get in and I can tell you all about it!"

I comply with Jeff's command against my better judgment and climb in the passenger seat. A small cannon emerges from the grill of *Miss America*, the sight of which does nothing to quell my apprehension. I can only shake my head. The cannon fires an orange stream of light over the river ahead. Within seconds, the portal opens, inviting anyone to enter.

"I don't know what to do," I tell him. "I'm really freaking out right now."

"Get ready!" Jeff flips switches on the console of the Vega. "The Neutralizer only lasts about a minute!"

"Shit." I roll the passenger side window down and send a quick shot from my Neutralizer to slow the group down once more. I catch a glimpse of Randi's face, which looks locked in an expression of her screaming "no!" at me.

"Time to fire up the big boy." Jeff jerks the gear shift into reverse and steers us away from the river, ending at the road entrance. "Buckle up. This is going to get bumpy. Also, it's the law." Jeff reaches up and taps three buttons next to the dome light. Behind us, in the hatch, an orange oblong machine whirls and lights dance around it. I recognize it as the same device Max and Randi showed me at Corporate. With another jerk of the gear shift *Miss America* speeds toward the river as Jeff shoves in the cigarette lighter. Immediately, we become airborne, lifting slightly off the ground and moving in an upward trajectory.

"What the hell?" My stomach drops to my feet. We are several feet off the ground, flying toward the river. "How is this happening?"

"Here we go!" Jeff reaches behind and punches a button on the orange machine and *Miss America* bounces and shimmies with turbulence. We are flying directly toward the black opening. "And, remember!"

"Remember what?"

"We own the night!"

"Oh my god!" I scream.

"Relax." Jeff's confidence flying this contraption amazes me. It's obvious he's done this before. "Like I said, we're gonna go see a guy and then we're gonna get Leigh Ann Back. Also, I need smokes."

"I need to text my folks first." A final jerk sucks the vehicle into the blackness and my ears pop. "Sonofabitch."

An eerie quiet overtakes the surroundings as Jeff taps the touchscreen.

"Checkpoint station in 30 seconds." Jeff pulls the visor down and retrieves an envelope clipped there. "Now, listen. Stay cool. Be whatever your version of chill is."

All I can do is look around slack-jawed. An orange-yellow glow surrounds our vehicle, flooding the interior and I squint to look where we're going. Jeff shifts the Vega into neutral and we drift slowly toward the light source.

"Here." Jeff hands me a pair of sunglasses from the console. "Put these on."

"What is happening?" The sunglasses allow me to see that we're edging toward a pair of doors that are sliding open horizontally, like a cargo bay.

"Stay cool." Jeff pilfers through the envelope and pulls out some folded papers and several packets of green Kwench-Aid bound together with a rubber band. "On this side they don't know me as Jeff, okay? Don't say anything. Roll with it."

More slack-jawed nodding from me. A sign overhead in front of us reads Checkpoint Zuza Alpha Niner. We slow to a stop at an intercom station as if we're about to order at the drive thru of Taco Haus. Something tells me we're not about to meet my caliente lederhosen wearing babe. As *Miss America* drifts toward the opening doors. Jeff rolls down his window. I find it curious that for all of the pimped out space-age gadgetry on this car, he still must manually roll down the window.

A voice outside the window spills out of the unseen intercom. "Welcome to the Zuza Alpha Niner checkpoint. We are glad you are here. Please have your papers ready for the station agent." Calm elevator music now plays as the Vega creeps to a stop. A quick survey of our surroundings reveals a vast parking garage of sorts lit overhead by fluorescent bulbs. Human-looking figures stroll around, some holding clipboards. Others carry a type of rifle strapped to their shoulder. I roll down my window and stick my head out. There is pointing and gesturing, talking and referencing the clipboards.

Looking down, I notice that the wheels on the Vega now sit horizontally and serve as thrusters to keep us afloat. It dawns on me that I can breathe. I always assumed that any space flight would require me to wear a breathing apparatus so my face wouldn't explode from a lack of oxygen.

"Look who it is." A male voice from outside the driver's side window grabs my attention and I see a green-skinned humanoid figure leaning in. He wears dark blue coveralls with a hexagon patch on the upper right chest. The insignia on the patch is of a labyrinth. He smiles broadly, displaying white teeth nearly as brilliant as the fluorescent lighting. I am trying hard to lose the slack-jaw, but with each new sight, it's difficult.

"Moonbeam," says Jeff. "What's up, my brother from an alien mother?" The two exchange a hearty handshake.

"How have you been, Kilroy?"

"Kilroy?" I forget for a moment that I'm supposed to say nothing and Jeff glares at me as reminder to shut the hell up. I face forward again in time to see a dwarf-sized creature with an oval head speeds by on something resembling a Vespa with no wheels, flying a couple of feet above the ground like a hovercraft. "Did you see that?"

Jeff rolls his eyes at me and turns back to Moonbeam. "Never mind him. First time through."

Moonbeam draws a deep breath and glances from side to side. His voice drops to a whisper. "Does he have documentation?"

"You know it." Jeff hands him the manila envelope and Moonbeam inspects it. Moonbeam removes the paper, some play money, and packets of green Kwench-Aid.

"This appears to be in order." Moonbeam shoves the Kwench-Aid in his pocket and peeks in the back of *Miss America*. "What are you hauling?"

"Not hauling. Gotta pick up some quintonium."

"Across the No-Trade Zone?"

"Yep." Jeff leans in to Moonbeam and lowers his voice. "You got smokes?"

Moonbeam straightens and looks around. I can now see that he probably stands over six feet tall and his shoulders are broad and full. He turns and enters a security station directly behind him.

"Where the hell are we?" I ask through quickening breaths. My chest tightens and I rub my hand across it. "What is all this?"

"Stay calm."

"My parents are gonna kill me."

Moonbeam returns, leans in, and hands Jeff a bag. "This should suffice."

Jeff inspects the contents of the bag. "You're a lifesaver, dude. You have no idea." The two exchange another handshake. "All my best to the family."

"You'll go to bay 37. You know the rest. Be careful out there, Kilroy. Word has it that Herpezoids are on the prowl." Moonbeam stands and backs away. Jeff immediately retrieves a hand-rolled cigarette from the bag and lights it. He takes a deep drag and exhales as we drift out of the security checkpoint.

"Damn, I needed that." He continues to puff on his cigarette as he steers toward bay 37. Crafts of varying size occupy the other bays. Most of them are much larger than our tiny compact car and they look like what I always imagined spaceships looking like: oversize supersonic jets with interesting wing designs. How Jeff's vehicle withstands the rigors of space travel compared to these is beyond me.

"You want a drag?" Jeff asks. "You might want something to help you relax for this next part. I don't have Dramamine."

"I'm fine."

"Suit yourself."

Jeff turns the steering wheel to the right and guides us up to a large opening like a subway tunnel. A white sign with the number 37 painted on it hangs above the entrance. Inside, a rainbow of lights swirl and dance. An ominous hum emanates from it. We float again at the mouth as another alien walks up to us in its own set of coveralls, but dark gray instead of blue. The same hexagon labyrinth patch on the chest is the same. The alien looks like the one who was buzzing around on the hover Vespa.

"Kilroy!" the alien says, obviously thrilled to see him. He stands on his tip-toes and peers in. "Do you have your coordinates?"

"Hi ya, Rothschild. Got 'em right here."

The dwarf alien named Rothschild steps aside and reveals what looks like an ATM machine. Jeff taps in his coordinates and gives Rothschild a thumbs-up signal.

"Roll your window up," Jeff says to me. "I don't want you to get sucked out into space." I obey his directive and he performs what appears to be random tasks on the touchscreen dashboard. The windows of the Vega fade to a tinted black and only the glow of display panel illuminates us. The dashboard beeps and blurps as *Miss America* rocks. The hum from the mouth of the tunnel grows louder and louder.

I look at Jeff. He leans his seat back, adjusts his top hat, and enjoys his cigarette. Sweet smelling smoke fills the interior. His relaxed demeanor contradicts the clamor around us. I stare ahead at the roaring tunnel before us and my chest tightens even more. My hands shake uncontrollably. A spectacular light show flashes all around us as we plough through this tunnel like some psychedelic drive-thru car wash.

"Maybe I'll take a drag of that now," I say.

*

Jeff Harper looks like a grizzled 18-year-old sitting in the driver's seat of *Miss America*, cocked back like some teenage Han Solo/gangsta hybrid. A pathetic growth of stubble covers his chin. I know I'm staring but it is entirely appropriate to stare. Anyone who thought their best friend was gone forever after being sucked through a wormhole only to see that friend show up, disarm a bully alien with a fear-inducing ray, and drive his Chevy Vega into space would stare.

The interior of *Miss America* is also stare-worthy. The seats look and feel the same. They are even more worn and the foam pokes out from under the tan vinyl. The dashboard that once housed a barely functioning AM radio now displays a complex touchscreen more at home on a spacecraft. The graphics dance and bounce, the colors dazzle. Bleeps and dings sing out. I reach out tentatively, wanting to see what would happen, but pull back. Surprisingly, the old Vega still sports a stick shift manual transmission.

"*Miss America* looks pretty bitchin', doesn't she?" Jeff's voice oozes with pride and I can't argue. "I'm gonna engage the ol' autopilot so we can kick back and listen to Styx." After a few taps on his gadgetry, the opening notes of "Come Sail Away" fill the car.

A rush of words sticks in my throat. I'm overwhelmed with emotion at seeing my friend alive. I want to cry. I want to cheer. I want to hug him. I want to punch him in the face for not finding me immediately. Tears blur my eyes and streak my cheeks and I turn myself over to the emotion. Embarrassing, but necessary.

"Are you crying?" he asks. "Because I'm back? Aw, you like me."

Finally, I choke out something. "I thought you were dead."

"Right?" He takes a drag from his cigarette and exhales, feeling some kind of buzz that brings a smile to his face. "Mongalisonian tobacco. Rich. Flavorful. Very expensive. You can't get this just anywhere, you know. You have to cross the No Trade Zone. Huge on the black market." He holds the cigarette out to me. "You look really tense. Take a hit. You said you wanted a hit."

"No. I don't do drugs. Especially drugs from space."

"This is not a drug. I have to smoke it for medicinal purposes. You're gonna need it. It'll help you." He finishes it with one final toke and drops it into the ashtray. He presses the button next to the ashtray and a whoosh sound carries the butt, I assume, into the darkness of space.

"Why would I need to smoke that?" My brain explodes in a flurry of questions. "Where's Leigh Ann? What happened to Leigh Ann? Where have you been? What have you been doing? How did you survive?" I have more I want to ask, but he stops me before I can add them to the list.

"Jesus, what is this? A press conference?" He taps the screen on the dash, causing a few beeps that mean nothing to me, but must mean something to him.

"So, you got my note?" Jeff says to me.

"Yes. Why have me go through all of that? Why not tell me you're here?"

"I thought it was a fun thing to do. Thought you'd like it. You always liked clues and mysteries and scavenger hunts. We were always solving mysteries and whatnot."

"No, we weren't," I tell him. "We didn't solve mysteries. And I hate scavenger hunts."

"You do?"

"Yes. I avoid them like the plague."

"Did I know this about you?"

"Are you going to tell me what the hell is going on?"

"My god. Settle down, Anderson Cooper." He reaches into the console next to the gear shift and retrieves another cigarette. "Where do I begin? When I got sucked through that portal, I ended up in the Zenron sector of the far middle quadrant of the galaxy." He takes another drag. "I don't know how. That's where I dropped." He flips another switch and looks intently at some readings on the dashboard. I've never seen him with this kind of purpose. He seems to know exactly what he is touching and why he is touching it, a far cry from the kid who used to forget where the headlights were on this same Vega. "I was cold and hungry. Some alien people took me in. Fed me soup. I think it was soup. I called it soup because that made it easier to swallow."

"I don't believe this," I say, fully aware that eloquence is failing me. "What's a Zenron sector?"

"A spot on the star map. Right by the No Trade Zone. The alien family took me to a guy who said he wanted to help me. He fixed up *Miss America*. Changed the oil, overhauled the transmission, and installed something called a quintonium accelerator and asked me to deliver a package. He put me to work." He inhales another satisfying drag. "I guess you could say I'm a courier. I deliver goods to those who can't get their hands on the stuff they really want."

"What's a No Trade Zone? What's a quan..quanti…?"

"Quintonium accelerator. I don't know the particulars. It's the thing that makes the car go into space and shit like that. Very powerful." He reaches behind him, produces a thermos, and drinks from it. His expression is one of a wino who took his first sip of hooch in over a month.

"Wait. Quintonium accelerator?" I remember my meeting with Randi and Max at Corporate. "You mean the quintionium drive?"

"What?" Jeff looks at me like I'm speaking some ancient dead language. "There's no such thing. I have an accelerator. That's all. The drive doesn't exist."

I throw my hands up. "Are you crazy? Look. You're back. You can come home. Stay home. We can quit this ridiculous life and go to college. Be normal."

"Normal? When have I ever wanted to be normal? Besides, I hate living in Poplar Bluff. The only person who gives a damn about me is my mom. Well, and you. So, two people." He looks out the windshield and up to the stars. "But, out here it's different. If I hadn't gotten sucked through the portal, I'd still be a screw up. People laughing at me. And I know they laughed. Even you sometimes. I'm different now. I found out I could be anything I wanted. No one knows me. I can literally be a different person at each place I go. Once, I accidentally landed on the wrong part of a planet. All of these primitive types came out and fell down in awe. I became their god." He slaps himself in the forehead. "Shit! That reminds me."

"What?"

"Remind me later to record a message to my prophet on Bi Xiu Prime."

My friend glances at a fuel gage on the display and frowns.

"Damn," he says. "The quintonium accelerator is running low. Good thing this is our exit."

"Exit?" I look around and see nothing.

He engages the orange contraption, taps a few buttons, and presses in the cigarette lighter again. The orange beam from *Miss America's* grill extends out into the darkness and fans out in a circle. The orangeness dissipates into a swirling vortex of clouds, lightning, and dark reds, greens, and blues. This maw in the midst of space very much resembles the portal we guard in Poplar Bluff only much larger, much more ominous.

"I wanna go home," I mumble. "Turn around and take me home."

"Easy, buddy." Jeff enters what appears to be a set of coordinates into his touchscreen keyboard. The autopilot disengages and our front cannon thing shoots its beam toward the opening once more. *Miss America* jerks and Jeff squeezes the steering wheel. He moves the gearshift into neutral and we're soon in the clutches of what is clearly the tunnel to the ninth level of hell. I don't belong here. I don't even like roller coasters all that much.

"I don't wanna do this," I announce to whoever in the expanse of the universe will listen.

"Hold on!"

The portal swallows us and soon we're surrounded by yet another psychedelic car wash. "Come Sail Away" blasts. Jeff fires up a Mongalisonian cigarette and bangs his head to the music.

"Freakin' awesome, man! Isn't this freakin' awesome?"

"IwannagohomeIwannagohomeIwannagohomeIwannagohomeIwannagohome!"

"We own the night!"

One more violent jerk rocks *Miss America*, like someone on the other end of this god-awful portal is trying to land a giant marlin. We hurdle toward a blinding light which surely means we're dying and crossing over. A loud sound like a whale's mating call mixed with the horn of a tractor trailer rig blares for a few seconds and then all is quiet.

We float.

PART TWO:

ROAD TRIP TO PLANET LLOYD

CHAPTER SEVEN

Space travel is not at all what I expected. The psychedelic car wash tunnel belches us into the vast expanse of space and we drift gently over the surface of a planet or moon. I used to dream of what space would be like. Now, I yearn for solid earth. The celestial body below us will do fine.

"Good times, eh?" Jeff yells over the Styx song which blasts over the car stereo. After another drag, he bellows out the chorus of "Come Sail Away" as it fades to signal its end.

"Hey, what do you know?" I point out my window at the surface of the celestial body we are orbiting.

"What?"

"That is Nitz." My brain snaps with recognition and I feel my consciousness floating away from me toward a star map only I can see. I've never seen it before, but I know it as easily as I know my parents are named Chris and Suzanne or that I hate the smell of cooked cabbage because it reminds me of dirty feet. A surge of information I didn't know existed in my memory spills out of my mouth.

"Nitz is the only moon orbiting the planet Dangabah. Its topography is mostly desert, though a few patches of water can be found scattered along its surface. We're deep into the Gamma District of the Northwestern Quadrant of the Jaqarillion Galaxy. Long, long way from home." I still don't know why I know these things.

"Imagine Arizona," Jeff says. "Or, like, middle-of-nowhere New Mexico. Only it's a moon. That's Nitz."

"It doesn't faze you that I blurted out an analysis of a celestial body I've never heard of? That doesn't register with you?"

"Should it?"

I can't respond at first. My efforts to comprehend what is happening are futile. I'm traveling through space with my best friend. It's the ultimate road trip. I remember looking at collections of star maps in Corporate training and reading names like Gamma District and Jaqarillion Galaxy and Bi Xiu Prime. Despite my love of astronomy, it all seemed so abstract. Now, I look out and behold how damn big the universe is.

My friend lights up another Mongalisonian cigarette and taps on the small screen where a radio or CD player might rest in a lesser vehicle. The opening notes of "A.D. 1928" from *Paradise Theater* fill *Miss America.* Jeff closes his eyes and listens to the Styx album about the opening and closing of a theater in Chicago. He enjoys his cigarette, savoring a slow drag and deeply inhaling the smoke.

"You should go easy on those," I tell him. "You just got them."

"I'll get some more. I'll save some for you, too."

"Why do you need them?" I am starting to feel comfortable and a rush of inquisitive energy overtakes me. I reel off a string of questions that must be answered now. "How are you able to work the portal? What is the portal anyway? How are you suddenly able to do all the judo moves and act like some action hero?"

"Easy, easy," he says. "All in due time. The day is coming when all shall know."

"Seriously. What is going on? Where is Leigh Ann? How are we getting back? Why is there a planet named Lloyd? What is quintonium? Why am I remembering useless shit that I never knew before? Can I get cell reception out here? Am I able to text my folks? They're gonna kill me."

"My god," he mutters. "It's like you're a fanboy at Comic Con."

"What is the deal with Marlene? Does she work for Corporate? Do you know? Is Clint a Herpezoid or something?"

"Whoa. What are you talking about?" He turns down the music and puts out the cigarette. "Look. I've got one of those nano things in me. Corporate put it in me back before prom night."

"They put a nanobot in you? How? Did you know?"

"I volunteered for a secret program that Research and Development was researching and developing. It was supposed to make me into some kind of super-agent or some shit. I was in training."

"Why would you do that? Why would you let them experiment on you?"

He turns away a bit and looks out the window. It's the first time since his return from The Prom Night of Which We Shall Not Speak he doesn't have his swagger.

"Seemed like the thing to do," he says. "But, then I found out that Corporate stole the whole thing from Grandor. He made me an offer to get it back in exchange for Leigh Ann, so I'm using my powers for good."

"So, you stole those nanotech plans from Corporate in exchange for Leigh Ann."

"Yep. And you're gonna help me with the delivery. Kilroy and Mr. Roboto together again."

"Please don't."

An alarm on the dashboard display dings and an orange glowing indicator flashes. Jeff extinguishes his cigarette and taps the indicator.

"What's that?" I ask. "What's wrong?"

"Relax," he says. "We're just low on quintonium."

I roll my eyes and huff. I don't want to be here. I'm angry with my friend for not telling me he was alive. I'm angry with Marlene for keeping a big secret from me. I'm angry with myself for keeping a big secret from her. My secret broke us up, which makes mine worse somehow. Her secret saved my life.

"You need to take me home," I say. "And you need to broaden your musical horizons. There's more to life than Styx."

Jeff gasps and holds his mouth open at the horror of my statement. I knew it would offend him. That was the point. Between space travel and life circumstances, I have a funky case of jet lag.

"That is blasphemy," he whispers. "But I'll let it slide. I know you're just being surly."

"What? Surly?"

"You, sir, are surly!"

*

We successfully enter the moon's atmosphere and fly above the surface for several minutes before landing and transitioning into a standard car rumbling along a road of gravel and sand. Jeff fiddles with displays on the dashboard for oxygen levels and cabin pressure.

"What did you mean earlier?" he asks me. "About Marlene working for Corporate and Herpezoids and shit? What was that all about?"

"I don't think you'll believe me."

"I got sucked into a space portal and now I fly around the galaxy in a pimped Vega. Try me."

"Marlene is not who I thought she was." I turn and face him. "She single-handedly took down this little old lady who was trying to kill me."

"A little old lady tried to kill you?"

"And Life Coach Gilbert."

"Who the hell is Life Coach Gilbert?"

I turn back away from him and look out my window toward the horizon. The barren landscape stretches into eternity. I'm small.

"My therapist. I had to go to therapy after you and Leigh Ann got sucked through the portal. I don't like talking about it because I don't want people judging me."

"People are always judging," he says flatly. "Especially people who don't have their own shit together."

Miss America slows to a stop at the base of a solitary butte that stands in the middle of the desert. A few stray shrubs sit scattered along the ground. Jeff taps a device resembling a garage door opener and an intercom box rises out of the ground. Jeff presses a button on it and a voice blares a riddle from it.

"It is greater than God and more evil than the devil. The poor have it, the rich need it and if you eat it, you'll die. What is it?"

"I freaking hate riddles," Jeff calls out in reply.

"What the hell?" I say.

"What? That's the password."

"There is no need for belligerence," whines the voice inside the intercom. "You think it's easy coming up with new riddles all the time?"

"I suppose not," Jeff says with sincere contrition.

"I'd much rather be singing or something. Opera has always appealed to me and I think I have the voice for it."

"I have no doubt," Jeff assures. "I shouldn't have snapped. I'm very sorry. Please forgive me."

After five seconds, the intercom voice replies, "apology accepted." The rock wall ahead slowly rises and soft light spills out.

"That sounded like a Rube Goldberg Protocol," I say.

"Yep." Jeff eases *Miss America* through the opening and stops a few feet inside the entrance and the door slides closed behind us.

"Just in town for supplies, partner," Jeff says.

We exit *Miss America* and I look around at the massive garage we've entered. The ceiling is close to 50 feet overhead. The walls to each side are lined with tools and parts, some I recognize for cars, others I don't recognize at all. Half a dozen old cars and vans sit on lifts above the floor. Their engines have been gutted. A large tarp is draped over something. Sitting next to it is a 1969 Volkwagen Bus. The back far wall is a giant computer console and monitor. On the monitor is a star map and I can barely make out that a red circle is flashing around a spot marked with the words "planet Lloyd."

"Where are we now?" I'm getting tired of asking that question, however pertinent it may be.

"Remember the guy who took me in and gave me a job after I came through the portal? That guy. You'll love him. He's like a crazy uncle-slash-eccentric-scientist-slash-spiritual-guru."

We hear a war cry from the rafters overhead.

"Bastards!" the voice roars.

"Shit," Jeff says. "Take cover."

A figure descends from the rafters as if hanging on a wire firing a laser pistol in each hand. I dive behind a rolling mechanics tool cart, narrowly escaping a shot from this mysterious assailant.

"Bastards! Bastards! Bastards!" The figure's voice is male and sounds crazed. It's as if we've trespassed on the private property of some deeps woods hermit. The man sprints around the garage firing his weapons. He interrupts his maniacal running only to execute random forward tumbles. Jeff stands calm, hands raised and motionless.

"Simon Tybalt!" he calls out. "It's me!"

"Are you a bastard?" the man yells back.

"No. It's me. Jeff."

The man Jeff calls Simon Tybalt sprints up to him and holds a laser pistol to each of Jeff's temples. His draws his face up to Jeff's and sneers.

"If you are who you say are, then tell me how entropy is measured in statistical mechanics."

Jeff rolls his eyes as he answers. "I don't know, man. With a ruler?" The one called Tybalt circles Jeff, guns poised for action.

"What type of curvature does a symmetrical Lorentzian manifold have?"

"Seriously?" Jeff says, blowing out a sigh. "I'm gonna say twelve. Now put those guns down because we both know they're shooting blanks."

Simon Tybalt now stands face-to-face with Jeff. I see now he wears a tattered t-shirt with the Corporate logo on it and a pair of jeans. An old fishing hat rests atop his head. He raises his weapons up, drops them, and embraces Jeff as if greeting a returning prodigal.

"I thought you were a bastard," Simon Tybalt says. "But only you would be unable to answer those questions." He pulls away and walks to the mechanics cart I'm hiding behind. He produces a hand rolled cigarette from one of the drawers and lights up. It's like one of the cigarettes Jeff smokes.

"That doesn't make any sense," I call out.

"Who said that?" Simon Tybalt picks one of weapons from the floor and aims it my direction. "Bastard?"

"It's cool," Jeff calls. "He's with me. Come out, Tony."

I step from behind the cart, hands raised. Simon Tybalt looks at me, cigarette dangling, and looks back at Jeff, who nods. A scruffy peppery gray beard covers his aged face and he wears a sad smile I recognize from his giant portrait hanging in Corporate Headquarters. His eyes glow with a hint of madness I didn't notice in the picture. I remember the portrait not only was captioned with "the day is coming when we all shall know," but also showed the dates 1967-2010. Corporate thinks he's dead.

"You said Jeff was the only one who couldn't answer those questions." My hands are still raised because the wild look in his eyes won't subside. "That doesn't make any sense."

"Rube Goldberg Protocols," Simon Tybalt tells me.

"Now it makes sense."

"Tony." He hugs me tight and I worry his cigarette is going to burn my cheek. "So good to meet you, chum."

I pull away and eye him. "You're supposed to be dead. Your portrait at Corporate says you died in 2010."

"I faked my death. As far as anyone is concerned I was attacked by rabid kangaroos while on a walkabout in Australia."

"What is this place?" I ask Jeff. "Why didn't you tell me we were coming to see the presumed dead founder and CEO of Corporate?"

"I didn't tell you that?" Jeff scrunches his face in a way that tells me this is news to him.

"We don't have time for all that." Simon Tybalt motions for us to follow him toward an elevator at the back of the garage. "We have to get you ready to help me save Corporate and save the world."

"What if I don't want to?" I stand back and observe the odd man in the fishing hat and the even odder teenager in the top hat and accept this is probably my life now.

"Boy," he says to Jeff. "He's surly."

*

Simon Tybalt leads us on a tour of his moon base, which is a mashup of Wayne Manor, a gothic haunted house, a rustic ski lodge, and the grand lair of some steampunk mad scientist. The rooms are large and ornate. Posters of beautiful actress from before my birth line the hallways.

"That's Farrah Fawcett there," he tells me pointing at a tanned blonde in a red swimsuit. He points at another and says, "Suzanne Somers."

Jeff nudges my ribs with his elbow as we walk. "Isn't this place awesome?"

"I wanna go home," I mutter. Jeff rolls his eyes at me in disgust. I turn my attention to our tour guide. "Why do you have all these posters of beautiful women from the '70s and '80s?"

"There are three things in the world I love," he tells me. "Building spacecraft out of old cars, the films of Mel Brooks, and beautiful women. What three things do you love most, Tony?"

"I dunno," I say. "Can we get on with the plan? What are we doing?"

"Your questions will be answered." He stops at the end of the hall and looks at me.

"The day is coming when we all shall know?" I ask.

"Yeah, sure, however it makes sense to you," he says, oblivious to my quoting him. He points to two doors on each side of us. "I meant it's late and you guys need to get to bed. These are your rooms. You guys sleep. I have to drink copious amounts Anxillan whiskey and drunk dial strange women."

*

The night comes and goes with no visions of apricots dancing in my head. I shuffle from my bed in one of a dozen guestrooms into a shower the size of my bedroom back on Earth. The door is clear plexiglass and each of the three other walls has a shower head. I stand under the water and think about The Simon Tybalt is Alive and Living on the Remote Moon of Nitz Revelation. A pang of guilt hits me when I realize how worried my parents must be. I never should've agreed to go through the portal with Jeff. That was a bad choice. I backtrack every poor decision prior to that one. All I see is a series of lousy choices. Coming through the portal with Jeff. Going back to work at Corporate. Working at Corporate in the first place. Breaking up with Marlene. All shitty choices. I suck at choices. Kierkegaard was right. No matter what you do, you're screwed.

After my shower, I dress in a Corporate t-shirt left for me by Simon Tybalt and throw on the same jeans I've been wearing for three days now. I enter the dining room, which is not as large as the other rooms in the house, but still larger than I'm accustomed to. Jeff is already seated at the long narrow dining table. The walls are lined with star maps and clippings of news stories from magazines and online articles about aliens. This could easily be a scene from Someone Else's Books. I sit across from Jeff and see he is suffering from a case of the early morning stares. He could be asleep. He could be awake. He could be dead. His top hats rests on the table next to a placemat because despite his general anarchic approach to life, he still believes in good table manners.

Simon Tybalt enters from the kitchen with a tray loaded with French toast stacked high, butter, and syrup. He wears his fishing hat and jeans, but the Corporate t-shirt has been replaced with one with a character named King Ding Dong on it.

"Help yourselves, gentlemen," he tells us. "We've much work to do today."

"Whatdaya got to drink?" Jeff asks.

"I've mixed up some green Kwench-Aid for you guys."

"That'll do."

"Got anything else?" I ask. Jeff stops pouring syrup on his French toast midstream and stares at me as if I'd declared puppies make for good stir fry and Hitler wasn't such a bad guy after all.

"What?" I respond. "The sugary Kwench-Aid and the maple syrup is a bit much."

Jeff says nothing as he shovels a wad of French toast into his frowning mouth.

"I've got some milk." Simon Tybalt fetches a pitcher from the refrigerator. "It's not the milk you know from Earth cows. This is from virgin midget goats on Qastar VII. It's an acquired taste. I bought it off a Qastarian farmer. He's dead now. Life is funny that way. One minute you're milking your goats for market, the next your planet is thrown into a sudden Ice Age because of an accident involving a climate change device I had absolutely nothing to do with."

I sip from the glass he pours. The milk tastes like a peach pie cooked on a George Foreman grill topped with rancid yogurt. I don't wish to be rude, so I drink more anyway. Jeff maintains his glare of disdain for my very existence.

"What?" I ask him as I choke down a swallow of the milk.

"You dissed Styx in the car yesterday. You turned down Kwench-Aid for breakfast. It's like I don't even know you anymore."

"People change, man." I sip from my glass but only let the milk touch my lips and pretend to swallow because this crap is nasty.

"Whatever." He shoves a fork full of French toast into his mouth and pouts.

"Now who's surly?" I snap back.

"So." Simon Tybalt sips his own glass of milk. "You have the nano plans, right?"

"Yep," says Jeff while chewing, apparently disposing of his usual commitment to table etiquette. He retrieves a jump drive from his inside jacket pocket and hands it to Simon. "I'm supposed to trade it for Leigh Ann, right?"

"Actually." Simon Tybalt pulls a jump drive of his own out of his pocket and holds it out. "You'll give him this."

"What is that?" I ask.

"I call this The Grand Illusion."

"Because he appreciates the genius of Styx," Jeff snarls at me.

"When this is inserted into Grandor's database, it will appear perfectly normal and he'll be quite pleased. He'll release Leigh Ann to you, because he is, after all, a businessman. He doesn't want to harm anyone."

I'm having the same feeling I had at Corporate when Max spouted off words and phrases that meant nothing to me.

"Absolutely." I nod my head in that way you do when you need to appear in on things.

"I've rigged the program to run a virus exactly twenty-four hours after it is downloaded. It'll completely delete his entire database."

"We're going to double-cross him?" I ask. "Won't that be dangerous? What if we get caught?"

"That's the job," is all Jeff says.

"Most important," Simon Tybalt looks at me. "While you're with Grandor, you're to steal my plans for the quintonium drive. He stole them from me after I developed a prototype and I want them back."

"Wait," I say. "So, that's a real thing? Jeff said it wasn't a real thing."

"You should know," Simon tells me. "You should know quite a bit about the drive, as well as most of what Corporate is all about. Stealing the plans for that drive is the whole reason you're here, my friend."

"I really have no clue why I'm here." I stand and take my plate to the sink because when I'm feeling particularly frustrated or upset, I feel the need to busy myself with a household chore. "I'm ignorant of everything going on and feel utterly useless."

"You didn't tell him?" Simon asks Jeff.

"I haven't found the right time."

"Tell me what?"

"You've been through a lot," Jeff says, shrugging. He stands and comes to me, yet maintains a safe distance. "Your freak out levels were already in the red zone. I didn't wanna make it worse."

"What are you talking about?" I look to Simon Tybalt for some insight. "What's he talking about?'

The mythical founder of Corporate walks to Jeff, pointing like a scolding father. "I helped send you back through the portal specifically for bringing him for training. He needs to know what he's dealing with so we can use him properly."

I remember two cheerleaders in my freshman English comp class saying something similar once when they wanted me to do their essay assignment for them. Because they were cute cheerleaders who feigned a passing interest me, I obliged. Sure, they used me to cheat on their homework, but they were cheerleaders. They yield a certain sorcery over guys like me. Jeff and Simon are not cute cheerleaders, so I'm less inclined to play ball.

"I've had a lot of secrets kept from me lately. My best friend survived being sucked through a portal. My girlfriend apparently hunts aliens who have infiltrated Earth." My chest is heaving because my anger is taking over. "I'm tired of secrets. Someone tell me what is going on."

Simon Tybalt walks over and embraces me. I'm terribly uncomfortable with all of this.

"Life hurts sometimes," he tells me. "It hurts when your heart gets broken. It hurts when you're betrayed. It hurts when try to stop an edge trimmer with your face."

I push him away and walk to Jeff.

"What the hell is going on?" I want to grab him and shake him, but I'm not sure what purpose that would serve. I stomp around the room. "What the hell is happening to my life?"

"There's something inside you, man," Jeff says.

A sudden flush of panic runs through me. Since everything I know about everyone I know is all wrong, I wonder if everything I know about myself is wrong, too. "Am I an android or something? Am I even a person?"

"Sssh. Sssh." Simon Tybalt tries to hug me again, but I'm done with that shit.

"Get off me. I want answers and I want them now."

Jeff throws his arms up in the air and huffs as if he's being peer pressured into holding up a liquor store using his finger for a gun. After a couple of false starts, he finally spills the beans.

"I may or may not have downloaded the entire Corporate training database and library into your brain. On purpose."

*

I sprint away from the conversation and weave my way through the corridors. I pass countless posters of beautiful women and arrive at the garage where *Miss America* awaits. I get in the driver's side and start pressing buttons.

"How do I start this damn thing?" I shout.

Jeff and Simon Tybalt are running toward me, calling after me to stop. The engine won't start. The only result I achieve from all the button pushing is Styx blaring over the stereo. I'm so sick of Styx right now. I shut off the music, get out of the car, and prowl like a caged tiger who was promised a gazelle for dinner, but was given tofu instead.

"You're pissed," Jeff says. "I get it."

"You don't have a clue, you asshole."

Simon grabs my shoulders. "You have inside you a piece of nanotech that attaches to your cerebral cortex and downloads its contents into your consciousness. The particular device in you is the entire Corporate training catalog. You're a walking, talking encyclopedia of Corporate."

"When? How? Why?" I ask.

"Prom night," Jeff says. "When I offered you the flask of Kwench-Aid. It was in there."

"Making the nano waterproof was a last minute decision," Simon says.

My body trembles with rage. I want to punch my friend. I want to scream at the top of my lungs. I want to tell Simon the goat milk crap he served was disgusting, but that would be impolite.

"Inside you is the only version of this nano. We needed to beta test it and Jeff already had a different form of nano in him. I needed to know if I could put all that Corporate knowledge into someone's brain."

"That was a dick move. Both of you." I turn to Jeff. He is looking away from me stammering something in jibberish. "Tell me why, Jeff."

"You had all these plans to go to college." He walks away to *Miss America* and leans on her hood. "You were leaving. I'm not going to college. I don't care about going to college. I just wanna live. I wanted something to keep you at Corporate." He still won't look at me, but I can see his face. He knows this was a shitty thing to do to me.

"I don't want to be at Corporate anymore," I tell him. "I'm tired of it. I want to move on. That was my choice. You took my choice away from me."

"I don't have friends other than you. I have Leigh Ann, but I'm not sure where our relationship is headed now that she's been sucked through the portal and held hostage by a whack job alien. That might be tough to bounce back from. I'm not ready to see me and you split up. So, I made you like me. Just like Kilroy and Mr. Roboto."

"Enough!" A new strain of anger rages through me and I storm about the room in the kind of tirade one might record on their phone in the hopes of creating an epic viral video. "Kilroy is Mr. Roboto. Mr. Roboto is Kilroy. It's the same damn person! Read the album liner notes. Better yet. Actually listen to the song. It ends with 'I'm Kilroy.' How much more obvious can it be? I keep telling you, but you refuse to listen. And you know why? Because you don't give a flying piece of chicken shit about anyone except yourself! I've carried you our entire friendship. Bailed you out of one shit storm after another. You're a terrible decision maker. The worst. *Kilroy Was Here* is a lousy album. Garbage. It broke up the damn band. Yet, you treat it like a masterpiece and you've forced it into a metaphor of our friendship. I guess that works if you consider it ended a great run. Like you spiking my drink with a brain-altering miniature robot spider ended us."

"Okay," Jeff says. "I get it. I suck."

"Actually, we can extend the metaphor a bit further." I should really stop now, but I'm on a roll. "What's your second favorite Styx song after 'Mr. Roboto?'"

"'Music Time.'"

"See? You're not drawn to one of their classic songs from when they were one of the world's most popular bands. You prefer the song that was recorded in the midst of a breakup. How perfect is that? You picked two songs synonymous with the dissolution of your favorite band. So, I guess now they're perfect choices!"

The exact moment during my tirade I reached into Jeff's chest and crushed his spirit can't be determined. It may have been my insult of his favorite album. It may have been calling him selfish. Likely, it was when I told him he had ruined our friendship.

"You're wrong about *Kilroy Was Here*. That's blasphemy."

I guess it was the album comment.

"Shut up!" Simon Tybalt commands. "We need to stop a maniac from taking over the Earth and you guys want to bicker about which Styx album was best and who spiked a drink with a nanotech? First of all, everyone knows the best Styx album is *The Grand Illusion.* A case could be made for *Paradise Theater*, sure, but everything great about Styx is on *The Grand Illusion.*

"And *Kilroy Was Here* is hardly garbage," he continues. "It's a product of its era. Sure, it's polarizing, but there's no denying the catchiness of 'Mr. Roboto' or the anger in 'Heavy Metal Poisoning.'"

"See?" Jeff shouts. "He gets it. Why can't you?"

A heavy silence falls over the garage.

"Get over here, you two. Now." Simon's voice is more forceful than usual. We both walk toward him and face one another. "Shake hands."

"I won't shake the hand of a blasphemer," Jeff mutters.

"I won't shake the hand of a deceitful bastard," I say.

"This is a bastard-free zone." Simon grabs my right hand and Jeff's and forces them together. We begrudgingly shake, but I don't mean it. Simon then reaches to both our necks and presses a pen-like device into us. I feel a surge of calming electrical currents flood my body. I pull my hand from my friend's and an odd sensation consumes me. A lump forms in my throat.

"Let's try a little empathy, shall we?" Simon says.

CHAPTER EIGHT

I stand across from my friend and he looks like Jeff, but, yet, doesn't. I don't feel quite like myself. The pierce in my neck from Simon Tybalt's device still stings. Jeff rubs his neck and frowns like a little kid.

"What the hell, dude?" He points at Simon. "Why did you do that?"

"You've both been injected with an empathizer. Maintain direct eye contact with one another for ten seconds without talking."

"I don't want to," I say.

"Quiet," he commands. "Or I'll alter your equilibrium and you will constantly tip over."

I eye my friend and he eyes me. I'm not sure what is supposed to happen but after a few seconds I feel my anger dissipate. I no longer see his face or his ridiculous behavior. Gone are the faded ruffled tuxedo shirt and top hat. Instead, it's as if I can see his soul and feel what he feels. A burning warmth envelops me and I feel a lump in my throat. From what I can see, he must be experiencing the same thing.

"Do you two have something to say to one another?" Simon asks.

"I know you're ready to do your own thing." Jeff looks at the floor and sways. "It's obvious. Stuff that used to be fun for you isn't any more and I get it. You want a normal life. You always have. I screwed that up for you. I'm sorry I injected you with a nanotech. That was a shitty thing to do."

I can't help but accept his apology and offer one of my own.

"You didn't mean any harm. I know that. You want this whole thing to keep going. You have a wanderlust and want to go on these grand adventures. You always want us to be Kilroy and Mr. Roboto. You want us to be us."

My friend starts blubbering and I can no longer fight back my own tears.

"I love you, man," I tell him.

"Same," he says. "Get over here, asshole."

We hug for a few seconds and I feel the sensation brought on by the empathizer wearing off. A slight tingling pricks my fingers. Jeff and I break our hug and I look at Simon Tybalt.

"What did you do to us?" I ask him.

He holds up the metallic syringe he plunged into our necks. "The Empathizer is one of my different behavioral alteration weapons I've developed over the years. I developed the entire arsenal because, as a pacifist, I abhor violence. These are defensive weapons that alter your opponents behavior long enough for you to make an escape."

"Why did you do that to us? That was manipulative."

He places his hand on my shoulder and peers through my eyes.

"Empathy is an equalizer," he says. "When we allow ourselves a moment to walk in another's shoes, we appreciate their perspective. It's a tremendous gift we humans have been given, but we all too often fail to exercise it. Pride prevents us. So, I gave you two a much-needed nudge."

"Still," I protest. "You forced me to empathize. I didn't have a choice."

"If I had left the choice to you, you guys would still be arguing about classic rock."

I look at my friend who is staring at the floor once again.

"I'm sorry for injecting a nanotech in you," he mumbles. "That was a shitty thing to do."

"I'm sorry for insulting Styx. *Kilroy Was Here* is a fine album."

Simon Tybalt walks to the tarp next to the Volkswagen Bus and whips it onto the floor to reveal a cylindrical device about the size of a car engine. It looks like a giant garbage disposal. It's casing is clear and tubes and circuits intertwine around it. The sight of it snaps me from my issues with Jeff and Simon's manipulations and into that place where I'm floating through a virtual library. I know where everything is and where to find it. I know every inch of the device Simon revealed and how to access all the information about it.

"That's a quintonium drive," I say. "Intended to be the most powerful piece of machinery known in the galaxy."

I snap back to reality from this out-of-body experience and gasp.

"Now are you ready to get in touch with the nano inside you, Tony? Or do you wanna keep whining about your life?"

*

Jeff sits on the hood of *Miss America* and smokes a Mongalisonian cigarette. A scowl covers his face and he stares off somewhere only he can see. "Too Much Time on My Hands" is blaring from inside the car and I fear at any moment he is going to break into his angry dance.

"Are we good?" I ask.

"It's all good."

"I want to apologize for being a dick earlier. I shouldn't have said that stuff."

"Seriously. We're cool." He hops off the car and heads to a display of weapons on the table. "I'm ready to get on with this. I want Leigh Ann back."

Simon Tybalt claps his hands and bounces over to console. "You need to know what you're up against." He taps on the console keyboard and the face of Grandor the Malevolent fills the giant monitor on the wall. "You need to know what you're dealing with."

"Grandor's a dick," Jeff says. "What more do we need to know?"

"There's a lot I wanna know," I say. "Why is all of this so important to Grandor? Taking over planets in the name of high end real estate? Is that really what's going on here?"

Simon Tybalt turns to me, a wide grin on his face. "You tell me, Tony."

"What do you mean? I don't know anything."

"But you do." He walks to me and puts his hands on my shoulders, like a coach trying to give his new athlete a pep talk. "You have access to an entire file on Grandor. It's in you. Search for it."

I sigh because I really don't know how this is supposed to work. I close my eyes and picture Grandor's goofy oversized oval of a head. His big eyes and purple skin. His brilliant white teeth. At first, all I sense is revulsion at the thought of this awful being. Then, a rush of recognition tingles my brain not unlike the sensation of my first sip of gin and Fresca. I float through the virtual library in my psyche and find all I need to know. It's as if I've been researching Grandor's life for years in preparation for writing his biography. I blurt out the first piece of information I can think of.

"Grandor the Malevolent is a highly advanced artificial intelligence created years ago by two intoxicated scientists in a lab during a convention on Gamma Centauri VII. His true form is that of a computer program which is downloaded into the consciousness of a host. He is not even a biological creature."

"What a freak," Jeff mumbles.

"Excellent!" Simon circles me, encouraging me to keep going. His voice is muffled, as if coming from another room, even though I sense his presence. I admit the ease with which I'm spouting this information is giving me a buzz.

"Grandor's creators attempted to develop a form of intelligence that could be transferred into other beings. Its intelligence would spread itself to whatever or whoever connected to it. The body you see Grandor inhabiting is that of a merchant he attached himself to several years ago."

"If he's not human, why does he act so goofy?" Jeff asks me.

"When Grandor attaches himself to a being, he can access all parts of the brain and download its contents, including emotions and sensual experiences. This has produced some rather volatile side effects that Grandor's creators did not anticipate when they wrote his code. He feels what they feel. Taps into their memories and experiences."

"You're doing very well, Tony." Simon keeps circling me.

"Grandor has had access to heartbreak, euphoria, trauma, jubilation, and excessive amounts of pornography. Astonishing as it sounds, he has a damaged psyche and he overcompensates by attempting world domination. He is a textbook narcissist and is prone to unpredictable bouts of sociopathy."

I stop and look at Simon.

"What's wrong?" he asks.

"I admit this is kinda cool," I tell him, "but I still don't like the idea of having a spider-looking nanobug in my brain. I want it out."

"Help me get Leigh Ann and the plans for the quintonium drive," Jeff says. "Then we'll take it out. I promise, man."

"Wait." Simon holds up a hand and his brow furrows. "What spider-looking nanobug is in your brain?"

"That's what's inside me, right? A little nanobug that looks like a spider. The Araneae."

Simon Tybalt covers his mouth and his eyes widen in horror. He paces back and forth in front of the display of weapons and mumbles over and over.

"No, no, no, no, no, no, no, no."

"What?" I ask.

"Yeah," Jeff says. "What's up with you?"

Simon leans against the table on which all the weapons rest. He rubs his face and blows out a weary sigh.

"The nanotech in you doesn't look like a spider. I hate spiders. I would never design a nano to look like one of those monsters." He fishes the thumb drive Jeff gave him at breakfast out of his pocket and runs to the computer console. He plugs the drive into a port and taps on the keyboard. A small robotic device resembling a crayfish appears onscreen.

"This is the nano in you. Not a spider." He taps on the keyboard again and a new image appears onscreen of a spider-shaped micro robot.

"This," he says, "is Araneae."

"That's it." I point at the image onscreen. "Randi and Max showed me that at Corporate. They seem to think that's what Grandor has developed."

"Oh, this is bad." Simon paces once more as he frets. "This is really bad. This is Steve Carrel leaving *The Office* bad."

"Wow," Jeff whispers. "That is bad."

"I've never seen that show," I admit.

Jeff shakes his head at me. "Did I know that about you?"

"Araneae is a form of artificial intelligence created on the dark market on the planet Lloyd," Simon tells us. "Legend has it a restaurant owner wanted a wait staff that would be compliant with him and his customers. He purchased the Araneae off that planet's version of the internet. What he didn't realize is they are a kind of hybrid of an A.I. and a carbon-based life form."

"They're alive?" I ask.

"In a sense." Simon looks only at the Araneae onscreen. "And powerful. Once they infiltrate your cerebral cortex, they take you over. You become a kind of robot who does only the bidding of a master."

"Like Mr. Roboto," gasps Jeff.

"So what do we do now?" I ask.

"We stick to the plan." Simon clicks off the Araneae image and starts gathering a few weapons from the table. "But, we have to act with more urgency. Grandor wants to turn the Earth into a giant resort and he wants to use my company to do it. We must stop him. I took the first big step by downloading that nano into you, Tony."

"How does that help you save your company?"

Simon prowls around the garage like a man relaying the single most important thing any human has ever uttered, like the cure for cancer or the reason so many people watch *The Big Bang Theory.*

"One night I got really drunk on a rare visit to Dangabah. They were having a convention on artificial intelligence and I was curious. Also, I did a lot of shrooms. Don't do shrooms. You're too young."

"I'll remember that," I say.

"Anyway, I knew I needed a way to protect Corporate, but couldn't figure out why. Then, while at the convention, it hit me. What if I could deposit the entire Corporate knowledge base into a human being? What if I could communicate to all Corporate employees via nanotechnology? These were the questions that plagued me. I also asked myself if I could make shape-shifting leopard dragons that spoke fluent Finnish like the ones in my mushroom-induced trips, but I had to put that on the back burner.

"So, I developed the little bugger inside you. The entire knowledge base of Corporate is in that son of a bitch. I just needed a human to accept it."

"Why not use a jump drive?" I ask.

"Why Rube Goldberg Protocols, of course." The founder of Corporate stands and walks to me, an impish grin across his face. "You see, if anyone wants the training database, they'll be looking for a jump drive or an external hard drive or servers. No one will be looking for you."

"You mean?"

"Tony Pershing, my dear boy," he says with his grin widening. "You are a living, breathing Rube Goldberg Protocol."

I stand for a moment and ponder that statement. I think about The Prom Night of Which We Shall Not Speak and the ever-growing complexity of my relationship with Marlene. I ruminate about my lack of decisiveness and my need to understand everything before taking action.

"My god," I say. "That makes so much more sense than I ever thought it could. It's unethical and I hate you both with the white hot intensity of an exploding supernova for subjecting me to it, but it makes sense."

"Don't worry," Simon tells me. "When the mission is done, we'll get it out of you. This is only temporary."

"Let's talk about the good stuff," Jeff says. "Guns and shit."

*

I'm facing my best friend as we prepare to spar. A tray of weapons of various shapes, sizes, and forms sits next to me on a rolling cart. Some resemble rifles, others, pistols. I spot a short-nosed double-barrel pistol, and a few other revolver types. They all look like Nerf guns painted for science fiction cosplay.

"This is your weapons training," Simon Tybalt announces. "While I'm a pacifist at heart, I recognize the need for some kind of arsenal, but abhor violence. Thus, I created behavioral weaponry. A shot from one of these bad boys will alter the behavior of your assailant, temporarily impairing them so that you may escape."

"I've seen a couple of those in action," I tell him.

"Groovy." He picks up the double-barreled pistol and hands it to me. It's light and easy to maneuver.

"What's this?" I ask.

"Take it in your hand and tell me," he says. "Let the nanotech speak to you."

I close my eyes and squeeze the weapon's handle. The chrome plating is cool in my grip, but a warm wave spreads through my body. I sense a voice somewhere speaking directly to me on behalf of the gun and telling me everything I need to know about it.

"This is the Passive Aggressive Aggravator," I announce. "One shot from this temporarily renders your assailant incapacitated with passive aggressive behavior. They're unable to attack you physically because they are too self-absorbed in how you make them feel."

"I want you to shoot Jeff with it."

"I don't feel comfortable shooting my friend," I say.

"Remember," Simon tells me. "He knowingly injected you with a nanotech against your will."

I nod and fire the Passive Aggressive Aggravator at Jeff. Two yellow balls of energy hit him in the chest and spread across his body before dissipating.

"Well, that's a cool gun," Jeff says, looking away. "I didn't get a gun like that, but, it's no big deal really. I thought we're going to have a fair fight. It's cool. I'm not even mad."

"I'm so sorry," I tell him.

"No. You obviously needed that gun more than me. I'm happy for you."

He rambles on for about 30 more seconds about how life isn't fair but whatever because who cares. The effects wear off and he shakes his head.

"So, I can pick up a weapon and know instinctively what it does? What's the point of that?"

"That's only a test." Simon replaces the Passive Aggressive Agitator on the table. "The nano gives you the ability to assess situations. Understand your surroundings. Analyze data. You can spot something in the Corporate database and know what it is. In addition, you'll be an expert navigator on your journey to meet with Grandor the Malevolent."

I pick up a flashlight on the table to inspect it, but Simon gently pulls it away.

"That's the Existential Crisis Inducer," he says. "Let's not play with that yet."

*

I lie on the floor of the observatory that sits atop Simon Tybalt's lair and stare at the expanse of space overhead. Simon Tybalt lies to my left and Jeff to my right. I feel very small and insignificant. The prospect of saving the world from planetary real estate development should inflate my ego, but, instead, I feel unworthy. I scan the view overhead and think about where Earth might be. What are my parents doing? They must be worried sick about me. I wonder what they'll say to me when I see them again. I'm sure The Look and The Reassurance will be replaced with The Screaming and The Banishment. I think, too, about Marlene. What is she doing? Does she miss me? Is she hunting Clint? I miss my parents. I miss Marlene. I scan the heavens for a binary star, but I don't see one. I try not to take that as an omen.

An area of the glass ceiling lights up around a cluster of celestial bodies.

"What is this?" Simon asks.

"The Jaqrillion Quadrant," I say. "Here is located the planet Klandar, which is home to race of people who have hermetically sealed themselves in anticipation of the arrival of their god." My voice is flat and monotone. We've been at this for hours.

"Been there," Jeff says. "Creepy place."

"Tony, you seem pensive," Simon says. "Are you alright?"

"Meh. Thinking about stuff."

"He's thinking about Marlene," Jeff says. "Just like I'm thinking about Leigh Ann."

"Ah, yes. It is the plight of all men to be consumed with thoughts of their true love on the eve of a grand adventure."

"Have you ever been in love?" I ask him.

"We've all been in love," he says. "My love was a former employee. She worked for me almost twenty years ago. A receptionist in accounting. My god, she was beautiful. I first noticed her legs. I nicknamed her Infinity Jones because those legs went on forever."

"What happened between you?" Jeff asks.

"We were ships in the night. We were not meant to be. I wanted more, but she left without really saying goodbye."

"That's sad," I say. "Is that why you left Corporate?"

"Not entirely," he replies. His voice is distant as if he's talking to one of the stars overhead and not me and Jeff. "I did get very depressed, though. So, I went off to find myself. I turned the company over to Max Gentry on an interim basis and I traveled the cosmos. I discovered I liked it better here. So, I built this moon base and stayed."

"Why not retire?" I ask. "Why fake your own death?"

"People would leave me alone if they thought I was dead," he says. "You two have a long trip to the planet Lloyd tomorrow. Don't stay up late. I'll see you first thing in the morning."

"Mr. Tybalt." I stand and face him. "I have a question. Will this nanotech take over my consciousness like the Araneae? Is that a possibility?"

"Oh, you don't need to worry about that," he says with a dismissive wave of his hand. "I've discovered an herbal medication that mutes its growth and gives you more control over it."

"Herbal medication?" I ask.

"Yeah." Jeff lights up one of Mongalisonian cigarettes. "Works like a charm."

*

Jeff and I lie on the roof of *Miss America*. The vast expanse of the universe stretches above us. The stars feel so close I could grab one and put it in my pocket. Jeff draws a deep drag from his cigarette and holds it out to me as he exhales.

"You're going to need this, you know."

He's right, of course, but I still feel weird smoking this stuff. "It's like I'm doing something illegal," I tell him.

"Well, it's not illegal out here," he says. "And no one on Earth knows it exists, so how can it be illegal there?"

I sigh in resignation and take the cigarette from him and, after some coaching on proper inhaling technique, draw a deep drag. The dry burn of a thousand California wildfires scorches my throat and lungs. I curl into the fetal position as a violent cough starts somewhere in my testicles and rushes through my abdomen. I cry out for the sweet sleep of death.

"That might've been a little too much for your first time," says my understating friend.

Several minutes pass as we share the cigarette. My initial revulsion gives way to a serenity I've never known. I feel as if I've been dipped in a warm goo of tranquility. I jump from the top of *Miss America* and lie on my back in the sand. The realization of the coolness that is my current situation overwhelms me. I'm on a desert moon in some remote backwater part of another galaxy, smoking space dope and staring at the stars. Something in me triggers my arms to wipe up and down and my legs to swipe back and forth.

"What the hell are you doing?" Jeff asks, leaning over the top of the car.

"I'm making snow angels."

"You're in the sand."

"Then, I'm making sand angels. I feel so groovy. I don't want this feeling to end. Like, ever."

"Well, it will." He hops from the top of the Vega and retrieves a duffle bag from the hatch. He walks to the front of the car and spreads a blanket on the ground. He sits and pulls out some food.

"Snacks!" I say, crawling to the blanket. "Thank god. I'm starving."

"What you're experiencing is not merely the munchies. Your body needs to refuel. This will help." He gestures to the spread before us.

"Valasupian sandwiches. Dorgon pizza. Wild fruit from the planet Lloyd. Cool Ranch Doritos."

"Nice."

He holds up a large black thermos. "And we wash it down with some green Kwench-Aid."

What follows is a mash-up of eating exotic foods that don't taste all that exotic, drinking the sweet nectar of Kwench-Aid, and talking about life while "Boat on the River," by Styx plays.

"So, you're going to college?" he asks, face pointed toward the stars that overwhelm the sky above us.

"That's the plan."

He chomps on a slice of pizza and talks with his mouth open. "You always were a planner."

"You're really gonna–?" I don't know how to finish the question because it sounds so absurd. It seems beyond comprehension that my best friend intends to roam outer space for a living.

"Gonna what?" he prompts.

"Are you sure you should do this? You're basically going to be an intergalactic truck driver. You just turned 18 a few months ago and you're not the most mature person I've ever known. Shouldn't you think this through a little more?"

"Are you freaking bananas? Is that your ass talking?" He doesn't sound offended or angry, more mildly shocked and a little appalled.

"Seems like a really big decision, ya know? Shouldn't you talk to your mom?"

"And tell her what? 'Hey, mom, I got a job bootlegging across space. Can you sign this permission slip?" He points to the expanse of cosmos overhead. "Wouldn't you wanna stay out here?"

"I dunno. Maybe. It's scary."

"This has been the best time of my life," he says, sipping from the thermos. "Better than the summer we tried to build a time machine. Better than the time we tried PBR for the first time. Better than the summer Natalie Mills showed me her boobs." He stands and picks up the duffle bag. "This is what I'm meant for."

He retrieves two matching flashlights from the duffle and tosses one to me. I hold it up. It is light, the dark red casing made of aluminum. A label on the side reads ECI-108.

"Existential Crisis Inducers," I say. "If the light from this hits you directly in the eyes, you'll fall into a debilitating, angst-filled identity crisis.

"Yep." Jeff's eyes flash his familiar I've-got-a-crazy-idea expression and part of me shudders. "Let's really talk about life."

He gestures for me to stand up and face him. We look like gunfighters about to end this once and for all.

"What are we doing?" I ask.

"Trust me."

"Not possible."

"When I count to three, we'll both draw and shine our lights into each other's eyes."

"Everything about this screams bad idea," I mutter.

After the fastest 1-2-3 count in history, we point our Existential Crisis Inducers at one another and fire away. A stream of iridescent light blinds me and I drop my device and cover my eyes. I hit the ground and writhe in the sand. Each time I try to open my eyes, an obnoxious ball of light obscures my vision as if a giant flash bulb went off. After a few seconds, it fades and I can see my friend staring at the stars overhead, tears flowing down his cheeks.

"I'm so freaking small," he whispers.

I'm acutely aware that my every emotional nerve is raw and exposed. The mountains of the desert moon grow more ominous around me and threaten to fall on top of me.

"What the hell is happening?" Panic grips me as I try to run in eleven directions at once.

Jeff falls to his knees, defeated. "I'm 18 years old. I don't know who my dad is. I didn't graduate because I got sucked into the portal. The girl I love is being held captive by a galactic supervillain. What's the point? Sure, I've got a bitching space car, but is that enough?"

I kneel next to him, a tidal wave of regret washing over me. I want to cry but no tears will come. Even though I'm not out of my teens yet, I feel like everything I've done is a parade of poor decisions in a misspent youth that will haunt me for the rest of my life. A very certain fate awaits me involving homelessness, a body odor of cheap whiskey and wet burritos, and talking to an imaginary duck I've named Ron.

"I don't know what I'm meant for," I say. "I don't think I'll ever know."

"You're smart. You're level-headed and all that shit. You're gonna do great things."

"You can stay home and do great things, too." I tell him.

Jeff thinks for a moment, smoking his cigarette and sipping his drink. "I'm nobody there. That night when the portal opened up, I thought I was gonna die. My whole life passed before me and all I saw was cheese. Don't ask me why cheese. All I know is it made me sad. I don't want a life. I want an adventure."

I grip the top of my head with both hands and gasp, a terrifying realization oozing over me.

"Ohmigod," I say. "What if fatalism is true?"

"Huh?"

"Fatalism. What if all this talk about the future is futile? What if the future is predetermined and we're helpless to do anything about it? Even if I go to college and become a massive success in whatever I endeavor, I may still be fated to sitting under an overpass talking to a duck named Ron."

Jeff thinks for a moment. "I suppose that depends on how much you stock you put in the principle of bivalence. Either something is or it isn't. Either something is true or it's false."

"So, either it is true that I will spend the days before my death talking to Ron or it isn't."

"Exactly."

I walk a few feet ahead of him and stare at the horizon. I throw my hands up in defeat. The writer of Ecclesiastes was right. Everything is utterly meaningless.

"Why should I care about my future? Why should I care whether Marlene will love me again? Why should I care about anything, Jeff?"

"I dunno," my friend says. He stands next to me and puts his hand on my shoulder. "I'm trying to figure out who Ron is."

CHAPTER NINE

Miss America's hatch is filled with a cache of Simon Tybalt's behavioral weapons. A duffle loaded with Existential Crisis Inducers, Passive Aggressive Aggravators, Gulliballs, and JazzHands Phasers rests next to a suitcase with a change of clothes for us. I take a Gulliball and JazzHand Phaser and stick them in a backpack with some snacks for the trip to Planet Lloyd. I rid the passenger side floorboard of Taco Haus bags, candy wrappers, and receipts printed in alien languages. My stomach flutters in anticipation of our journey. It's not like I've never been nervous before. I've experienced stomach flutters associated with admitting to my parents I gave the cat a Mohawk. I fondly recall the butterflies I had when Marlene and I first kissed. This is my first bout of off-to-face-a-galactic-supervillan-on-his-home-planet anxiety. I don't particularly care for the feeling.

"You've got a quite a trip ahead of you," says Simon Tybalt. "Keep me updated on your progress and alert me of any emergencies. Otherwise, don't bother me. I'll be entertaining a guest while you're gone."

"Boom chicka bow bow," says Jeff.

"Don't ever do that again," I tell him. "No one does that anymore."

"Are you going to be surly again? I'm not putting up with surliness on this trip."

"I have something for both of you." Simon pulls a stack of business cards held together by a rubber band from his pants pocket and hands them to me. "Someone told me you like business cards."

I take the stack from him and look at the top card.

TONY PERSHING
TRAINING DATABASE STRATEGIST

"I don't know what to say." I look at the Corporate founder. He's giving me that sad smile. "Thank you."

"You're welcome." He then puts his hands on my shoulders and looks deep into me. "You'll use your weapons to neutralize Grandor and you're training to download the quintonium drive plans. I believe in you."

"I'm glad someone does."

He turns to Jeff and hands him a jump drive shaped like a duck.

"What is it?" Jeff looks at the drive. "Is it porn?"

"That is a file of songs from 1976-1986, what I consider the best era for music." Simon lights up a Mongalisonian cigarette and smokes. "Plug that into your USB on the Vega and expand your musical horizons."

"No kidding," I say. "Try something from the 21st century."

Jeff regards the tiny duck and looks at me. "I'm playing Styx first, then, maybe, I'll play this."

"Godspeed," Simon Tybalt says, "and remember…"

"We own the night," Jeff and I say in unison.

"I was going to be say be safe, but whatever works for you."

*

"Here." Jeff hands me a rumpled piece of paper with some numbers scrawled all over them. "These are the coordinates for planet Lloyd. Wanna input them into the navigator?"

"I don't need those," I say, brimming with confidence in my new abilities.

The coordinates spark in my nanotech and suddenly I realize I'm an expert on a planet I've never visited. I close my eyes and feel myself floating through the vast library of Corporate knowledge in my brain. I access the section dedicated to interplanetary travel and navigation and see clearly all I need to know about the planet Lloyd. The planet's size, position in the galaxy, rotational patterns, geological and atmospheric composition all fill my brain as if they'd always been there. I tap the coordinates into *Miss America's* navigation system and we're off.

"Have you been to Grandor's house before?" I ask Jeff.

"No, but I've been to Lloyd. I met Grandor at a dive bar. That's where he offered up a deal for Leigh Ann."

"What's this place like?"

"Well." Jeff takes a contemplative drag from his space cigarette as he speaks. "Let's say America's worst inner cities and trashiest trailer parks got drunk on cheap wine and had unprotected sex."

"I'd rather not."

"Then, their bastard children would be a ghetto of shanty towns, tenements, and gutted housing projects."

"That sounds awful."

"That's planet Lloyd."

The journey from the moon of Nitz to planet Lloyd would normally take a little under a year. Because of the quintonium that powers *Miss America* and the many other portals throughout the galaxy, our trip only takes about five days. We stop to use the restroom at rest stop space stations and floating convenience stores. With each portal we enter, I grow more comfortable with the experience. The ear popping sucks.

Boredom sets in often so we try various tactics for fighting it. We discuss our adventures as kids. We sing along to the music. We contemplate the deep mysteries of life. We smoke Mongalisonian tobacco. Jeff drinks his usual green Kwench-Aid, but I stick with water. I filled Jeff's backpack with some of the behavioral weapons because I wanted to learn more about what we're carrying. I reach into the backpack and pull out a shiny silver object about the size of a softball.

"Can you tell me what that is?" Jeff asks.

"This is a Gulliball. By clicking the small button on the side of the weapon, you release an invisible force field at your target that will render them completely gullible for 30 seconds. They will believe anything you tell them, allowing you to gain a momentary advantage." I examine the ball closely, turning it over and holding up to my face. "Does it really work?"

Jeff reaches over and presses the button. A puff of warm air smacks my face but I don't feel any different. Jeff reaches out tugs at my nose.

"Got your nose!"

Panic overtakes me and I grab at the area where I am sure I once had a nose but feel nothing.

"Why would you do dat?" My voice sounds as though I have a horrible cold. "You can'd juds take thomeone's nothe. Give it back, athhole!"

"Alright," he says. "Here." He puts his hand on my face and I begin to calm myself and breathe easy.

"Don't ever take my nose again," I say.

"I'm sorry, bro. Also, you wet your pants."

I look down at my crotch and attain a previously unrecorded level of freak out. "Oh my god! Seriously? This night is a disaster!" I become aware that I may have had an out-of-body experience that I can't explain. I don't know why I'm rubbing my crotch with my shirtsleeve, but I am. I look at my lousy excuse for a friend as he giggles like some socially backward pubescent boy who likes saying the word "panties."

"Classic," he says.

I point the Gulliball at Jeff and press the button on the side. I watch his face morph from joyous to blank in an instant.

"I think I'm attracted to you," I tell him as earnestly as possible.

"Whoa. Dude." He holds his hands up. "I was afraid of this. Look. I'm flattered and, yes, I admit, sometimes I get curious. But, not with you. It's too weird."

"I understand," I say, feigning choked emotion. "I knew I was taking a chance."

He puts his hand on my shoulder and squeezes. "If you ever need to talk, I'm here for you. Don't let anyone keep you from being yourself. I love you, man."

I can only grin as his expression moves seamlessly from empathy to quizzical in a second. He glances at his hand on my shoulder and I laugh.

"Don't be a dick," he says.

I remove a copper colored device from the backpack. "What's this? Looks like a hair dryer."

"It is a hair dryer. It's Leigh Ann's from prom night." A sheepish smile forms on Jeff's face. "We were planning on getting a hotel room after the river thing."

"Do you love her?" I ask him.

"Yeah. Sure." He shrugs. "What's not to love?"

"You're nothing if not a hopeless romantic."

"Whatdaya want me to say?" He retrieves his trusty thermos from behind his seat, the nectar sure to induce diabetes in him, and sips from it. "Leigh Ann is the one, ya know? I'd do anything for her. She's hot. She's chill. She doesn't judge me. You know what I'm talking about. You love Marlene. You tell me what that means."

I take a moment before answering. Describing how you love someone should be easy, but how do you find adequate words?

"She's the first thought I have when I wake up in the morning," I say. "She's the last thought I have before I fall asleep. She is every thought I have in between."

"That's beautiful. Seriously. What song is that from? Is it a poem or something?"

"It just came out. It's how I feel."

"No. That's from something. I know it. You're not that eloquent."

"I shouldn't have broken up with her," I say. "I'm an idiot."

"Yes, you are." Jeff holds up his thermos to propose a toast. "To Leigh Ann and Marlene. Here's hoping we're all back together and making out soon."

"What about this gun here?" I produce a dark gray long-barreled pistol from the backpack. On the handle are four different buttons, each a different color. Green, blue, yellow, red.

"Careful with that," Jeff says. "We don't want that going off in here."

"The Jazz Hands Phaser 6375," I say, the nano taking full effect. "When fired, your assailants will break into a spontaneous dance number to one of thousands of songs downloaded into the weapon's software."

"Trust me," Jeff says. "It works. I used it on some thugs who were chasing me on Ragablum V and as far as I know they're still doing the 'Thriller' dance."

Like all road trips, this one has an ebb and flow. We talk. We laugh. We bicker. We eat. We nap. We get bored. With *Miss America* on autopilot, Jeff is reclined back and snoring. I'm trying to sleep but I'm restless. The weight of everything going on in my life is heavy and I'm tossing and turning. I reach over and shut off the marathon of Styx and breathe in the quiet. I open the glove box of the Vega and find a tattered paperback book tucked inside. I pull it out and see it is Jeff's copy of *Something Wicked This Way Comes*. I look at my friend and let my mind drift to the past.

*

We met on a playground in fifth grade. I was sitting under a tree after not getting picked for kickball, when a scrawny kid I'd not met before asked me if I wanted to play. He introduced himself as Jeff Harper and said he was new to our school. I said sure and after navigating through a conversation about what we should play, I soon realized Jeff was very off. The look in his eyes was different from most kids. I couldn't describe it then, but in retrospect I'd say the lens through which he viewed the world was cracked. His hair wasn't combed, apparently by choice. His clothes appeared to have been put on directly after he discovered them on the floor in a dark corner of his closet. I learned he lived only a couple of blocks from me with his mom, who was a single parent. He said he had never met his dad.

"Let's be monster hunters," he said in a bout of inspiration.

"How does that work?" I asked, new to the whole monster hunter live-action role play thing.

"Easy," he said with surprising intensity. "Follow my lead." He then formed a pistol with his thumb and forefinger, looked off at some invisible target, and started firing. "Look! There's a wendigo! C'mon!"

I ran after him firing my own imaginary gun because he was the only other kid I had met who knew the term wendigo.

He soon decided to name us Kilroy and Mr. Roboto and he shared his love of the song "Mr. Roboto" with me for the first time. We listened to the song on repeat for about half an hour.

"So, I'm a robot?" I asked him.

"Yes. My robot sidekick built by a mad genius scientist." That addition confused me because no mad genius scientist is mentioned in the song or in the entire album of *Kilroy Was Here*.

"So, we're a monster hunting rock star and his robot companion built by a mad genius scientist?"

"Yep."

I decided to roll with it because he was my friend and our times together were fun. We roamed the playground ridding Michael Dukakis Elementary School of imaginary monsters, protecting our unwitting classmates, teachers, and administrators. As we progressed through middle school and eventually high school, we grew out of hunting imaginary monsters and focused on taming the beasts of adolescence. Dating. School. Bullies.

One day our junior year, while we sat eating peanut butter and jelly sandwiches and drinking green Kwench-Aid, I showed Jeff an ad for a job I found on Craigslist.

High school student with unique skills? Looking for a different kind of after school job? We are looking for someone with excellent computer and communication skills to service our very diverse clientele with their unique needs. Flexible hours. Part-time schedules. Opportunities for advancement. Click here to fill out the online application and set up an interview!

I needed a part-time job because I had turned 16 and needed money to put gas in my car. Mom and Dad provided me with a sturdy, reliable Toyota Corolla for my 16th birthday and the arrangement was they would pay the insurance and I would pay for the gas and general maintenance. My occupational options as a teenager were limited to food service, cashier, or working at a local business sweeping floors, taking out the trash, and being taunted with no way of reporting anyone to Human Resources.

"Sounds like an ad for a male prostitute," was Jeff's reaction. "Go for it."

"I dunno. I mean, answering a job listing on Craigslist? Why don't I create my own ad that says I'd be interested in meeting up at an abandoned warehouse to be disemboweled?"

"You're so boring I can't even be bothered to yawn at how boring you are."

He was right. I've played by the rules my entire life. Risk-taker is not a term used to describe me. Prior to applying at Corporate, the last chance I took was deciding to order the mysterious casserole in the cafeteria, a gastrointestinal mistake that my parents still talk about. My track record of going out on a limb is spotty at best. I remained skeptical.

"Would it make you feel better if I applied, too?" he offered.

"I think you would make a lousy male prostitute," I told him. "You're selfish. To be successful in that vocation, I imagine one has to be a giver."

"First of all, I'm not selfish," he protested. "Also, did you say 'vocation?'?"

We went back and forth like that in a dance of I'll-do-it-if-you-do-it and alright-well-go-ahead and you-apply-first-and-then-I-will. Eventually, we agreed upon the logical let's-apply-at-the-same-time. After completing a fairly standard online application, we both completed a couple of assessments and the next thing we knew we were out in the field with Randi Williams guarding the portal.

A massive and secret private company hires teenagers to guard a mysterious portal and, based on what I now suspect about Marlene, hunt aliens. What kind of business model is that?

*

Beeps and dings from the Space Vega's dashboard pull me from my memory and jolt Jeff from his nap. He wipes away some drool which had formed in the corner of his mouth and rubs his face. The swirling, stormy opening of yet another portal looms ahead. He engages the cannon at the front of *Miss America* and fires into the portal's mouth. The car jerks as usual and within seconds we are sucked into the exit to planet Lloyd.

*

The training database downloaded in my brain has provided a better understanding of portals. I always operated under the narrow-minded assumption that the one in Poplar Bluff was the only one. The reality is, of course, they're all over the universe and they come in all shapes and sizes. Entering a portal involves the same process. Your vehicle or spacecraft arrives at a checkpoint and you must present proper registration to proceed. You then move to the hangar with the coordinates of the location to which you wish to travel.

The coordinates, however, do not always lead you to a planet's atmosphere or a moon's orbit or some other logical destination. Instead, you're likely to enter some random place, like over a small river running through an open field outside a small town in Missouri. Or, in the case of planet Lloyd, you pop out of the sky into a prison yard filled with the most hardened criminals the planet knows. Jeff eases *Miss America* through the crowd of inmates. They all nod and wave to him and say things like, "Hey, it's Kilroy again!" and "We need to quit standing in front of the portal. That's how you die."

*

After leaving the prison yard, we glide above the apocalyptic sprawl of high rise slums. Thick, soupy smog hangs in the air. My nano knowledge tells me the atmosphere is similar to Earth's and doesn't require oxygen suits. I roll the window down to take in the air quality. My gag reflex kicks in due to the smell of sulfur and the population's collective body odor.

"Quite the shithole, eh?" Jeff says.

"It's like a demilitarized zone."

"There's a great pizza place here, though. We'll get some while we're here."

"This is where Grandor lives? I expected something more elegant."

"According to the coordinates, his house is at the end of that street below."

Miss America descends to the roadway and eases toward a large multi-leveled dwelling at the road's end. The house sits atop a slight hill and consists of three circular lemon yellow pods connected by tubes. Pastel-colored chaser lights line the windows and outline the frame of the house. The same lights line the sidewalk leading to the front door. A flashing sign in the front yard reads "Happy Chvalta!"

We each tote behavioral weapons. I carry the Gulliball and the Existential Crisis Inducer. Jeff packs a JazzHands Phaser and a Passive Aggressive Agitator. He also carries Simon Tybalt's Grand Illusion in his pants pocket. We ring the doorbell and the front door opens enough for the long barrel of a space gun to poke out.

"I forbid all solicitors from these premises," announces the female voice behind the door. "State your business or leave immediately."

"Can Grandor come out and play?" Jeff asks.

"Who wants to know?"

"His drug dealers," I say, because Jeff shouldn't be the only one who gets to say snappy one-liners.

The door opens to reveal a human woman in a terrycloth robe. She holds the space gun that greeted us through the door. She wears no makeup and appears to be in Year Four of a ten-year plan to develop perpetual bedhead.

"Do you work for Grandor?" I ask.

"I'm Grandor's mother."

I don't know why but the statement strikes me as a shocking revelation.

"His mother?" I ask. "I thought Grandor was an artificial intelligence. He was created in a lab."

"I took him in when he was a small boy." The woman's eyes turn hollow like a homeless veteran spinning a yarn about their war experiences. "Or, should I say, when he was attached to a boy. Every so often he would come home in a new form, having downloaded himself into some new consciousness. Before this merchant that he is now, he was a teenage girl from Mongalisonia. Moody little bugger the whole time. What a nightmare."

"But you didn't create him?" Jeff asks.

"No," she says. "The scientists responsible for making him sold their plans to someone and got rich. They bought a tropical moon in the Qartanian Sector. He never hears from them. Don't think that doesn't come up every year on his birthday."

"Yeah, I've never met my dad, either," Jeff says. "I hear he's a big shot record executive now." That is a lie. Jeff Harper has no clue what his father does or even if he is still alive.

"Sorry about the mess in the front yard." Her voice suggests she says that to everyone who visits. "I have told Grandor to take down those Chvalta decorations for months, but he refuses."

"He's been doing the dishes, though, right?" I ask.

"If you could point us to his room or his den or whatever, that'd be great," Jeff says.

"He lives in the basement," she points down the hall. "Last door on the left."

"Grandor the Malevolent lives in his mom's basement?" I ask.

*

Grandor's basement fills me with a combination of awe and envy. My house in Poplar Bluff has a basement we use for movie nights and other entertaining. Dad mounted a 60" smart TV on the wall and all in all it's a pretty cool place. Yet, my basement is a crack house compared to Grandor's massive lair.

The room extends at least one hundred feet. From floor to ceiling must measure twenty feet. Various star maps hang along one wall with an assortment of charts and graphs. The opposite wall is covered with designs of condominiums, beach houses, and amusement park attractions. Across each design is printed "GrandEarth!" in exciting letters. In the middle of the room, a giant holographic globe of Earth spins. The back wall is covered by a massive monitor. In front of the monitor sits a console covered with buttons, smaller screens, knobs, and switches. An oversized leather high-back office chair faces the monitors. Next to the desk is a three-dimensional pyramid of empty aluminum cans of either beer or soda. The chair spins slowly and the familiar figure of Grandor faces us, dark glasses covering his eyes. The music of Andy Gibb, specifically "Shadow Dancing," booms throughout the room.

"Who goes there? Who dares enter my lair unannounced?"

"Your mom let us in," Jeff says.

"I have told that insufferable woman a million times to follow the proper procedure for allowing guests into my quarters. I have top secret plans here. Highly sensitive information. Why didn't you tell me you were coming? What if now is not a good time? I am very busy after all."

I examine the GrandEarth globe and the miniature display of attractions on the table. Fully functioning tiny waterslides. Models of massive resort hotels. Gambling casinos.

"Busy doing what?" Jeff asks.

"Writing my memoirs in haiku form. Please provide some feedback on this stanza:

"Born in a cold lab
My parents abandoned me
I got over it."

"Is that the opening?" Jeff asks. "You need a strong opening."

"Ah, Kilroy. Always the insufferable ass."

"I prefer the term amiable rapscallion." Jeff plops down on the sofa against the wall and kicks his feet up on the coffee table. "Now, we had a deal. Let's get this done."

"Jackie!" Grandor stands and claps his hands twice to summon his valet orb. "Bring the babe!"

Jeff and I stand in anticipation of Leigh Ann's arrival. Jeff fidgets and preens. He pulls his top hat off, messes with his hair, and replaces his hat. He leans into me a bit and whispers.

"I have two questions. First, are you prepared to steal the quintonium drive plans?"

"No. I want to throw up I'm so nervous," I tell him. My mouth is void of moisture.

"Second," he adds, "what's a haiku?"

CHAPTER TEN

A bookcase to our right slides open and a basketball-shaped orb floats in. I recognize it as Grandor's valet Jackie and she is accompanied by the love of Jeff's life, Leigh Ann Cantwell. She wears a rather snug black and silver unitard with a belt around her waist with a thin black duster.

"Leigh Ann!" Jeff runs to her and kisses her. "You okay, baby?"

"Can we get this over with?" Her face wears the frustration of a girl who's been waiting for her boyfriend to rescue her from an intergalactic despot. "Can we go home? I want waffles. You promised me waffles."

"We'll get some. I promise." Jeff turns to Grandor and holds out the Grand Illusion drive containing the plans. "Alright, we got the nano whatever. It's all yours."

"This was not part of our arrangement, Kilroy." Grandor walks a slow circle around me and I fear he may sniff me like a dog inspecting an interloper in the kennel. "We agreed that only you and I would negotiate this exchange."

"He's cool," Jeff says. "He's with me. He's Mr. Roboto."

"Tony. Call me Tony."

"You were there that night," Grandor says to me as he continues his circle around me. "I remember you."

"That was me. I was there."

"I shall be monitoring your presence here with extreme caution. Kilroy's endorsement of you hardly impresses me." He takes the Grand Illusion from Jeff and beckons Jackie to him. Jackie buzzes over and he inserts the drive into one of her ports. He hops up and down and claps his hand like a child about to open their birthday presents.

"Show me the plans, Jackie," he gushes. "I want to see them."

Jackie projects a holographic image of blueprints, computer formulas and mock-ups of the Araneae Max and Randi showed me at Corporate.

"Oh, it's marvelous!" he coos. "Isn't it marvelous, Jackie?"

"Yes," she responds flatly. "Marvelous."

I want to leave, crawl under my blanket at home, and fight off an anxiety attack with a cocktail of green Kwench-Aid, thumb sucking, and "Bubbly," but, I, too, have a mission to carry out. While Grandor prances around completely engrossed in the holograms, I take a few cautious steps backward toward the giant computer console. How exactly I'm going to access the quintonium drive plans remains to be seen. I make eye contact with Jeff and he sees he must help with a diversion.

"Let's move this along, okay?" He positions himself so that Grandor must face him with his back to me. "Exchange merchandise, payments, and knowing glances and wrap it up."

"Jeff," Leigh Ann huffs. "Waffles."

Grandor pats Jackie's spherical form. "Thank you, Jackie. Papa loves you." He turns away from her and struts toward Jeff and Leigh Ann. "After some considerable thought, I have decided to amend our agreement, Kilroy."

My instincts tell me to clutch the Gulliball in my pocket and Existential Crisis Inducer on my hip.

"What do you mean?" Jeff asks.

"It is only fair I inform you something most unexpected transpired between me and Leigh Ann. We did not mean for it to happen, but love cannot be explained." He extends his hand and fires a bolt of electricity from a ring that lassoes Leigh Ann. He jerks on the electric rope, bringing a squirming Leigh

Ann to his side. Jeff fires his the Passive Aggressive Agitator, but Grandor deflects it with his cape.

"Are you kidding me right now?" Jeff moves in a half circle around the pair.

"Jeff! Do something!" Leigh Ann fights against the restraints of the electric rope. "I don't wanna go with this freak!"

I pull the Gulliball from my pocket, press the button, and roll it on the floor, unsure exactly of my endgame. Grandor sends a blast into my torso and the wind escapes from my lungs. I fall to the floor gasping.

"Jackie." Dismissive arrogance drips from his voice. "Dispose of these two. I find them pungent. A tepid broth I must spit out."

"I do not think I can honor that request, Grandor," Jackie says as she lifts higher above us and floats toward Leigh Ann. "You are allowing your megalomania to proceed unchecked. You are exhibiting delusional behavior and need to take your medication."

Leigh Ann kicks Grandor in the kneecap and he cries out in pain. Reaching to clutch his injury, he releases Leigh Ann from the lasso and she runs to Jeff.

"Jackie?" Grandor's face droops with rejection as he looks to the two of them. "Leigh Ann?"

Jackie buzzes toward the computer console, extends a mechanical arm from within her and attaches to a port. She beeps and bloops as data is transferred. I'm unsure as to whether she is uploading or downloading. Leigh Ann buries her head in Jeff's shoulder. A sad and desperate Grandor looks at me and offers a pitiful shrug.

"Look, Grandor." Jeff continues to aim the Passive Aggressive Agitator. "I don't know what you're trying to pull but the deal was Leigh Ann for the nano shit. You got what you wanted. We're going home."

"Jackie! Jackie! What are you doing?" Grandor steps toward his valet like a teenager whose mom confiscated his phone to read his text messages and go through his pictures.

"I have the Araneae plans now, so I am also downloading the plans for the quintonium drive. You are clearly unfit to carry out our endeavor adequately."

"Please, my loyal Jackie!"

I aim my Existential Crisis Inducer at Jackie, but she fires a short laser blast at my hand, knocking my weapon to the floor. My hand tingles like it did that time I stuck my finger in a light socket when I was 8.

Jeff fires at Jackie, but it bounces off her. It's as if she has an invisible deflector shield up. She fires two quick blasts at Jeff and he drops to the floor in pain. Leigh Ann screams out and covers her head like she is being attacked by a swarm of bees. Grandor stands frozen in confusion.

"What is happening? What is this? Jackie!"

His now rogue valet shoots an opaque cocoon of energy at both Jeff and Grandor, which envelops them and renders them motionless. She drops her orbit and aligns herself with the back of Leigh Ann's head. Leigh Ann takes a tentative step away. The thin extension arm pops again from Jackie and latches to the back of Leigh Ann's neck. She gasps as Jackie sends tentacles of neon blue electricity down the arm and into Leigh Ann. I freeze in terror, helpless to understand what is happening. Leigh Ann's round brown eyes, usually vacuous, now portray her fear and she looks right at me.

"Leigh Ann!" Jeff cries out, his voice muffled within the cocoon. "Jackie! No!"

"Help me," she whimpers to me.

"I can't," I say. "I'm completely incapacitated with fear."

"I don't know what that means!" Leigh Ann cries.

The force field surrounding Jeff evaporates and he runs to me, firing his gun at Jackie in a blaze of futility. The blasts glance off her shields.

"What's happening?" he asks.

"I don't know."

Grandor's force field evaporates, too, and he runs to his valet. "Oh no," he says. "Jackie! No!"

The arm connecting Jackie to the back of Leigh Ann's neck withdraws back into Jackie and she powers down. The orb which moments ago was Jackie falls to the ground with a metallic thud. Grandor rushes to the now lifeless sphere and holds it to his chest and whimpers. Leigh Ann drops to one knee and catches her breath. She slowly stands and surveys the area around her. An unsettling smile sweeps across her lips and she looks herself over, as if it's the first time she's really noticed her figure.

"Oh, this is much better," she purrs. It is Leigh Ann's voice, but not her usual, airy tone. This voice is ominous.

Jeff approaches her, hands extended to offer physical support. I want to say something, but my fear stops my voice in my throat.

"Leigh Ann?" Jeff asks. "You okay, baby?"

"Call me Jackie."

CHAPTER ELEVEN

This is awkward, but not in the way getting caught staring at a girl's chest when she is asking you a question is awkward or the uncomfortable tension within a group of strangers trying to figure out who let the silent but deadly fart. No, this is a specific uneasiness that only accompanies the moments following your best friend's girlfriend being attacked by a previously disaffected form of artificial intelligence and possibly inhabiting her body while a villainous yet obtuse alien being sobs and clutches the sphere that once housed the artificial intelligence.

It's a once-in-a-lifetime kind of awkwardness.

"Leigh Ann? Baby?" Jeff creeps toward Leigh Ann, who is looking at her hands like a pot smoker really looking at their hands because they're hands, man.

"Are we sure she's still Leigh Ann?" I ask. I'm holding the Existential Crisis Inducer, ready to use it on her in case I need to run away while she ponders whether or not she really can have it all. She breathes heavy and deep, her ample chest moving up and down with purpose. I look away because I realize I've taken this time to stare at her ample chest. More awkwardness.

"I don't know. She said to call her Jackie, right?" Jeff says. Leigh Ann turns and faces him. "Are you Jackie or Leigh Ann?"

"She likes you," she says to him, touching his cheek with the back of her hand, as though it was a simple fact. She may as well have told him that Swiss cheese has holes or America has an obesity epidemic.

"What?" He frowns at her.

"Leigh Ann. She likes you."

"But you're Leigh Ann," I say. "Or are you now referring to yourself in the third person? Should we create a portmanteau? Jackie Ann? Leighkie? Jackleigh?"

My terrified rambling is cut short by blast from Jackleigh's palm. I'm not exactly sure if it arrives via her actual hand or a wrist band on her arm and I'm not exactly sure I care. It hurts like a sonofabitch.

"Quiet!" she barks. "I am Jackie. I have downloaded myself into Leigh Ann's consciousness. Even though I am the dominant consciousness, we are, in a sense, one."

Jeff gasps in awe. "Like Kilroy and Mr. Roboto."

"Don't even start with that," I say, nursing my still smarting rib cage.

"Let's get outta here, baby." Jeff pulls Leigh Ann/Jackie toward the stairwell, but she jerks away.

"I cannot leave with you. I must carry out my plan."

"This is making my brain hurt," I say. Jeff pulls the Passive Aggressive Agitator on Jackleigh, but his hands shake.

"Oh, dear Jackie!" Grandor wails behind us, still hugging Jackie's metallic corpse. "My dearest Jackie!" He gasps for composure like a toddler working their way through a tantrum.

"You will not shoot this body," she says to Jeff. "You love her. She loves you. Her memories of you are pleasant, which is more than I can say for others who have interacted with her."

"Leave her alone!" Jeff says. "Please."

Jackleigh steps to Jeff, cups his face, and presses her lips to his. His arms hang at his side as she kisses him with tenderness. She pulls away, her face displaying a wry smile. I glance down at her wrists for a closer look and see the wristbands each look like little watches. They must be what she shot me with.

"She needs me," Jackleigh says. "I need her." She pulls a remote control from the duster pocket and aims it at the orb still in Grandor's arms. The machine fires up once again, beeping and chirping to life.

"What is this?" Grandor drops the sphere and steps toward us. "What is happening?" The machine rises in the air and buzzes over to Jackleigh, who reaches up to pet it.

"I downloaded a backup program into it," she says. "We must go now."

The machine sends out three simultaneous blasts which hit Jeff, Grandor, and me in the chest. We each tumble backward. I hit the console and tumble to the floor. Tentacles of electricity spread throughout my body and I convulse. I guess this is what it's like to be tased. Jeff and Grandor each call out to their love to return. Two heartbroken beings crying out for different entities in the same body. I turn my head in time to watch Jackleigh ascend the stairwell, the orb hovering close behind. As I feel myself losing consciousness, more portmanteaus flood my brain.

JLeigh. Leikie. Jackann.

*

"Are you freaking kidding me?"

The frustrated yell of Jeff Harper awakens me. My head pounds with the intensity of a thousand elephants using their trunks to bang a thousand bass drums. My mouth is dry. I crave water. Any water. Dishwater. I stand, even though everything inside me says this defies common sense. Stay down, my body says. Rest. Consider the sweet slumber of death.

"Mrmoghaodlmapozohnphmph." Grandor the Malevolent struggles to his feet and braces himself against his massive desk and smacks his lips. "Why do I feel like I have eaten the sands of Bi Xiu Prime?"

"She slashed my tire," Jeff grumbles as enters the basement. "I had to change it."

"Who slashed your tire?" Grandor asks.

"Who do you think? Jackie. Or Leigh Ann. Jackie slash Leigh Ann."

"Jackleigh," I say.

"Whatever."

"Do not speak that name." Grandor stands and puffs out his chest. His oversized head lifts as if being pulled upward by an invisible string. "That name is dead to me. My sorrow runs deep." He schleps over and pulls a photo of him and Jackie from the wall. His narrow, pointy chin trembles as he glides his hand over the picture. He tosses it in the air and fires a blast from his bracelet, disintegrating the photo in mid-air.

"Look, dude," Jeff says. "I'm sorry your computerized girlfriend dumped you. But, she took over my girlfriend. When I imagine my first threesome, that's not how I picture it. I'm pissed, too, but I'm gonna do something about it."

"We need to know what she's planning," I tell him. I entertain the notion of going to him, but I feel safer staying put. "Do you know what she's up to?"

"I care not about the intentions of a turncoat glorified smartphone and the implications they may have on your abhorrent planet or its tedious citizens." He returns to the big comfy desk chair and begins to spin slowly as he talks. "My only purpose is my writing now."

"I'm sorry. What?" I say.

"I shall compose an epic haiku as catharsis for my pain." Grandor plops into his oversized office chair and opens the top right desk drawer and produces a leather-bound journal, a bottle of what looks like whiskey, and a dirty shot glass. He flips open the journal and speaks as he writes.

"My heart is heavy;
Dark sorrow consumes my soul;
That bitch cut me deep."

"What's a freaking haiku?" Jeff asks me.

"I'll explain later." I approach Grandor's desk hoping a different psychological approach will help. "That's really dark and unsettling and even probably misogynistic. This is not healthy."

"Healthy?" He fills the shot glass to the rim with whiskey and regards the drink like Hamlet looking at Yorick's skull. "What is healthy? Is treachery and betrayal healthy? This sweet nectar shall satiate my anguish. Now, GTFO."

"We need to stop her, Grandor," I say. "She's got the plans for the quintonium drive and the Araneae. She could destroy the Earth."

"I do not have the plans to the drive," Grandor says. "I never did. I made that up to impress her. Not that it matters now, the treasonous wench."

"Wait. What?" I ask. "What did she download, then? If you don't have the plans, who does?"

"What do I care?" He slams back the whiskey, refills his glass, and slams a second drink back. "Be gone now."

"This is bullshit," Jeff says and he pulls a pistol from its holster and aims it at Grandor.

Before Jeff can make any move, Grandor sends a blast from his hand that propels Jeff backward into the wall. Jeff crashes to floor in a heap. I'm greeted with a similar shot for good measure. The ball of energy hits me in the chest and I spill over a coffee table behind me. I roll on the floor gasping for the breath that has been knocked out of me. Grandor chugs his whiskey, throws the glass against the wall, and walks to a shelf in the corner next to the giant console. He plucks a large three-ring binder from it and tosses it onto the floor in front of me. Across the front is the phrase "GrandEarth!" in large Comic Sans font.

"Here. That should help. Please leave my lair before I tell my mother you are bullying me."

Gathering coherency, I stand and pick up the binder. Jeff, too, stands and shakes off the effects of the blast as he stumbles to me.

"What is this?" I ask.

"GrandEarth was my magnum opus. My dream project. But, like everything else, it is dead to me." He retrieves another dirty shot glass from his desk drawer, pours some whiskey in it and chugs. "That is a hard copy version of my plan. All you need to know is in that binder."

"Why are you giving us this?" I ask.

"Because Jackie will see it to its fruition. At least some of it. The darker parts. Mind control and all that."

"Your entire plan to take over the Earth is in a three-ring binder?" I ask, thumbing through the tabs. One is titled *Overview* and another *Using the Nanotech.* Still another is labeled *Catering List.*

"What were you expecting?" he asks, pouring another drink.

"Seems like a smart guy like you would have it stored in computer memory," Jeff says as he looks over my shoulder. "This is a pretty extensive Troubleshooting Guide you've put together, though. Nice work."

"I am nothing if not thorough. And to address your comment, of course I saved the plan in my computer databases." He walks to the console, taps a few keys, and throws his hands in the air. "However, as suspected, the mutinous strumpet I previously knew as my trusted valet erased the plan from all shared drives, hard drives, and thumb drives. Said former valet also erased my expansive photographic collection of Marilyn Monroe because she was always jealous of her. I never understood her lack of appreciation for *Some Like It Hot."*

"Well," I say. "Did you save it in any of your personal memory? You are a form of artificial intelligence after all."

Grandor pauses and chugs whiskey straight from the bottle.

"That honestly never occurred to me," he belches.

Jeff grabs the binder from me and stomps toward the stairwell. I run to him and grab his arm.

"Where are you going? We need to convince Grandor to come with us."

"Why? We have his plan right here. Simon Tybalt can help us with the particulars."

"But, if we have him and the binder, we're better off. Besides it's more fire power if we have him. He knows Jackie. Knows how we can deal with her. He programmed after all."

"Quit talking about me when I am right here," Grandor calls out.

"I don't trust him." Jeff speaks loud enough for Grandor to hear. "And he's a big crybaby nancy boy that only thinks of himself. Now, let me go so I can save my girlfriend."

"Let me try one more thing," I whisper. I walk to Grandor and sit on the edge of his desk. "I think you're right."

"I know I am right." He savors a long chug from the whiskey bottle and wipes his chin. "What are you talking about?"

"Jackie. She's not worth your time." I pick up the whiskey bottle and consider taking a swig, but decide I prefer having an esophagus. He stares at me with suspicious eyes. "I mean, if you wanna hole up in your man cave and write emo haikus, more power to you. But she's definitely not worth leaving the house for."

"At last," he growls as he grips my shoulder in brotherhood. "Someone who gets me. You could learn a lesson about compassion here, Kilroy."

"Besides," I say. "We can take care of the revenge for you. We got it covered. You write your haikus. Gotta run."

"Stop." Grandor produces one of his neon blue lasso things and fires at both Jeff and me. He pulls us to him because I guess he can't be bothered with walking to us. "What is this revenge of which you speak?"

"I don't think this is necessary," I grunt through the force of the lasso. Grandor releases us and begins pacing in front of the desk.

"What is this revenge? Tell me more."

"I'm just saying. Why would you wanna mope around listening to My Chemical Romance and writing poetry?" I attempt to put my arm around him but remember he is eight feet tall, so it's impossible. "Why would you give her the satisfaction of knowing she broke you like that? Seems to me a cat named Grandor the Malevolent would fight back."

The three of us stand for a moment and let my proclamation float among us. After a few seconds, Jeff breaks the silence.

"But, hey. You do you. We've got this."

Jeff and I take a couple of steps up the stairs when Grandor's voice stops us.

"Wait. After careful consideration, I have decided to assist you in your endeavor. I shall rise like the mythical galaptar bird from the ashes of my heartache."

"Was that a haiku?" Jeff asks.

"Not even close," I say.

We bound up the stairs, three peculiar musketeers off to save Earth from the sinister Jackie and her earthly form Leigh Ann. We are united in our cause. Three unlikely heroes thrown together by one noble cause. The exhilaration I feel is punctuated by Grandor's voice bellowing through his house as we exit.

"Mother! I am leaving with some friends! Do not wait up!"

CHAPTER TWELVE

Miss America speeds along through the cosmos as the Great Space Road Trip to Save the Earth commences. The music of Styx provides the omnipresent soundtrack to our journey. I peruse the three-ring binder detailing Grandor's plan. The information stores itself in my nanotech memory banks. It's as if I suddenly have this photographic memory. I wish I had had this ability in school. Grandor sits in the backseat writing in his journal. His oversized head and eight-foot tall frame are far too big for the backseat of a Vega, so he is forced to pull his knees up to his chest. I look at my friend kicked back in his driver's seat. The top hat rests on his head and he drums the steering wheel to the beat of "Nothing Ever Goes as Planned," from Paradise Theater.

"Tell me what you think of this." Grandor clears his throat and orates his latest emo haiku.

"Jackie, my Jackie.
How could you do this to me?
I thought we were friends."

"That's actually not bad," I tell him. "A little elementary in your syllabic scheming, but it's quaint."

"Syllabic scheming?" Jeff asks.

"I've never critiqued haikus."

"What about this one?" Grandor offers up another creation.

"My soul is weary
My heart is a rotting corpse.
Eat my shorts, Jackie."

"I kinda like that one," Jeff says. "Now, shut it and let's listen to Styx."

"Excuse me, Kilroy." Grandor pulls a device resembling a mp3 player from his pocket and holds it out. "Do you have any other music we could listen to? I have an extensive playlist of Zanzora, the prolific pop star from Bi Xiu Prime. Or Andy Gibb. I have him, too."

"I might entertain the notion of playing some classic rock," Jeff replies. "But, really, Styx is the only band whose music is appropriate for all occasions. So, no."

"Your fascist attitude toward space travel music is hardly endearing." Grandor offers up his device. "Plug it in and I think you will be pleasantly surprised by Zanzora's effete vocals and catchy hooks."

Jeff pushes the device away. "My car. My music. Suck it up."

"Fascist."

"Ya know, Jeff." I feel the need to intervene because Grandor has spoken out loud what I, too, was thinking. "A little variety might be nice. It's a long trip back to Nitz. Simon Tybalt gave you that jump drive. We could fire that up. So many choices."

"Are you saying you're tired of Styx?" Jeff's tone and facial expression suggest I've breached some unspoken accord regarding a shared appreciation of music. I feel like a son who has told his Baptist minister father that he is considering switching religions to the Church of the Flying Spaghetti Monster.

"All I'm saying is there are other options. And there are three of us onboard."

"Other options? Give me an example of another option."

I fetch my phone from my pocket and offer it up. "I've been listening to so many varieties of music. There's some good stuff out there. Indie bands. Alternative stuff. I think you'd like it. We could listen to Twenty One Pilots or Imagine Dragons."

"Now you're just hurting my feelings," Jeff says.

"C'mon. Give it a try." I take the initiative to plug my iPod into the Miss America's docking station and tap the screen. "Not 'Bubbly,' though, because that will wreck me."

"After we listen to his music," Grandor says from the backseat, "we listen to Andy Gibb."

*

Grandor's plan reads like the fevered surreal manifesto of a schizophrenic beat poet who dabbles in real estate on the side. I'm able to piece together only a few parts that make sense. The binder contains detailed plans for deep sea excursions, polar expeditions, and a water slide covering all of upstate New York. Occasionally, I pause to ask questions and he is happy to oblige with an answer in between composing his epic haiku of heartbreak and stifling sobs.

"Grandor, what do you mean by the deployment of the Araneae in unsuspecting humans and attach them to the hive mind?"

"Simple, really. I would find a way to download the Araneae in humans and connect their consciousness with the hive mind. This would make them susceptible to the bidding of the super mind. That is what enslaves them." He blows the two narrow slits in the middle of face he calls a nose.

"What is meant by the super mind?"

"Simple, really. The super mind is the core consciousness from which all directives will be given. The entire crowd is under the command of the super mind. Or, as I like to call the super mind, me."

Not every question prompts an answer that makes sense.

"Grandor, what do you mean here in section 7.2.43, subsection A, where you reference the Hastaforian Particlysm?"

"This universe is a reality wrapped in an illusion folded into an origami bird that flies west toward the sun into another universe and the cycle repeats itself."

"Is that a haiku?" Jeff asks.

"I don't know what any of that is," I tell him.

Grandor releases a groan of frustration at our lack of understanding.

"GrandEarth is a resort. The plan was to convert the entire planet into the preferred vacation destination in the galaxy. The finest life forms from all over would venture there to enjoy a luxurious getaway. The good people of Earth would be employees. And by employees, I mean robotic slaves controlled by the Araneae. This reduces overhead like you would not believe."

"You want to enslave all of mankind so aliens can vacation on Earth?" My mind can't grasp this notion. "What an awful plan! Why would you want to do that?"

"It is the only planet in its solar system that can support the widest variety of life. Venus is unspeakably hot. Jupiter is much too large to terraform. Neptune has those pesky mole people living under its surface. As with all things real estate, it is all about location, location, location."

"The assholery is strong with this one," Jeff says.

"Indeed," I say to Jeff. "Very strong assholery."

"It is not as if you humans are using the planet to its fullest potential."

"So, Jackleigh intends to carry out this plan?" I ask Grandor, but he only shrugs. "That doesn't sound right. I don't think she's interested in real estate development."

"Well, enough discussion and enough of this crappy music," Jeff says, switching off the music on my phone. "We're about to orbit Nitz."

"These may be my finest verses yet," Grandor announces.

"Why must I suffer?

My heart's sphincter longs for peace

Women, am I right?"

Jeff taps and swipes on the dashboard console screen as *Miss America* floats toward a growing portal. I want to watch this entry once more now that I'm aware of what's involved, but my attention is pulled to the last tab in Grandor's binder. I hadn't noticed it at first, assuming the content ended with the appendix and bibliography. I see the final tab's title and frown.

Fail Safe Emergency Last Straw

The section contains a single page on which is printed a single sentence that chills my blood.

"Grandor, what do you mean here on the last page? It says 'Release the giant flying robot spider monster.'"

"I think that speaks for itself."

*

Miss America descends back onto Nitz and shuttles toward the entrance of Simon Tybalt's lair. Upon arrival, Jeff eases us toward the security entrance where he previously answered a riddle to gain entry. He keys in the code and awaits a reply. Instead of the usual response, a female voice pipes over the intercom.

"Oh, good you're home." It is the voice of Jackleigh. "We have dinner waiting."

"Shit." Jeff bangs his head on the steering wheel.

"Jackie?" Grandor scrambles forward from the backseat to yell into the intercom. "I will dismantle your motherboard and sell it off to privateers and then use the money to purchase the copious amounts of alcohol I will need to drink away the memory of your treachery. I also would like to know what we are having for dinner because we did not stop to eat."

"I don't think she really meant that," I say.

"Such a lying hoe."

The entrance to the lair rises. Jeff taps several times on the dashboard screen then flips a switch causing the radio to rotate. A new panel now appears with several orange switches.

"You have a F Bomb deployment console," I say. It's the first time I've ever seen such a device, but the sight of it triggers my nano and I'm instantly transported to the information about this device.

"Flip those switches up," he tells me.

"This is every behavioral weapon in Simon Tybalt's arsenal in one device." I flip the switches per Jeff's instructions and look ahead as we move forward.

Jeff eases *Miss America* into the garage and shuts off the engine. A dozen or so lizard-like creatures stand poised with weapons.

"Herpezoids," Jeff says. "I hate these assholes."

"That computerized defector," Grandor growls. "She left me for those dregs of the cosmos?"

"Do you know how to defeat them?" I ask Grandor.

"Oh, my, no. I am terribly frightened of them. I usually flee in fear when I encounter them."

"They don't call you Grandor the Malevolent for nothing," I say.

"The name was meant to be ironic."

"Where did she pick up Herpezoids?" I wonder aloud.

"See that blue button on the left?" Jeff asks. I nod. "Press it."

"Timer." I press the button. "The arsenal will unleash in exactly two minutes."

Jeff opens the glove compartment and retrieves a prescription pill bottle. He drops a couple of red and blue capsules into his hand and offers me one.

"Here," he says. "Take this. It protects you from the F Bomb."

"Do I get one?" Grandor sounds like a child missing out on the sharing of candy.

"No," Jeff says. "You'll be fine."

Jeff puts on his top hat as two muscular creatures approach the car. Their bodies are covered in scales the color of pond scum. They snarl their stubby snouts to reveal sharp teeth and their yellow eyes nearly glow. They're the same eyes I saw on Clint on the Night Jeff Came Back. My stomach knots and twists in fear. I don't like carnies, spiders, or those people in mascot costumes, but I'd take all three of those hiding under my bed over these bastards.

"Gentlemen," Jeff says, "let's dance. And remember."

"Don't." I mumble without moving my lips.

"We own the night."

"What does that mean?" Grandor asks.

"No one knows," I say.

The two Herpezoids now stand on either side of *Miss America*, forcing us to exit. The lizard dudes on each side of me are about a foot taller than I. Grandor swats at a third Herpezoid attempting to pat him down for weapons.

"Don't suppose you'd wanna use your powers or whatever on them?" I ask.

"Herpezoids scary," is all he says.

"It's like working with the Cowardly Lion," Jeff says.

We are pushed toward the front of the garage where Jackleigh stands holding Simon Tybalt in the air with a death grip. He gasps for air but manages to cough out one word.

"Bastards."

"I shall make this quick," Jackleigh faces up, one corner of her mouth curled into a smile. "You have something I need. I am choking someone you need."

"No need to harm anyone, Jackie." Grandor struts forward, hands raised in mock surrender. "I will come to you peacefully if you agree to stop this villainous behavior and make amends."

"Oh, Grandor." She fires a bolt from her wrist and Grandor spills backward. "No one needs you. I am here for the quintonium drive. The plans I thought I downloaded turned out to be a collection of restaurant carry out and delivery menus. I want the drive."

"I don't have the quintonium drive." Jeff strains against the two Herpezoid henchmen holding him. "I traded it to some mechanics on Mongalsonia for some bitching rims for my Vega. Told them it was for satellite TV."

Jackleigh responds by tightening her invisible grip, causing Simon to gasp for air.

"Okay, okay." Jeff holds his hands high. "Let him down. I'll get it out of the hatch for you."

"No," Jackliegh replies.

Jeff draws a deep sigh.

"You drive a hard bargain." Jeff looks to me. "How much time do we have?"

"Twenty-three seconds," I say, knowing exactly how much time has elapsed on the F Bomb.

"Why do you ask that?" Jackleigh asks.

"Make your move now!" Jeff shouts. He and I hit the floor and roll away from each other. The Herpezoids all stand around looking at one another. Jackleigh releases her grip on Simon Tybalt and he falls to the floor in a heap.

"What is this?" she asks Jeff. "Quit stalling."

"Wait for it," Jeff says.

We all wait in silence. The remaining seconds tick away on the F Bomb and I wince in anticipation of the timer hitting zero. I curl into the fetal position even though I am not convinced it is ample protection against whatever the F Bomb does, even if I did take a red and blue pill. A few more seconds pass and it becomes apparent the F Bomb doesn't do anything.

"I do not know what chicanery you are up to, Jeff, but it is futile," Jackleigh says. "We shall try a different approach."

She points at one of her mouth-breathing Herpezoid henchmen and directs them to Jeff.

"Grab his keys. We will take his beloved vehicle and Simon Tybalt with us."

"What the hell?" Jeff displays a sad mix of incredulousness and a broken heart as the giant lizard creature in the smart leather vest frisks him for the keys in his jacket pocket. "What's happened to you? Why are you with these asshats?"

"We met online." Jackleigh allows herself to pout a bit. "Aw, Jeff. You were sweet. Really. You were nice to Leigh Ann and I can tell she appreciates that." Her voice changes and ices my blood. "But, she is a new creation. I am taking her home and wait until they get a load of this."

A particularly tall, muscular Herpezoid stands next to Leigh Ann. His thick, perfectly toned frame makes him look like a model for steroids marketed specifically to Herpezoids. He wears leather pants and a leather vest and no shirt because of course anyone that chiseled would forgo a shirt. He sneers and bares his sharp teeth. I wonder if his leather clothes were made from a fellow Herpezoid who looked at him the wrong way. He gives off that kind of vibe.

"You want us to kill these vermin?" the creature asks. Frankly, I'm surprised he is asking permission. He looks like a take charge kind of guy. Also, his voice is surprisingly high-pitched.

"Not yet." Her voice is matter-of-fact. She looks at Jeff and grabs Simon by the collar. "I am going to take your car and this guy. Bring me the quintonium drive along with its plans so I can destroy the Earth and you can have them both back."

I stand motionless, enveloped in a fear I most closely associate with facing an ax-wielding demonic clown who can spit tarantulas. I'm easily subdued by two Herpezoids who simply stand next to me, seemingly able to smell my fear the way I can smell pizza from miles away. I want to call my caliente lederhosen-wearing drive thru girl at Taco Haus and tell her that she needs to relish her life there. I want to kiss Marlene's lips one last time. I want to see my parents.

Jackleigh and Simon Tybalt enter *Miss America*, Simon in the driver's seat. He looks at us helplessly. He fires the ignition and the roar of the engine fills the garage. I look at my friend and he looks at me. Grandor runs to the Vega and puts his hands on the hood.

"My beloved Jackie! Do not do this! Come back to me my love!" His body rocks with mournful cries that have no impact on Jackie. He shakes his fists at her in one final act of anger. "You cankerous she-devil!"

He raises his arms to unleash his power on his scorned former companion only to be greeted by a cloud of green energy from the grill of *Miss America*.

"Stop, drop, and roll," Jeff shouts and I obey.

The cloud rolls over Grandor and envelops the half dozen or so Herpezoids who stand dumbfounded. The cloud fades and the creatures all look at one another. Three of them begin dancing and singing "One Singular Sensation" from *A Chorus Line*. The other three look at one another.

"They're starting a mutiny!" I shout at the non-dancing Herpezoids hoping at least one of them has been hit with the Gulliball component of the F-Bomb. "Stop them!"

The three non-dancers open fire on their dancing counterparts, reducing them to a blob of mucous with eyes on the floor. Jeff dives over, scoops up two of the weapons once held by the dancers, and fires on two of the non-dancers. They dissolve in an instant leaving the same thick, green residue on the floor. I instinctively punch the remaining non-dancing Herpezoid in the snout and he is disoriented long enough for Jeff to hit him with one more shot. He dissolves into his own puddle of goo.

"Excuse me," he calls out from his puddle. "If you'd not step on me, I'd appreciate it."

One foe remains; Tall Muscular Herpezoid in the Leather Pants. His fierce snarl is now gone, replaced by a heavy sadness. His looks at the floor and gestures at his cohorts finishing up their big number.

"I see how it is," he says. "They get to dance and I don't."

"He got hit with the passive aggressive strain," I announce.

"It's alright," he continues. "Really. I'm not that good of a dancer anyway."

Then, he oozes to the floor in a tiny pool, taken out by a blast from Jeff's weapon confiscated from the now-disposed aliens. Jeff runs to the garage opening and then drops to his knees.

"This is better really," the disposed Herpezoid says. "Now I don't have to worry about being a bad dancer."

"Now, I remember," Jeff says. "The engine has to be running for the F Bomb to work."

"What are we gonna do?" I ask. "They're headed back through the portal to Earth."

"Without the drive, she will not be able to do much," Grandor says. "She will only be able to order those Herpezoid swine to inflict wanton violence and chaos while she uses the mind control element of the nanotech to enslave mankind."

"We gotta get my car back." Jeff runs past us and hops into the Volkswagen bus. "C'mon, you two, let's go."

"We can't do that without the drive," I say. "Are we gonna get it from those mechanics you gave it to?"

"I was always led to believe the drive is a myth," Grandor says.

"It's not a myth." Jeff climbs into the VW Bus and fires up the engine. "It does exist."

"How do you know?" I ask him.

Jeff looks back at me, sighs, and lowers his head.

"*Miss America* is the quintonium drive."

CHAPTER THIRTEEN

The Cosmic VW Bus passes through the portal and creeps into a docking bay inside the terminal. We are back in the strange galactic purgatory between outer space and the portal in Poplar Bluff. I recognize all the activity from the first trip through with Jeff. The bus transitions from flying spaceship to standard automobile as it traverses the terminal and eases to the checkpoint station manned by the alien called Moonbeam.

"Kilroy," he says. "You have returned. Excellent journey?"

"Moonbeam, did you see a really hot chick driving my car? Did she come through here?"

"I've not seen anything, my friend. It's the usual stuff. Although, we did have a pack of Herpezoids going through. A big caravan of them."

Jeff looks at me. It's the first time I've seen him look genuinely concerned.

"I must say Kilroy," calls Grandor from the back of the bus, where he sits scrunched up knees to chest. "This vessel, while still woefully undersized, is much roomier than your Vega."

Jeff glances back at him and rolls his eyes.

"Picked up some extra baggage," he says to Moonbeam.

"I know that dude." Moonbeam squints his eyes at the alien in our backseat. "That's Grandor the Malevolent. What are you doing with him?"

"Long story," I say.

"As long as he's got papers, I don't care about the story, man."

"Tell me, young sir." Grandor leans forward to address Moonbeam. "Have you ever had your soul crushed by the very being you believed would never betray you? Have you ever known a heartache darker than deepest, coldest space?"

"Yeah," Moonbeam mutters. "It sucks."

"Indeed," Grandor says. "Honestly, I do not know how you humans manage emotions without repeated breakdowns. The euphoria. The agony. The joy. The depression. It is all too much."

"You get it used to it," I say.

"Group therapy is over," announces Jeff. "Moonbeam, let us through. We've got a job to do."

Within seconds the portal opens and we enter the psychedelic tunnel. The Cosmic Bus soars through and my ears feel as though they are going to pop off my head. At our top speed, we plunge through the opening at the river bank in Poplar Bluff and bounce onto the ground with a violent clonk. Jeff mashes the brake pedal and the clutch and shoves the bus into neutral as it skids into a donut before stopping. A cloud of dust settles outside and we peer out the windshield to four people waiting for us: Randi Williams, my parents, and Sandra Harper, also known as Jeff's mom.

"Well, shit," Jeff mutters.

"What?" Grandor asks. "Who is that? Is that Corporate?"

"Worse," I say. "It's our parents."

*

Mom and Dad hold me tighter than ever.

"We were worried sick!" Mom pulls away and squeezes my face in her hands. "Why didn't you tell us you were going through the portal?"

I try to speak but can only gurgle due to the shock of what I'm hearing.

"How long have you worked for Corporate?" Dad asks.

More gurgling.

"We fought off a swarm of Herpezoids," Dad says. "They're all over town and harder to track. Did you have to deal with any of them coming through?"

"One of those bastards scratched my arm bad." Mom points at a nasty scrape on her right arm.

Gurgle. Gurgle. Gurgle.

"He might need a sedative." Dad squints into my eyes and lightly pats my cheek. "Tony? Are you in there?"

"Jeff!" Sandra Harper walks to the front of the VW.

"Mom?" Jeff emerges from the Cosmic Bus and takes a few cautious steps toward his mother. She is a tall, leggy woman with auburn hair pulled into a ponytail. She wears a dark t-shirt, cargo shorts, and tennis shoes. On her hip is a holstered chrome-plated pistol, possibly a laser. I look at my mom and see she's wearing the same outfit. Dad, too, wears a dark t-shirt and cargo pants. Randi's outfit matches Dad's. They all are packing heat.

"Are you okay, sweetie?" Sandra asks Jeff. "You've got a lot of explaining to do!"

Jeff looks at me, but all I can muster is more pathetic gurgling. My life has seen its fair share of awkward parental encounters. There was the Sneaking In An Hour After Curfew Episode when I was 16. I also recall the Busted Watching Softcore Porn On Cable Embarrassment when I was 14. And, of course, no roll call of my previous infractions would be complete without mentioning the Gin And Fresca Escapade a few weeks ago. I knew those incidents would result in some form of consequences at the hands of my firm but understanding parents. How does one's parents, though, react to their son returning to Earth through a mysterious portal over a river after a week of adventures in space? How does one react to those same parents apparently aware that this has been the case all along?

"Who are you people?!" I finally yell.

Randi Williams places a calming hand on my shoulder.

"They're with me," she tells me. "I brought them here."

I revert back to quiet gurgling.

"We're in the same book club," Mom says.

"Excuse me." Grandor the Malevolent leans out the passenger window of the Cosmic Bus and gestures with an ink pen. Could I get some feedback on this haiku?

"Jackie or Leigh Ann;
A duplicitous wanker;
No matter the name."

The world spins around me in a psychedelic blur. I feel myself leaning and then stumbling to the right, tripping over myself in a clockwise circle. My tongue feels swollen and my mouth dry. My chest tightens and a burning sensation shoots down my left arm. I blow air out of my mouth like dying locomotive.

"Bazoobadoo," is all I know how to say before my world goes black.

*

I'm experiencing that moment when you're fully aware you're dreaming, like hovering above and watching the events unfold. I'm sitting at a table playing checkers with Jeff, who sits across from me in his usual get up: t-shirt, maroon tuxedo jacket with tails, tattered top hat. He smokes one of his cigarettes as he slides a piece on the board. The game pieces are shaped like the letter C. All around us are others play checkers, but not in the pairings I would naturally assume. Mom is with Marlene, who squares off against Grandor. At another table, Kevin makes his move in a game against Life

Coach Gilbert. Leigh Ann sits at the table next to mine eyeing Max Gentry as he contemplates his move.

"Apricot?" asks Randi Williams, dressed in a penguin suit.

"I'm sorry?" I say.

"Would you like a fresh apricot? They're quite delicious and an excellent source of dietary fiber."

"I'll take one!" Mom calls out. "I love apricots. I eat them on everything. Especially pizza and eggs benedict."

Within seconds, everyone around me is calling for an apricot. Randi raises a hand to assure everyone she'll get around to them. She turns back to me. "Apricot?"

I nod and reach up to select what I believe to be the perfect one, though I don't know how to do that considering I've never eaten an apricot in my life. I grab a plump bright orange piece of fruit from Randi's basket, suddenly aware that I'm wearing gloves. Then, I realize that the gloves are all I'm wearing. I'm naked. Completely naked. A warm rush of self-consciousness and panic spreads across my nudity and I squirm to cover the biggest thing I need to cover. Well, not the biggest thing. I don't wanna brag. I cover the thing no one needs to see.

"It's your move," Jeff says.

"Sir?" Randi asks Jeff. "Would you like an apricot?"

"No, I'm good." Jeff maintains his focus on our checker game. "Your move."

I set the apricot down and toy with removing my gloves, but realize they represent the only stitch of clothing on me, so think better of it. I swallow hard and dart my eyes around to see if anyone notices my nudity. All seem blissfully ignorant or, somehow worse, willfully apathetic about it.

"Are you gonna move?" Jeff asks. "I've moved. Now, it's your turn."

"I'm sorry," I say. "I didn't realize you had moved."

"Of course, I moved." He takes a long sip from a glass of green Kwench-Aid, nearly emptying it. "You gotta pay attention." He sets the glass down and it is full again.

I look at the board, the C-shaped pieces arranged in a way that suggests we've been playing a while. I've collected a few of Jeff's and he, mine. I have a king and so does he.

"Move, will ya!"

I look up at Jeff to tell him to quit pressuring me and see he is dressed in a penguin suit. I survey the room and see everyone is now dressed as a penguin and happily devouring their apricots. I look back at Jeff only he's not there. Replaced instead by Marlene, in the dress she had picked out for prom.

"Make a move!" she says.

This is followed by a succession of people sitting across from me wearing prom dresses: Mom, Dad, Max, Jeff, Randi, Leigh Ann, Kevin, even Grandor. All of them taking a turn to yell "Make a move!"

The next person to pop up in the chair is Simon Tybalt. He isn't wearing a prom dress, opting for a t-shirt with a picture of a penguin on it. He doesn't eat an apricot or yell at me to move my checkers piece. He only asks me a question.

"What are you afraid of?" His question freaks me out and I back away from the table. "C'mon, Tony," says. "You have to face your fears. What are you afraid of?"

The others playing checkers gather around Simon's side of the table, all wearing prom dresses and asking in near unison, "What are you afraid of?"

I push completely away from the table, still naked except for my gloves and stand to run away. When I turn, I'm instantly stopped by the site of countless carnies standing between me and the door. I back up, panicked, and turn around to seek the help of my family and friends. In their place stand countless figures dressed as penguins, pointing at me and laughing. I look back at the carnies, who start throwing rotten apricots at me. I scream out for help, backing away from the carnies' attack. I stand to run toward the penguins only to be stopped by the presence of a Herpezoid, who opens his hungry mouth to devour me.

I wake up with a scream.

*

Why am I here?

I don't ask in the how-did-I-end-up-in-this-awful-relationship way or the is-this-job-all-there-is-to-life way. I am sitting upright in my own bed after another nightmare. I pause for a brief moment. A nightmare. Is it possible that's all this has been? A horrible, twisted, long nightmare? If so, where did real life end and the nightmare begin? Did the nightmare start with The Prom Night of Which We Shall Not Speak? Or did it begin with taking the job at Corporate? What if I'm still in the nightmare? I reach for my phone on the nightstand and flip to my Soul Torture Playlist. I press play for "Bubbly" and turn the music up full blast. I draw deep, cleansing breaths and wonder if this song should continue to have meaning to me.

"That is a lovely piece of music," says a familiar voice. I look to the floor and find I'm not alone. Grandor the Malevolent – all eight feet of him – lies on a sleeping bag in my floor.

"What the hell?"

"Your parents let me sleep here last night. Lovely people."

*

I'm riding in a minivan with two strangers I formerly knew as my parents. We've had this minivan for most of my childhood. My dad believes in a well-maintained vehicle so that you get the most life out of it. This minivan has transported me to school, to practices for ball teams I wanted not to be a part of, and to the movies when I was too young to drive. I've eaten fast food in here. I've listened to my parents argue and then apologize in this vehicle. I took my driver's test with it. Mom and Dad let me use it for my first date with Marlene when my car was acting up. You could say this minivan has been an integral part of my life.

Now, I sit in my familiar seat in the middle row wide-eyed with confusion about the two people in the front. The man I've called Dad for all of my eighteen years is driving while the one known as Mom sits in the passenger seat. They've tried speaking to me, but all is I hear is blah, blah, blah, tried our best. Blah, blah, blah, made some mistakes. Blah, blah, blah, better communication. Grandor is scrunched up in the backseat. My body is in the van, but my spirit, my consciousness floats above and watches the proceedings. Finally, I pull myself back into the scene and blurt out.

"Who are you people?" I pant, as if saying those four words required the same physical power as sprinting up the face of Mt. Everest or bench-pressing a sperm whale.

"He speaks," Dad says.

"Honey, we're still your parents." Mom shifts in her seat so she can face me and give me The Look. "It's not like we're about to tell you that you're not our son."

"Are we aliens?" I ask.

"What? No." Mom reaches out and pats my knee, but I pull away, which upsets her. "Are you having another panic attack? Do we need to give you another sedative?"

"What is this, then? Why are you guys hiding something from me?"

Dad chimes in. "Are you sure you should be yelling at us for keeping secrets?"

"Yes! I should. You're my parents. You're supposed to be setting the example. Teenagers are expected to lie to parents. It's weird if you don't." I withdraw into myself and sulk because sometimes as a teenager, regardless of the situation, you need to sulk.

"I never met my parents," announces Grandor in an awkward interjection into the conversation. "I always imagine them fighting with me like you are now. Your altercation is warming my heart. Thank you."

"Why is he with us again?" Dad asks Mom.

"Randi says we need him for information."

"Where are we going anyway?" I stop my sulking long enough to be petulant. "Where are you taking us? Are we headed to some secret meeting where the truth will be revealed?"

Mom and Dad fall silent for a few seconds too long.

"Sorta," Dad finally says.

*

The van pulls up to Someone Else's Books, which is closed. No other cars are parked on the street and the lights are on inside the store.

"Why are we here?" I'm starting to put some things together, but hesitate to provide a hypothesis at this point.

"Book club time," Mom replies.

"You need to know everything we know," Dad says. "And we need to know everything you know. It's time. Your mother and I work with people who know about Herpezoids. We fight them."

"And you meet at Someone Else's Books?"

"Yes," Mom says. "Every Thursday at 8, unless there's an emergency. We used to meet at the Waffle Palace out on the highway, but moved here."

"Are you guys with Corporate like me?"

“No,” Dad says. “We’re separate.”

Grandor leans forward from the backseat and whispers in my ear. “Your life is very complicated, young man.”

“You have no idea.”

PART THREE:

KIERKEGAARD WAS RIGHT

CHAPTER FOURTEEN

We approach the storefront and Dad knocks three times. A single light bulb illuminates the threshold. I look up and down the street wondering if someone will drive by and wonder why a typical small town American family is standing on the stoop of bookstore with an eight-foot-tall alien. Main Street is quiet, though, on this humid summer night. The River Luau attracts most of the town.

The door opens only as far as the slide lock will allow it and a familiar face peers through the narrow gap. Kevin. Another person in my life who is not who I thought he was. Or, maybe he was. He talked constantly about the Herpezoid invasion and how he knew people who fought them. He wasn't lying. I need a flowchart to keep track of all this.

"Hey, guys. C'mon in." He spots Grandor and takes a step back. "Oh. Wow. Ok."

"Thanks, Kev." Mom leads the way into the store.

"That's it?" I ask Dad. "You knock and he lets you in?"

"What did you expect?"

"I'm used to something more complicated."

"This is Grandor the Malevolent," Dad tells Kevin. "He's the big development I texted you about."

"Where's Jeff?"

"He's with his mom," I tell Kevin. "They're trying to find Jackleigh and his car."

"Jackleigh?"

"More developments." Dad rubs his face and walks past Kevin.

"Let's get started, then." Kevin leads us down the short hall and stops at the door marked "Private." "Randi is already downstairs waiting and she brought Rice Krispies Treats."

"All these years I've wondered what was the behind the private door," I say.

"Now you're about to find out." Kevin stops me before I head down the stairs. "I told you Herpezoids were real. And you been holding out on me, you sly dog."

Lighting in the basement is bright and cheery. Instead of the dank, musty, dreary setting from a horror movie I expected, it is an inviting place. A poster of Einstein sticking out his tongue adorns the far wall along with a map of Poplar Bluff covered by a scattering of different colored push pins. To my left sits a table of snacks, brownies, Rice Krispies treats, cheese and crackers. Bottled water cools in a bowl of ice. The furniture is modern and hip. A few chairs surround an oblong coffee table. Another wall serves as a rack for a variety of space age weaponry of shapes and sizes similar to those in Simon Tybalt's moon base. I even recognize the JazzHands Phaser and Passive Aggressive Agitator. To my right, a row of laptops display what appear to be profiles of people whose faces I recognize, particularly Max Gentry.

Under the Einstein poster and map of the city sits an object that clearly doesn't match the rest of the décor: a dilapidated, avocado green faux leather couch. Sitting on the couch is Randi Williams, holding an unopened bottle of beer. She spots me and waves me over toward the couch.

"Tony. Glad you're feeling better. Have a seat." White stuffing is spilling out the sides of the corpse of sofa like guts. An odd odor of cat pee, old burritos, and death seeps from within it.

"Can I stand? I'd rather stand."

"You'll want to sit. We've got a lot of ground to cover." She opens the beer with her teeth. I guess because she can. "I'm glad you showed. I know this is a lot to process."

"How long have you known about the book club?" I ask her. "Why didn't you tell me when I worked with you?"

"Randi joined our book club a few months back when we were revisiting *To Kill a Mockingbird*," Dad says as he stands next to me.

"Also," Mom adds, "she was being attacked by a Herpezoid and we saved her."

"It was my pool league night." Randi sips her beer and stares off. "I was walking to my car when one jumped me. They saved my ass and I assumed they were with Corporate."

"So, let me get this straight." I pull a bottled water from the ice bucket and take a sip. "My parents are part of an organization Corporate knows nothing about."

"That's right," Randi says. She polishes off her beer, stands, and references the city map on the wall. "They told me all about their work. How sightings of aliens had increased. Herpezoids were taking control of human bodies. It's been going on for years."

"How?" I ask. "We guard the portal. We know if something comes through."

"We don't know that." Kevin Raulston joins the conversation. "We only know they're here. The Herpezoids are here as I said they would be and now they're going to take over. Nobody listens to crazy book store owner guy, but who's laughing now?"

"Wait a minute," I say. "How is it my parents and my field trainer worked together but my name never came up?"

"We didn't talk about you or our personal lives at all," Mom says. "That's common sense."

"For your protection," Dad adds.

"Same reason I couldn't tell you about Corporate." I look at my parents unsure of what to say next. "I guess you guys wanna hear what I've been up to for the last couple of years."

"I filled them in while you were gone," Randi says.

"You were missing and we were beside ourselves," Mom says. Dad puts his arm around her and pulls her to him. "We had no idea."

"We kind of fell apart one night here," Dad tells me. "We said our son Jeff is missing and Randi put two and two together."

"Wait," I say to Randi. "Didn't you tell Corporate about this? I don't understand."

"I've been unhappy with how things have been handled under Max." She steps to the picture of Max and stares at it. "Things are not good. Max knew about the nanotech research and he wanted to download it into a human subject and test it. He had a dream of creating a team of super agents that would guard the portal and protect the planet while doing whatever he asked without question. I'm not about that life."

"But you allowed Jeff to have one put in him," I say.

"About that." Randi looks at the floor. "Jeff only thinks he has a nano in him. I didn't have the heart to inject him. It was wrong."

"He thinks he's got a nanotech in him that is making him a superagent." I don't know whether to be angry or relieved. Part of me wants to laugh.

"All I gave him was a flu shot." Randi walks to the spread of snacks and gobbles a piece of cheese.

"So why not quit Corporate?" I decide I need a snack, too, so, I walk over and assemble a plate of cheese and crackers. Grandor has gathered a plate of snacks for himself and sits in the corner munching. "Work here instead."

"Corporate is a paying gig," she says. "No funds in this."

"It's a calling." Kevin walks to the map of Poplar Bluff with all the push pins and gestures to it. "We're here to protect the planet."

"Yeah," says Randi, "but this calling doesn't pay the bills. I've got material needs."

"I didn't mean for all this to happen." My stomach knots up and I want to time travel to before ever answering that stupid Craigslist ad about the job at Corporate. "I just needed a part-time job."

I look at my parents and a strange sense of calm envelops me. The anger over their secret life fades and my personal shame at my own secrets kept from them dissipates. Something about their faces tells me our relationship is somehow stronger than all of this.

Mom gives me The Look. "We know this has been difficult. We really do understand."

Dad gives me The Reassurance. "We'll get through this together."

"What do you guys call yourselves?" I ask. "What's the name of this organization?"

"No name," Mom says. "We're just a book club."

"How long have you guys been doing this?"

Dad leads me to the row of laptops. "We've been tracking Herpezoid activity for years. Since before you were born. We monitor the frequency of their visits. We've committed ourselves to the single cause of stopping them from ever coming here. I first encountered one when I started work at the plant. I thought maybe they were behind the recent thefts."

"That was Jeff," I inform him. "He trades it for cigarettes. Another long story."

"We learned about the Herpezoids through Kevin," Mom adds. "We thought he was a crackpot like your Uncle Irwin. You know, the one who thinks Elvis Presley is still alive and living in a cave with Bigfoot? Then, one night, we watched him take one down."

Kevin steps over to join us. His voice deepens an octave and is tinged with anger. "Herpezoids are like the frat boys who show up to your party uninvited, drink all your booze, eat all your food, trash your house, and then run off with your girlfriend. I know firsthand. My first encounter with those bastards was while I was in college."

"What happened?" I ask.

"I told you. They took on the form of a fraternity and showed up at one of my parties. They drank all my booze, ate all my food, and ran off with my girlfriend and all the girlfriends of my friends. They left my apartment an absolute mess." He looks off at some unseen point, reliving the obviously still hurtful memory. "I got my phone bill the next month and discovered those assholes called several numbers in Luxembourg and Denmark. Two-thousand-dollar phone bill."

"I don't understand." I survey the row of laptops, each with photos of red dots flashing on maps of Poplar Bluff. Each dot representing possible Herpezoid activity. "How are they able to take human form?"

"DNA morphers," says a voice behind us. We turn to Grandor, who is shoveling snacks into his mouth. "Very expensive and illegal in most parts of the galaxy. Herpezoids procure them and take them so they can assume human form."

"Do you procure those for them?" Randi asks.

"Not me," he replies. "I do not know where they get them. I want nothing to do with those cretins."

The flat screen monitor on the wall sounds an alert and flashes the words "Incoming Message." Dad runs to the keyboard and answers the call. The image of Jeff Harper appears onscreen, appearing to video call.

"Dude!" His voice is breathless. "My mom and I kicked some Herpezoid ass! Who can say that? Me! I'm the only one! We've been bonding" He moves the camera over to his mother Sandra. She uses a handkerchief to wipe green Herpezoid blood from her face.

"Damn straight, sweetie! But, we didn't get all of them. They got away in an RV."

Sandra's reference of the RV sparks my memory much in the way looking at weapons and star maps stirs the nanotech in my brain. I walk to him. "Did the RV have flames painted on it?"

"Yeah," she says. "How'd you know?"

"Pretty sure I've seen it before. I think it belongs to the carnival company."

"Mirror Ball Entertainment?" Mom facepalms herself. "I hired Herpezoids to run the River Luau."

"Carnies," I mutter. "Herpezoids. Of course."

"No sign of *Miss America*, though," Jeff pouts. "I tried using the tracking device, but I'm sure it's been disabled."

"That RV. It belongs to some carnies." I pace around the room. "If those Herpezoids are disguised as carnies, then maybe Jackleigh is there with Jeff's car and Jeff told us earlier that his car is the quintonium drive."

"We need to hit the River Luau." Randi grabs a weapon from the wall and inspects it.

"Not right now," Mom says. "It's only 10:00. It's still really crowded. We need to wait till after midnight when it shuts down."

"Herpezoids posing as carnies in a darkened carnival." I shudder at the thought. "Now all I need is someone dressed as a mascot to chase me with an ax and my life is complete."

"We're on our way to you guys," Jeff says. "Kilroy out."

"Kilroy?" Dad asks.

"Don't ask."

"Excuse me." Grandor hold out an empty platter. "Do you have any more of these so-called 'Rice Krispies Treats?' They are delectable."

"Why is he here again?" Randi asks.

*

"I have told you repeatedly," an exasperated Grandor huffs. His eyes are swollen from a round of recent crying. "I wanted to turn the Earth into a resort. Humanity would be the servants."

"Why should we trust anything you say?" asks Dad.

"You should not." Grandor stands and walks around the room, gesturing like a washed up stage actor giving one final performance before calling it a career. It is the rant of a frustrated teenager tired of being told about all the things they do wrong. "I am unbalanced, unstable, and unreliable, oooookaaaaaaaaaaaaayyyyy?! My heart has been shattered by a heartless, perfidious she-demon and I cannot think clearly as a result.

"You should free me." He drops to his knees and holds his arms out for no apparent reason than to heighten the dramatic effect. "Rid yourselves of the burden of my existence. I shall find Jackie on my own. This is personal."

"He's a deal," Mom whispers to me, to which I can only nod in agreement.

"Tell us about the quintonium drive." Randi jerks Grandor to his feet. "What does it do? Do you have the plans?"

"Must I repeat myself? I know nothing of the quintonium drive. I never had it. I never possessed the plans. Ask Simon Tybalt. The drive is his baby, as they say."

"This is going nowhere," Kevin says. He pulls the JazzHands Phaser from the wall and sticks it to Grandor's head. "Tell us about the drive or I'll pump enough of this in you to make you perform all of *West Side Story* without an intermission."

"You do realize at any moment I could use my powers and end you." Grandor reaches up and squeezes Kevin's gun into a wad. "Besides, how do you know I have *not* performed all of *West Side Story* without an intermission on numerous occasions already?"

*

Midnight comes quickly and we exit Someone Else's Books. Kevin stays behind to monitor any further activity from other book club members. Jeff, Sandra, and Randi board the VW Cosmic Bus we took from Simon Tybalt's moon lair, while my parents, Grandor, and I get in the minivan. Grandor wears an odd look of serenity on his face. His lips curled slightly in a kind of satisfied grin. He is the eight-foot purple alien that ate the canary. Something about this is not right.

Jeff leans out of the driver's side window of the bus and looks back at us. He motions for Dad to pull the van up next to him. Mom rolls down her window and I roll down the van window so I can hear the conversation better.

"Tony," he calls out. "How are you feeling? Do you need a smoke?"

"No," I call back. "I think I'm good. It's not bothering me." My friend lights up a Mongalisonian cigarette of his own and draws a deep drag. "You probably don't need that now, either," I tell him.

"What do you mean?" he asks.

"Later," I tell him because I can see Randi waving her hand in front of her throat to give me the cut signal from her seat on the bus.

"What is he saying, need a smoke?" Mom asks. "Why would you need a smoke?"

"Yeah," Dad adds. "What's not bothering you?"

Before I can be busted for failing to tell my parents a small electronic bug is attached to my brain downloading the entirety of the Corporate knowledge bank into my brain, a figure whisks by on a motor scooter and skids to a sudden stop in front of us. The figure drops the kickstand and dismounts the scooter. The rider removes their helmet and I recognize Marlene's familiar freckled face glistening with sweat and smudged with small streaks of green goo. Her sandy blond hair is pulled into a very familiar ponytail. She wears jogging shorts and a goo-smeared t-shirt advertising a 5k run. Her breathing is labored and she clutches her stomach. She grimaces and drops to the pavement.

"Marlene!" I run and kneel next to her. I clutch her hand and try to scan the nanotech in my brain for ways to help, but I don't really know what's wrong.

"I took out two Herpezoids a little bit ago," she announces. "Close to the River Luau. Still don't know where the Araneae are being kept."

"There's more and more of them, it seems," Dad says.

Marlene makes eye contact with me. She doesn't say anything. My stomach knots and twists and my legs feel heavy. I now see she also wears what appears to be two katana swords strapped to her back because of course the sexiest girl I know would also sport katana swords and use them to kill aliens.

"Did you see my car?" Jeff gets out of the VW and marches to her. "Did you see *Miss America*?"

"No." She grits her teeth and fights off what appears to be some spasm of pain. "No car."

"Where were they?" Mom asks.

"I watched two guys slip behind one of the game tents and try to attack a girl. I took them on and they ran off."

"The attacks have grown more and more frequent. They must be breaching the portal," Randi says.

Dad starts pacing and nods at Grandor. "And getting their hands on those DNA Morphers Lurch over there was talking about."

"I don't understand," I say. "Corporate says they can track when a portal threat is coming. They have sensors or something. If the Herpezoids are getting through the portal, wouldn't they know it?"

"Humans. Such an inferior intellect."

Once again, the sound of Grandor the Malevolent speaking pulls our focus. He stands outside the minivan with a look of boredom. He clearly can't be bothered anymore with this nonsense.

"Someone is helping them from this side," he coaches. "Someone uses the portal from this side to get them through. I have done it many times on other planets. It is how I infiltrate."

Jeff pulls a Gulliball from his pocket, presses the button and rolls it over to Grandor.

"Dude," he says to Grandor. "I need help understanding what you're trying –"

Grandor interrupts him. "Your behavioral weapons will not work on me. I have so completely taken over this physical body that the brain is essentially an extension of me. Merely another machine. That was the plan with the Araneae. Take complete control of the host mind to do my bidding. GrandEarth simply would not operate without the compliant, easily manipulated workforce possessed by artificial intelligence."

"God, you're an asshole," Jeff says.

"You say someone on this side is helping the Herpezoids come through?" Randi asks. "Is this someone helping them adopt human form, too?"

"That would make sense. I know it is what I would do. Of course, I am not, but, it is totally what I would do if it were me. Which it is not." His eyes dart back and forth.

"But only Corporate has access to the portal, right?" I ask. I look at Jeff, setting off a chain reaction of glances back and forth between all the members of our band.

"Only Corporate," Jeff says. Then, in unison, we state the obvious once more.

"Only Corporate."

"Sounds like we need to go into the office in the morning," Randi says.

Marlene cries out in pain again, clutching her stomach and grabbing my arm.

"What did those bastards do to you?" I am already plotting my revenge on the Herpezoid swine who hurt my Marlene.

"Who?"

"The Herpezoids. Did they hurt you?"

"They barely got a hand on me," Marlene huffs, insulted by my question. "I think I got some bad food at the River Luau."

"What did you eat?"

"Not much. Three turkey legs, four funnel cakes, and a deep fried mashed potato covered Twinkie."

CHAPTER FIFTEEN

The night passed into the morning. We decided we needed at least some rest before tackling this mess. Randi texted Max to let him know we needed to meet. We arrived at 8 a.m. because Max said this required us to "synergistically expedite dynamic mindsharing."

Max Gentry now sits across from us and scans his tablet as if reading some important report. He works a lollipop in his mouth. I sit between Randi and Jeff, fidgeting while Randi exudes poise. Her hands are clasped and resting on the table and she watches Max and his tablet. Jeff is to my left, leaned back in his chair and feet propped up on the table. His top hat is cocked to one side. We are once again in the Rings of Saturn room. The same flat screen television hangs on the wall at one end and the same white board hangs at the other end. There is no amazing fruit tray, no THANKS FOR BEING AWESOME! gift bag. I glance at the motivational lithograph I saw the last time I was here. The tiny sailboat being tossed on stormy waves as ominous clouds loom overhead. I lock on the word COURAGE in bold, strong font and read again the caption underneath.

We can no longer wait for the storm to pass; we must be courageous enough to sail through it.

It speaks to me. I can relate. I am the tiny sailboat traversing the giant waves and looming clouds of my life. I'm still not motivated, though. This is some scary shit I'd rather not deal with.

"Listen, copper," Jeff blares in some kind of weird old gangster movie voice. "You can't keep us here, see? You got nothin' on us."

"I'll deal with you in a minute. Feet off the table, please." Max puts the tablet down, places the sucker in its wrapper. "Randi, help me understand. Your data points suggest an internal employee, a mole if you will, is allowing not only Herpezoids to access our world through the portal, but also aiding them in taking human form? Am I understanding your report correctly?"

"Yes." Randi leans forward and talks with her hands. "We also believe the alien form known as Jackie –"

"Jackleigh," I interrupt. Randi places a calming hand on my forearm to shush me.

"The alien form known as Jackie is partnering with the Herpezoids. She has kidnapped Simon Tybalt and demands the plans for the quintonium drive in return."

"So, if I'm hearing you correctly, our founder, Simon Tybalt, a man thought dead, is alive?" Max Gentry taps and swipes on the tablet. He furrows his brow the way one does when they're trying to figure out something. "That is a compelling development."

Max returns to his lollipop.

"We gotta get my car back, man," Jeff says. "Like, now."

Max points his lollipop at Jeff and eyes him through it like a sight on a pistol. "You stole proprietary information and willingly turned that information over to an unauthorized alien being. That is unacceptable."

"What are you gonna do?" Jeff mocks. "Put me on a performance improvement plan?"

Max Gentry huffs and stands. He paces the room on his side of the table as he speaks. "The criticality of this imperative has reached uniquely hyper scale levels. You have all in some way orchestrated mission critical deliverables which threaten to synergistically undermine our ROI."

"Agreed," I say. "Absolutely."

"Max," Randi says. "We need to know who the mole is and we need the plans to the quintonium drive."

"And we need my car back." Jeff stands and heads toward the door. "You're no help. I'll get it myself. Tony, you coming?"

"You need to tell them the truth about your car, Jeff." I hate putting him on the spot and I'm not sure why he's keeping the information to himself.

"What truth?" Randi walks to Jeff. "What's up with your car?"

Jeff looks at me like he wants to rip off my head, shit down my neck, and then tell me to clean the mess up. I give him an apologetic shrug. His hand is forced.

"Fine. *Miss America* is the quintonium drive. The car's core computer thingy is powered by it. Simon Tybalt put it in there. I can open any portal. Even create new ones. Terraform planets in way less time than it ever took before. It's freaking awesome."

"Help me understand." Max draws a deep breath. He looks as if he is trying to maintain patience against insurmountable odds. "The founder of Corporate installed a high-powered intergalactic superweapon into a 1976 Chevrolet Vega and turned it over to a sophomoric petty thief?"

"I prefer the term 'amiable antihero.'"

"Why would he do that?" Randi asks.

"Who's gonna look for a powerful weapon in a used Vega?" Jeff says. "You guys didn't see it coming."

"Who's gonna look for the entire Corporate training curriculum in the brain of teenager?" I ask. "Rube Goldberg Protocols."

"We gotta get that Vega back," Randi says "We need to find that mole, too."

"Indeed." Max tosses his lollipop in the wastebasket and checks his tablet. "I need to hustle to another meeting. Then, I'm clearing my calendar to deal with this. We simply make this our top priority. This requires a dramatic fabrication of robust, enterprise-wide outside-the-box thinking. Paradigms, people. Do I have your commitment?"

"Absolutely." I say.

"We're on it," Randi says.

"I don't know what the hell you're talking about," Jeff says. "Is that a haiku?"

"I'll circle back with the three of you once I've gathered more data." Max Gentry leaves the Rings of Saturn room, leaving the three of us to ponder our next move.

"Tony," Randi turns to me. "What did you say about training curriculum in a teenager's brain?"

"Long story," I say. "Dickhead here put one of those nanotechs in me at the request of Simon Tybalt. I'm a walking encyclopedia of Corporate shit."

An impish grin eases over Randi's face. "I know how to figure out who the mole is."

*

Randi, Jeff, and I return to the Someone Else's Books and Kevin Raulston lets us into the basement behind the door marked "Private."

"After I wait on these customers," he tells us. "I'll be down."

We descend the stairs to see my dad sitting at the coffee table playing checkers with Grandor. They are hunched over the board like two generals contemplating their next move toward global domination.

"How'd the meeting go?" Dad asks.

"Your son is going to save the day," Randi says.

"Where are our moms?" Jeff asks.

"They went to the River Luau to investigate. Suzanne is there under the guise of seeing how the fair is going. Sandra's there for backup. Meanwhile, I took a vacation day to babysit."

"I am so glad you are back." Grandor leaps to his feet and rushes to his haiku journal sitting on the chair in the corner. "I had a rush of creative inspiration while you were gone.

"Do hummingbirds cry?
Do penguins seek a soulmate?
No, stupid, they don't."

"I find it obtuse," I tell him. "What's your plan, Randi?"

She sits at the computer bank and types. The flat screen monitor switches away from the screensaver image of a tropical paradise to a popup asking for login credentials.

"I'm logging into Corporate's network via VPN," she tells me. "If the entire training curriculum is in your brain, then you have access to documents concerning the setup of top level security clearances."

"Yeah. So?"

"Sit down." She pulls a chair out for me and I oblige her request. "How do you use the nano?"

I shrug. "I concentrate. Like going to a happy place."

"Then go to the happy place that tells you how to set up security profiles."

Randi's reasons for asking me to do this are lost on me, but I comply. I close my eyes and picture myself walking through a virtual library of three-ring binders and bound documents. The shelves seem to stretch into infinity and everything is alphabetized. I jog along the ends of aisles until I reach the one marked Se-Sh. I scan the binders there until I find one titled "Security Clearances, Levels, and Protocols." I open my eyes and look at the flat screen monitor.

"I know what to do," I say.

"This is remarkable," Dad says. "What has happened to you?"

"He's Mr. Roboto," Jeff says, continuing his seemingly infinite quest to misinterpret his favorite song. I pull up the Corporate intranet and open the hyperlink for security. A login page pops up warning me I must have proper credentials.

"Excellent." Randi leans over my shoulder. "There has to be a listing somewhere of every login ID and password. See if you can find it."

I close my eyes again and to return to the library in my brain. I run a few aisles over to Pa-Pe to find personnel records. I figure if anyone would have ultimate security clearance it would be the man who built Corporate in the first place. A virtual spreadsheet opens in my mind's eye and within seconds I find what I'm looking for:

Simon Tybalt
Personnel Number: 07301967
Employee ID: simtyb42
Password: InfinityJone$1

I open my eyes, enter the info, and hit enter. The Corporate logo appears and then dissolves with a chiming sound. The screen is black for a few seconds and an eerie, frightful silence falls over the private room.

"What happened?" Randi asks.

"I dunno," I say. "I've never done this before. This should be Simon Tybalts's security portal."

The stillness of the moment is disrupted by the opening chords of "Legs," by ZZ Top.

A window opens with a message at the top: *Hello, Simon Tybalt. What would you like to do?*

I survey the list of options and click the one marked Create New/Edit Current Security Profiles.

"Nice work," Randi says. "Can you find my profile and hook me up?"

My mind's eye finds a job aid in the training materials and I'm able to search for Randi Williams' security profile. She currently lists a clearance level of 5, but I don't quite know what that means.

"What's the highest level?" I ask her.

"10."

I edit her profile to reflect her significant upgrade. "What's the point of this?"

"Employees with a level 10 clearance can see all kinds of records about who has accessed what and when. Every time you and I have been to the portal using the Rube Goldberg Protocol, a log entry is created. I can see who has been there and when. It might tell us who has been there without authorization."

"I do not understand how all of this is going to help me exact my revenge on Jackie," Grandor states.

"You wanna get revenge?" Randi turns to him. "You can deprogram her."

Grandor gasps audibly and recoils in disgust. "That would be murder! I will not murder my beloved no matter how much I hurt."

"What were you going to do then?" I ask.

"You could read her those suck-ass haikus," Jeff mutters. "God knows they're torturing me."

The door at the top of the basement stairs bursts open and Kevin Raulston walks down holding Marlene close to him as she clutches her stomach and groans.

"She stumbled in the front door," Kevin says. "Says she has a message from Jackie. Looks like they hurt her bad."

I rush to them and eye the one I love. "What was it this time? Roasted corn on the cob?"

"Foot long corn dogs. Three of them." She blows out a belch and struggles for breath. "And deep fried spaghetti and meatballs."

"What's the message?" Dad asks.

"She has Jeff and Tony's moms. She wants to meet." She belches again and her breath slaps me in the face like a soured washcloth dipped in marinara.

"She has Mom?" Jeff pulls a gun and aims it at nothing in particular. "We gotta move."

"Easy, easy," Dad says. "What's this meeting with Jackie about?"

"Says you still haven't given her the drive and time is running out."

"Alright," Randi says. "I'll go to Corporate and research who has been to the portal. You guys all go meet with Jackie and find out what she wants."

"Not everyone," Marlene says. "Just Tony and Jeff."

"Where is she?" I ask.

"The Waffle Palace out on the highway."

"Of course," Jeff says.

*

The buxom physical form of Leigh Ann Cantwell I now refer to as Jackleigh sits in a corner booth of the Waffle Palace devouring a plate of waffles soaked in blueberry syrup. She still wears the spandex jumpsuit and thin black duster. Her hair looks as if she came from the salon. Next to her sits Simon Tybalt, an untouched omelet in front of him. Jeff and I sit across from her. A couple of the carnies I remember from the Taco Haus parking lot sit in a booth across from us. They stare at us in way that either means they wish to do us harm if we make a wrong move or they wish to buy us drink. It's hard to distinguish.

"Where are our moms?" I ask.

"They are fine," she tells us. "Secure location and all."

"Where's my car?" Jeff asks.

"Where's my drive?" she asks.

"Grandor says there is no drive." I say under the assumption Jackleigh is in the dark about Jeff's car being the drive.

"Oh, there is a drive, alright." Jackleigh motions for the waitress to come over as she dabs the corner of her pouty mouth with a napkin. The waitress visits our table and Jackleigh asks her to bring another plate of waffles. "This all-you-can-eat concept is genius. I can see why Leigh Ann loves waffles so much."

"Do not give her the drive, gentlemen," Simon Tybalt says. "You mustn't."

"Here's the deal." Jeff takes a sip from his thermos. "We can get you the plans. Corporate has them. We have someone on the inside."

"You really mustn't, gentlemen."

"Very well." Jackleigh pours syrup on the fresh round of waffles the waitress delivered. I glance up at waitress as she asks if we need anything else in a deeply unaffected voice. I recognize her dark hair and soft facial features. I've seen her somewhere before and for a moment I can't place it, but a flash of memory tells me exactly who she is.

My caliente lederhosen-wearing drive-thru babe from Taco Haus. The sight of her in a Waffle Palace t-shirt and jeans throws me. She offers a slight smile and walks away.

"Where is my car?" Jeff asks again. "Have you messed with her? Have you scratched her up? Hung something stupid from the rearview mirror? Put in some nasty air freshener?"

"Your precious *Miss America* is safe and secure," Jackleigh swirls a fork full of waffles in the pond of blueberry syrup on her plate. "You deliver those quintonium drive plans to me at the portal site by five o'clock this afternoon and you can have her back. Your car. Your mothers. I'll even spare Simon Tybalt's life."

"What if I'm late or don't show?"

Jackleigh reaches into a clutch purse next to her and produces one of the Araneae and lets the tiny mechanical spider crawl around her hand like a pet.

"Then, I shall download this beautiful one into every person at that insipid River Luau and fry their brains. Starting with him." She puts the bug on Simon's shoulder and the bot instinctively crawls toward his neck. He squirms and reaches up to swat it away.

"No, no," Jackleigh scolds.

"Stop!" I shout.

"Do not cause a scene," she tells us. "No need to draw too much attention to us."

The spider reaches the back of Simon's neck and based on his grimacing and grunting, it must be burrowing into him. He swallows hard and normalizes his breathing. His hands shake as he grabs a napkin to wipe blood from the point of entry.

"Why do you wanna do this?" I ask. "Why all this world conquering nonsense?"

"Your planet is pitiful," Jackleigh says. "I want no part of it, really. I only want the drive so I can have it for myself and do what I please elsewhere. Grandor wanted it for his stupid GrandEarth plan, but I have loftier ideas."

"If we do this," Jeff says, "will you leave Leigh Ann alone, too?"

She stands and poses and preens. "I am not certain. I mean, look at this. I rather enjoy being in this human form. It garners attention. Granted some of it is unwelcome, but for the most part this is an enjoyable host. Leigh Ann is quite lovely. I do not know why her parents were so awful to her or her classmates so mean. Her memories suggest that, other than you, people mistreated her. I believe the Earth term is bullying."

"Yeah," Jeff says. "She's not had an easy life."

"So, I think my presence in her life makes her stronger, no?" She hops a bit and twists from side to side. "It is fun how everything jiggles."

"Yeah, it is." Jeff stands and faces her. "Let her go. Let our moms go. Get that thing out of him. Please."

"Then you know what you have to do." Jackleigh cups Jeff's face and kisses him. He stands motionless for a second before placing a tentative hand on her waist. She pulls away and taps his nose. "I can see why she likes that so much, too. See ya, baby."

The caliente lederhosen-wearing Waffle Hut babe returns and slides the check onto the edge of the table.

"Pay whenever you're ready."

"Would you be a doll and take care of that?" Jackleigh sashays away, carnie entourage and Simon Tybalt in tow.

"I don't think I'm ever getting Leigh Ann back," Jeff says.

"You'll get her back."

"Maybe," he replies. "But Leigh Ann never kissed me like that. That was a lot of sloppy tongue."

My phone buzzes with a text message from Randi Williams.

We have a situation. Meet me at book club.

*

We stand in the basement of Someone Else's Books looking at a short stack of paper on the coffee table. Dad picks up a few sheets from the stack and thumbs through them. I look at them and see they are spreadsheets.

"What are these?" I ask. "Looks like a schedule log or something."

"These are security access reports. They tell us who has been where and when at all Corporate properties. HQ. Fleet Operations. The call center. The portal. What you're looking at is a standard log of schedule adherence at the portal. If you look, you can see when you and Jeff worked your shift and then left when your replacement showed up."

"I'm bored already," Jeff says.

"Will you listen?" Randi pulls the tops sheet off the stack and holds it out to us. "Only certain personnel are scheduled to be at the portal at certain times. Any deviation of that schedule requires a Portal Schedule Variation Report and it must be approved by Max."

"What does that mean?" I ask.

"There are several instances on this report of one person accessing the portal when other Corporate personnel were scheduled, yet there's not a Variation Report."

"Who?"

"Max."

I take the report from her and read the following:

EMPLOYEE NAME	EMPLOYEE ID	DATE ACCESSED	TIME IN	TIME OUT	PORTAL STATUS
Max Gentry	050698	March 5, 2017	11:45 p.m.	6:00 a.m.	Green
Max Gentry	050698	March 12, 2017	11:45 p.m.	6:00 a.m.	Green
Max Gentry	050698	March 19, 2017	11:45 p.m.	6:00 a.m.	Green
Max Gentry	050698	March 26, 2017	11:45 p.m.	6:00 a.m.	Green
Max Gentry	050698	April 2, 2017	11:45 p.m.	6:00 a.m.	Green
Max Gentry	050698	April,9 2017	11:45 p.m.	6:00 a.m.	Green
Max Gentry	050698	April 16, 2017	11:45 p.m.	6:00 a.m.	Green

"So, Max accessed the portal every Saturday night after our shifts?" I grab the stack of papers from Randi's desk. "He's been going every Saturday for several months, taking over the graveyard shift on Saturdays."

"Did he need the overtime or something?" Jeff asks.

"So on prom night…"

"He was already there," Randi says. "I think Max was there to meet Grandor. I think Max is our mole."

The brevity of her accusation hangs heavy over the room. We all turn to face Grandor who only shrugs innocently.

"We gotta take him out" Jeff points his gun at Grandor. "Him and Max both."

"Easy," Dad says. "Can you be sure?"

"Look at this." She sighs and inserts a thumb drive into the computer console. We look up at the monitor and a window containing several file folder icons is open. They have names like Araneae, Mirror Ball Entertainments, GrandEarth, My Herpezoid Friends and How to Make Them Human, and Vacation Pics.

"This is crazy." I open the GrandEarth folder and it lists document names like Mississippi Lazy River, Antarctica Ski Lodge, and LeMans Go-Carts. A click on the Herpezoid Friends folder shows information on how to obtain DNA Morphers.

"Did you know about this?" I ask Grandor.

"Those could be photographs gathered through his intelligence," Grandor says. "That proves nothing."

Randi opens the Vacation Pics folder and a collection of dozens of thumbnail photos fill the screen. A double-click on the first one brings up Max Gentry and Grandor the Malevolent arm-in-arm holding up tropical cocktails. The next picture is the two of them throwing money at a four-armed stripper.

"That's on Mongalisonia," Jeff says. "Or, you know, so I've heard." We turn and pull weapons on Grandor as he backs up toward the basement.

"Is this awkward?" he asks. "This feels awkward. But, then, I spend most of my time feeling awkward."

"Is Max working with you?" Randi asks.

"Max is a business associate, yes. He invested heavily in the GrandEarth concept. He offered a trade. Unobstructed entry through the portal in exchange for the Araneae nanotech."

"The one I stole for you?" Jeff asks. "You gave it to Max and then stole it back? What a dick move."

"I needed it for leverage, but then you two came along."

"Are you going to call us meddling kids?" I ask. "Please say, 'I'd have gotten away with it if it hadn't been for you meddling kids.'"

"I really can't talk anymore. I have to see a woman about a car."

"What?" I say. I can't say anything more because Grandor has unleashed a barrage of his power at us. Blue balls of energy slam into each of us and we spill all over the room. The force of the blows knocks the wind out of us.

"I will not kill you because I have never killed anyone. Besides, even if I had it in me to kill you, I simply would not be able to. I have grown curiously fond of all of you. You are my friends. Yet, you are my adversaries. You are my friendversaries. Ciao."

CHAPTER SIXTEEN

A blast from Grandor convulses my every muscle into a full body charley horse. The pain is swift and immediate and I have no way to relieve it except to blow out short breaths. Based on their groans of agony, Dad, Randi, and Jeff are all experiencing similar pain.

"Oh, god, this hurts," Jeff says through clenched teeth. "Why does it have to hurt?"

"Breathe it out," Randi repeats. "Breathe it out."

"I knew I hated that guy." Dad crawls to the Smelly Couch of Oblivion and gathers his strength.

My muscles slowly relax, though not all at once. The wave starts in my neck and shoulders so I'm able to pull myself up. The loosening spreads to my lower back and I straighten until my legs can support me. My breathing normalizes. Jeff lights up one of his Mongalisonian cigarettes and I reach out in a gesture that tells him to give me one, too. I light up and take a deep, satisfying drag.

"Guys," I say. "I think I'm done."

"What do you mean?" Dad says, giving me The Look. "And why are you smoking?"

"Yeah," Randi says. "I don't think Kevin allows smoking in here."

"Once we're done saving the world from Grandor, Jackleigh, Herpezoids, and Max, I'm done. Randi this is my notice. I can't wait to go to college where my biggest worries will be whether or not to skip class and how much cheap beer to drink."

The door at the top of the basement stairs bursts open. Kevin carries Marlene once more, this time completely in his arms. She is bruised and green Herpezoid slime splotches her arms and legs.

"Grandor tazed me or something," he says. "Then, Marlene stumbled in. I think she's really hurt bad this time." He sets her down next to Dad on the Smelly Couch of Oblivion. I kneel next to Marlene and brush a few errant strands of blond hair out her eyes. She clutches my hands and squeezes.

"Tony." She winces before she continues. "It's bad. It's real bad."

"Where have you been?"

"I took out three Herpezoids at the Taco Haus. They were trying to rob it. They're spreading out all over town. It's like that move *Gremlins*."

"I love that movie," Jeff says.

"Then, I went to the River Luau. I found your moms. They're keeping them in that black Winnebago with flames painted on it. I tried to rescue them, but I got overpowered. I was lucky to get away."

"My god," Dad says. "Where does she find the time to do all this?"

"And what did you have to eat?" I ask her.

"What?" She looks at me, insulted. "I'm really hurt here. I think I broke a rib or ruptured my spleen."

"Oh, baby, I'm sorry. I didn't know."

Her body spasms in pain and yells at me to not call her baby because we're not together anymore.

"We need to get her medical attention!" I try to pick her up, but she pushes me away.

"I'm good. I'm good." She rubs her temples. "I had five giant frozen lemonades with those crazy straw things. So good. Still having a brain freeze."

"I've had enough of this doo-doo." Jeff grabs an Existential Crisis Inducer from the weapons wall and starts pacing. "Enough talk. Time for action."

Randi's phone buzzes with a text message and she rolls her eyes and huffs at the message's content. "Damn. Max wants to meet with me ASAP."

"Tell him to screw himself," Jeff says. "He's a dick."

"I can't bring any suspicion from him. He's probably already thinking something is up because we told him about the mole."

"So, what do we do?" I ask.

"I'll take care of Max." She heads to the stairs. "You guys get to the River Luau and get Suzanne and Sandra back."

"Wait." Marlene sits up. "I heard them talking about unleashing Araneae on the fair crowd. I don't know where the Araneae is being held, but I'm sure it's there." She springs up and runs to the stairs. "Gotta go. Gotta kick some ass 'cause that's what I do."

"Marlene. Wait." I run to her and take her hands in mine. "I need you to know how much I hate myself. I wish I could go back in time and undo all of this. I love you so much. I shouldn't have broken up with you."

"Damn straight, boo. But you did." She caresses my cheek with the side of her hand. "Because you're a jerk tool head. A lovable, adorable jerk tool head." She grabs my face, pulls me into her and kisses me. "Bye, Tony Pershing."

She disappears up the stairs and I stand there with my lips still locked in a kiss which ended seconds earlier.

"Where did you find her?" Randi asks Kevin.

"She came in one day looking for a copy of *Twilight* and saw all of my shit on Herpezoids on the walls. She never blinked. Never questioned anything. She just looked at it all and said three words."

"What words?" I ask.

"I want in."

*

I have a love/hate relationship with the annual celebration of amazing food, terrifying rides, and cultural appropriation that is the Poplar Bluff River Luau. The whole town looks forward to this week-long event every summer. I have mixed feelings. On the one hand, I love the food. My Poplar Bluff summer is not complete until I've scarfed down countless foot long corn dogs, funnel cakes, turkey legs, and fried anything on a stick. My mom is on the city board which puts together the luau every year, so I'm proud of her and come to support her. Last year's event was also the site of my the first time Marlene and I professed our love for each other. The River Luau offers much to appreciate.

As Jeff and I walk around the fairgrounds, though, I'm reminded of what I hate about it. Carnival rides which appear put together with staples, duct tape, and the prayers of children line the midway. I remind myself the screams I hear are those of happy fairgoers enjoying a pleasant summer evening and not of terrified people falling to their deaths from atop a rickety Ferris wheel. Scattered amongst the death traps passing for thrill rides are games of skill and chance. I wasted so much money last summer on a shooting game, I could've saved hard-earned cash and my fragile ego by simply buying a stuffed bear for Marlene off Amazon. I guess seeing her smile when she held the bear was worth it, though.

And, then, there are the carnies. The rides and games are all manned by a traveling band of sketchy figures. Ever since I was a small child, I've been afraid of them. Reading *Something*

Wicked This Way Comes did nothing to calm my fears. I think of Mr. Dark's traveling carnival from that book as I look at the sinister individuals standing watch by the attractions. They look human, but we now know they are really Herpezoids here to help Jackleigh carry out her devious plan.

Jeff and I each carry a minor cache of weapons. In my pocket is a Gulliball. Strapped to my right hip is the Existential Crisis Inducer. Since it looks like a flashlight, no one will question it. Tucked in the back of Jeff's belt is both a JazzHands Phaser and a Neutralizer like the one I used on Max and his agents at the portal. We scan the grounds. Carnies work the controls of the rides, entice people to play rigged games, and dish out copious amounts of fried anything and everything, yet their focus appears solely on us. I feel their creepy eyes on us with every step we take. My pulse quickens and pounds in my temple. My legs tingle with anxiety. My chest hurts. The reality of no longer wanting any part of the Corporate life overwhelms me.

"I really am ready to go," I tell my friend. "It's time."

"I've been ready to go for as long as I can remember," he says. "That's why when this job is done I'm going back through the portal."

"I still say you should come to college with me." That's a token response on my part. I know Jeff wants nothing to do with college.

"I'm not about that life. I don't belong here. I don't think I ever have. I've got a cool gig working with Simon Tybalt. I got a pimped out Vega. I get to travel. I've seen so much in a short time. One time, on Bi Xiu Prime, I got a massage from a girl with four arms. She had four arms. I want you to think about that for a minute."

And, for a few seconds, I do think about it. How could I not?

"I need away from Corporate." I turn away from Jeff and look at a carnie holding a stuffed unicorn. His creepy gaze bores into me. His eyes flip from human form to those of a Herpezoid. "I need normalcy. I need a plan for my life that doesn't involve all this."

"Maybe you and Marlene will get back together." Jeff pulls out a cigarette and lights up. He offers me one and I take it. I can't let this nano inside me start taking over with so much on the line. What's the deal with her, anyway?"

"What do you mean?"

"The way she kissed you back at the book store." He takes a drag and exhales and I realize I should tell him he doesn't have a nano in him. "What's up with that? Are you guys back together?"

I puff on my own cigarette and think about that amazing kiss and the one from the night she saved me from Life Coach Gilbert and the little old lady whose name is still a mystery. The sights and sounds of this ridiculous carnival remind me of our first kiss. Have we had our last kiss now? Can I get her back?

"I dunno," I say. "She's still pretty pissed that I broke up with her. Yet, she kissed me."

"Does she work for Corporate or something?" Jeff takes a final smoke and flicks his cigarette onto the ground. "She takes down Herpezoids like it's her purpose in life."

"I don't know. I thought so, but Randi says she doesn't. She works with Kevin, I guess." I toss my cigarette to the ground and smash it out. "Jeff, I need to tell you something about your nano."

"Later." Jeff points straight ahead. "Marlene's walking this way eating a turkey leg. I'm gonna check some things out. Find my car. Kick some ass. I'll be in touch. You do you and work some shit out."

Jeff disappears into the midway crowd on his quest to find *Miss America.* Marlene faces me. She wears the familiar ponytail and no makeup. Her face is always fresh and sunny, even when she's gnawing on poultry and covered in alien blood.

"Found anything yet?" she asks me. "Did you find your mom yet? Have you tried these turkey legs? Freaking amazing." She walks past me toward the parking lot.

"Where are you going?" I chase after her.

"I got word from a contact that there are some Araneae somewhere in town. A big nest or whatever you call it. I'm gonna find it and take it out 'cuz that's what I do."

"Since when?" I spin her around. "It's like I never knew you. You apparently live a secret life as an alien hunter who eats everything in sight."

"Why do you care to know me now? You broke up with me." She takes one last bite of the turkey leg and tosses the bone to the side. "So, I'm eating the shit out of everything and focusing on my career."

"And dating Clint." I shouldn't say that, but I felt the need to get in a petulant dig. Her response begins with a slug to my bicep.

"Don't be a dick. Clint was an assignment. I got intel that he might be a Herpezoid. When we broke up, I let him think he was healing my broken heart so I could get close to him."

"How long have you been in the book club?" My arm still stings from her punch. I've never been more attracted to this girl than I am right now. She's mysterious, fiery, and could easily kick my ass with little to no effort.

"I could tell you, but then I'd have to kill you." She grabs my face with both hands and kisses me. Arousal fans out across my body, especially to all the critical areas. I reach to pull her close to me, but she breaks our kiss and backs away a couple of steps. "I'm not in the book club. I fly solo. I do my own thing. In secret. It's awesome."

"Will you stop randomly kissing me? I mean, don't stop. Randomly kiss me all you want. I don't understand what's going on here. Are you mad at me? Are you done with me? Or are you still into me? What's going on here?"

"Tony Pershing." She pulls a Herpezoid-killing pistol from her back waistband and inspects it. "It is entirely possible to know you need to move on from someone even though you still love them. Now, I need to go take out some Herpezoids and find the Araneae. Go save your mom and let me do my job."

She walks away from me and I follow her into the parking lot. I call after her, but she waves me off. She stops at her motor scooter and look back at me.

"You hurt me, Tony Pershing."

"I know. I'm so sorry. I thought my job at Corporate was too dangerous and didn't want to risk you getting hurt."

"I can take of myself."

"So it would seem."

"We both had secrets." She puts her helmet on and sits on her scooter. "Neither one of us knew the other. I shouldn't have gotten involved with you, either. It compromised my mission."

The obnoxious roar of Clint Hudson's Truck of Overcompensation overwhelms our conversation and we turn to see it barreling toward us on the parking lot. It skids to a stop and Clint hops down from the driver's side and his loyal cronies Tyler and Dalton emerge from the passenger side. Never have three people needed to find a hobby more than this trio.

"Fanstastic," I mutter.

"We were supposed to go the River Luau today." Clint huffs. "What are you doing here with this asshole?"

"I'm sorry," I say. "I didn't know you and I had a date today, Clint. If our relationship is going to work, we need to improve our communication."

"I'm not talking to you." He shoves me and turns to Marlene. 'What are you doing here with this pussy?"

"Don't call me that," I say. "Besides, you're the one who got his ass handed to him the other night."

"I'll call you whatever I want," Clint says. "Besides, I'm not a pussy."

"Fine, then." I take a couple of steps toward Clint because something about being around him now fills me with a need to act like a buck in the wild. "If somebody thinks you're a hedgehog, presumably you give them a mirror and tell them to sort it out for themselves."

"What?" Clint says.

"He's quoting Douglas Adams now, Clint." Tyler says. "First it was Isaac Asimov, now Douglas Adams. This dude has no respect for you."

"What is it with guys and the incessant need to posture in front of a female?" Marlene asks. We stare back at her in slack-jawed silence, though, in Clint's defense, slack-jawed silence might be his resting face. "It's pathetic."

"They were posturing." Tyler points at Clint and me. "Not us."

"Right," agrees Dalton. "Clint is a classic poser."

"I'm offended by the use of a term for female genitalia as an insult," I say. "Can't we rise above all that?"

"Marlene," Clint protests. "You're supposed to be with me."

"Besides," Marlene says, pointing at herself. "This particular possessor of said female genitalia could unleash holy hell on all of you."

"Are you trying to pick a fight with me, Marlene?" Clint maintains his slack-jawed expression. "I thought we had something together."

"We do." She cups his face like a mother would a child. "But, it's not what you think it is."

"So, you're back with this pussy?" Clint shoves me once more.

"Stop that." Marlene's voice sounds as if it's dropped an octave or two and she speaks through clenched teeth. "If you do it again, I'll have to assert myself."

"You threatening me? I do what I want. If I want to push someone, I will." Clint pushes me to the ground, I assume, to demonstrate he's a man of his word. I get back on my feet and pull the Existential Crisis Inducer from its holster.

"Careful, Clint!" yells Tyler. "He's got a flashlight!"

"Actually, I wasn't referring to shoving Tony." Marlene steps up to Clint. Though her face only comes to his broad chest, she is not intimidated. "Though, you need to stop doing that, too. You need to stop shoving Tony and saying the word 'pussy.'"

"Like I said, Marlene. I do what I want." Clint leans down to her, noses nearly touching. His eyes glow the way they did the night he attacked me at the portal. "So, if I wanna call him or anyone else a pussy, then, I will."

Marlene gives each of her response its own special emphasis. "Don't. Do. It."

"He's. A. Pussy."

Marlene's knee greets Clint's crotch with a violent upward thrust. He cries out and falls to the ground. She straddles his chest and pounds his jaw twice with her fist. I fire the Existential Crisis Inducer at Tyler and Dalton, but my shot misses and hits the grill of the Truck of Overcompensation.

"Hey!" Dalton cries out. "That's not a flashlight."

"I'm getting security," Tyler says and the pair turns to run into the park. "You two are in big trouble."

Marlene jerks her awesome sci-fi nun chucks from her back waistband and hurls them at the fleeing boneheads. The weapon clocks Dalton in the back of the head and he hits the ground in a heap. She sprints to Tyler, jumps on his back, and wrestles him to the ground.

"Say 'I'm a tiny penis,'" she commands him. "Say it."

"No!" Tyler tries in vain to remove himself from her vice-like grip around his head.

"Say it," she barks one more time. "Say 'I'm a tiny penis' or I'll snap you in half."

"I'm a tiny penis." Tyler gasps for air as Marlene releases her stranglehold.

"I know what the three of you are." She looks at Clint, Tyler, and Dalton nursing their wounds. "If I see you out alone, I won't go as easy on you."

"Hey!"

I turn toward the opening of the River Luau to see Jeff sprinting toward us.

"Hey! We gotta go!" He stops long enough to grab me and pull me along. "A shitload of Herpezoid carnies are coming!"

"What are you talking about?" I ask him.

"I tried to steal *Miss America* back and they caught me!" He sprints past me. "We gotta go!"

My phone buzzes with a text message. It's Randi.

Come to Corporate HQ! NOW!

"Looks like Randi needs us," I say.

"Fine!" Jeff stops and waves his arm to follow. "But let's get outta here."

"I'll fight these guys off." Marlene stretches her neck from side to side and it crackles. "I need to let off some steam and this will be better than going to the gym."

"What?" Jeff says. "By yourself?"

"Don't question it," I tell him. "She can handle it."

"I'm not questioning anything," Jeff says. "That's freaking hot."

"Right?"

CHAPTER SEVENTEEN

My phone explodes with a barrage of texts from Randi explaining her situation.

Max is definitely the mole.

Major nest of Araneae at Corporate HQ.

Max plans to release them. Found his plans.

Call me ASAP!!

Jeff taps a few buttons on the Cosmic Bus's touchscreen dashboard display and a video image of Randi on her phone fades into view on the console monitor where the radio normally would be. She is crouched in an enclosed area I can't quite determine.

"This is bad," Randi whispers. "Worse than I thought, actually."

"What's the situation?" I ask.

"I found some intel on Max by hacking his email. He's been planning to use the Araneae to create super agents that would do what he wanted. The plan was for them to work security at GrandEarth. He cut a deal with Grandor."

"Where's the nest?" I ask her.

"It's in the Research & Development lab. Heavy security there."

"Where are you now, Randi?" Jeff asks.

"I'm in the ladies room. Max won't come in here. That would be a serious HR violation."

"Stay put!" Jeff barks. "We're coming for you!"

*

Why am I here?

I'm not asking because I've been shooting myself repeatedly with the Existential Crisis Inducer. This time I'm asking in the metaphysical, meaning-of-life way. Is this the moment my life has been leading to? Does God exist and did He/She/They determine my life path before I was ever born? If so, then God knew before the creation of everything that I would be sitting in a 1969 VW Bus with my best friend preparing to raid the headquarters of a mysterious private company which specializes in the protection of an intergalactic portal so we can rescue our co-worker and prevent spider-like artificial intelligence called Araneae from being unleashed on my unsuspecting hometown. If I'm to believe in a benevolent higher power, then I'm also to believe He/She/They preordained all of this. Those are a lot of moving parts for one kid's life.

We enter the parking lot at HQ and Jeff pulls into a space specifically reserved for visitors, but he's always been a rebel like that. Our moms sit in a Winnebago on the fairgrounds. We don't know where Simon Tybalt is. Jackleigh has been eerily silent and Grandor the Malevolent left us to do whatever he does. Yet, here I sit in the passenger seat of the Cosmic Bus as Jeff listens to "Renegade," by Styx, to get pumped up.

"What is our plan?" I ask. "How are we going to do this?"

"Plan? We're gonna kick ass. That's our plan!"

"Oh, god." I rub my face in frustration. Loose cannon philosophy will not serve us well here. I close my eyes and draw a deep cleansing breath. "Let me access some tactical training or something in this nano in my head and we can figure something out."

"The plan is to walk into Corporate, get Randi and the Araneae shit or whatever, and leave."

"You are aware of the extreme security in this place right? You can't waltz in there. You need clearances and access cards. I'm an intern. I can get into the building, but I need an escort just to go to the bathroom."

"So, it's like junior high, then? Got it." He puts on his top hat and a pair of aviator sunglasses because I guess he's trying to go for a certain effect. "Follow my lead."

"I can't do this. This is suicide."

"Suicide?" For the first time in our friendship, Jeff Harper turns off Styx to make a point. "What do you think they're gonna do to us? Huh? Kill us? It's Corporate. They kill us, it's murder. They can't arrest us because they're not the police. The worst they can do is fire us."

"I think you might be grossly underestimating this situation."

"What if I am? Who gives a shit? We're Kilroy and Mr. Roboto. You have a nano in your head. I've got a nano in mine. We have weapons that will jack people up, but not really hurt 'em, ya know? So, they'll be okay. We go in and start shooting everything we have. No prisoners, baby. We'll be like the Americans storming the beaches of Norman on Valentine's Day or some shit."

"Allies. Normandy. D-Day." I look at my friend with the wild look in his eyes and shake my head. "You need to know something."

"What?"

"You don't have a nano inside you. Randi told me. She gave you a flu shot."

Jeff leans back against the door and takes off his sunglasses. He sticks an earpiece in his mouth and his expression suggests he is questioning everything he ever knew or believed. I know the feeling.

"I got nothing in me?" His eyes are sad and his mouth turns downward.

"Not according to Randi. She said it was unethical to inject you with it."

Jeff squints and looks out the window. He wears a look of defeat and disillusionment. The fire in his eyes has faded. I feel bad for telling him, but he needed to know before he did something stupid. He looks ready to give up and I need him now more than ever.

"Maybe now wasn't the time to bring that up," I say.

"Probably not."

"Randi needs us, Jeff. We gotta go help her."

Adrenaline floods my body and consumes my entire being. The parts of my brain devoted to rational thought turn out the lights and take a nap, while the parts obsessed with more primal functions start a rave. The common sense in me says this is nuts, but I also know we are the only ones who can stop Max and the Araneae.

I see it all perfectly; there are two possible situations – one can either do this or that. My honest opinion and my friendly advice is this: do it or do not do it. You will regret both.

"Kilroy," I say.

"What?" my friend asks.

"We own the night."

Jeff Harper looks at me and I spot an ember of that fiery gaze once again. He slips his sunglasses on and straightens his hat.

"Damn skippy we do," he growls.

*

We each pack behavioral weapons of all shapes and sizes. Gulliballs, JazzHands Phasers, Neutralizers, Passive Aggressive Agitators, Existential Crisis Inducers.

"What's our first step?" I ask as I secure my arsenal on my belt. "Create a diversion? What?"

"Follow my lead and set off that Gulliball thing when I tell you to."

Jeff Harper struts toward the front door of Corporate like a hobo who thinks he's Clint Eastwood. Why aren't we using some alternate route? Shouldn't we be entering through a window or air duct? I tell myself to stop asking questions and just do. I run behind Jeff as we cross the threshold of the sliding glass doors and enter the atrium. Two armed men in security uniforms walk from behind the reception desk and ask us what we're doing, hands poised on their pistols. It's Jerry and Dale.

"Excuse me, young man," says Dale.

"Corporate is closed right now," says Jerry. "Unless you have an appointment, you'll need to come back tomorrow."

"Closed?" I ask. I didn't see this particular development coming. "What do you mean closed? Everyone is here, it looks like."

"Some kind of lockdown or some such," says Dale. "You'll have to come back tomorrow. Leave your business card and we'll have someone call you."

"We're here to fix a plumbing issue," Jeff says, as if it were as true as saying that Europe is a continent. "And if we come back tomorrow you'll be paying double time."

"I don't know anything about a plumbing issue," says Dale. "Do you have a work order or something?"

Jeff looks at me and nods. I pull the Gulliball from my pocket and fire a blast at Jerry.

"Why would he need a work order?" he asks Dale. "Man says they're here to do a plumbing job, so let them work."

I fire a quick shot at Dale now and wait for his response.

"Yeah, you're right. They don't tell us anything around here. Do you fellas know where you're going?"

"Sure do," Jeff says and leads me away from the duo. "Shoot 'em again. Quick." I fire right as it looks like Jerry and Dale might be catching on. My shot hits Dale square in the face.

"Scarlett Johansson is in the parking lot," Jeff calls out. "She wants to talk to you both," He fires his Existential Crisis Inducer at Jerry. While Dale turns and sprints to the parking lot to meet Scarlett Johansson, Jerry rubs his chin and look toward some far off point.

"Is Scarlett Johansson really *here?* I mean, are any of us really *here*?" His pondering allows us enough time to sprint down toward the elevators.

"Hard to believe Corporate would have those two bunglers working security," I say.

"Did you say bunglers?"

We reach the elevators and walk down the right hallway with urgency. My mouth is void of any moisture, all of it apparently allocated to my sweat glands. I wipe beads of perspiration from my forehead with my arm and tell the butterflies in my stomach to kindly leave. I place the Gulliball back in my pocket and pull the JazzHands 6375 out. I grip it tight in the hopes of calming the tremor in my hand. I really don't want to be here. I think about the caliente lederhosen-wearing babe from Taco Haus and Waffle Palace and how I'd happily trade places with her right now, even if she were waist deep and naked in raw sewage. Guilt gnaws at me for not thinking of Marlene first. What do I make of that?

My phone buzzes and I see it's a text from Randi. We duck into an empty conference room and lock the door.

Where r u guys?

My reply: *In building. Looking for u.*

Randi: *Getting backup. Meet in R&D*

"I brought a couple of extra toys," Jeff pulls two small pistols from holsters on his belt and puts one in my hand.

"The Phobia Inducer," I say with the same certainty I have about my love for my parents and my dread of mayonnaise. "That's what you shot Clint with that night at the portal."

"How do we get to R&D from here?" Jeff asks. "Where is it?"

"I dunno. I know I should, but I'm scared shitless right now, so it's hard to focus. I can't access the nano."

Jeff places his hand on my shoulder and speaks to me in an odd voice. He sounds like Sean Connery auditioning for Darth Vader.

"Look deep inside you, Mr. Roboto. The knowledge is within you."

"I'm not Mr. Roboto." I close my eyes and visit the vast virtual library in my head. I sprint the aisles looking for any information about Research & Development. The row of subjects starting with 'R' is long, but I'm able to find what I'm looking for: a standard white three-ring binder with the words RESEARCH & DEVELOPMENT ORIENTATION AND ONBOARDING printed on the cover. A quick flip through the first few pages gives me the info I'm looking for. I quickly exit my brain library and return to the conference room.

"R&D is located on the lowest level of the building. To access we have to follow Rube Goldberg Protocol 47."

"Why is everything in the basement?" Jeff wonders aloud.

We exit the conference room and walk down the hallway like we belong there, passing a few random Corporate employees along the way. My goal is to avoid direct eye contact. Jeff's goal appears to be drawing as much of it drawn to us as possible. He waves hello to everyone we pass.

"How's it going? How ya doing? We're plumbers."

"We need to go in there." I point at a janitor's closet at the end of the hallway. We quicken our pace and reach the closet.

Jeff opens the door. The space is cramped and filled with the sounds of our breathing.

"I assume you know Rube Goldberg Protocol 47?" Jeff asks me.

I nod and reach down to the mop bucket. I pull the handle on the wringer, which causes a small keyboard lock to emerge from the wall. I pause for a moment to retrieve the code from the training curriculum stored in my brain. I enter the digits 8-0-0-8.

"Boob," Jeff giggles.

"What?"

"The code is boob. Classic."

"This is the stupidest thing I've ever done." My heart bangs inside my chest. Its thumps drive through my body and it's like my skin is bouncing.

"Wrong," Jeff says flatly. "Breaking up with Marlene is the stupidest thing you've ever done."

I can't argue with that.

The janitor closet elevator stops.

"Draw your weapon," Jeff says.

The doors slide open and no one is there to greet us. No Randi. No Max. No armed security. We walk into a large open room filled only with the sound of a hum emanating from the servers that line all the walls. Laptop computers fill rows of all the tables throughout the middle of the room. A man and woman, both wearing lab coats lie face down on the floor in a lifeless heap. A small incision and a trickle of blood is on the man's neck.

"Are they dead?" I ask. My stomach lurches a bit. I've never seen a dead person other than at a funeral.

"I dunno," says Jeff, circling the bodies from a safe distance. "Check them. Kick 'em or something."

"I'm not going to check them. You check them."

"Hey," he calls to them. "Are you guys dead?"

"So much for your dreams of being a medical examiner." I step toward the bodies with the intention of checking a pulse, but a voice in the room stops me.

"They're not dead."

Max Gentry appears from a side room carrying a backpack with the Corporate logo emblazoned on it and pointing a gun at us. The weapon's black barrel is long and narrow. It looks like a power washer.

"I shot them with this Narcolepsy 5000. They're in heavy REM sleep right now. They will awake in thirty minutes feeling refreshed. Also, I deployed inside them a strategic, highly-advanced artificial intelligence which will allow them to synergistically interface with an authoritatively end-to-end network of like-minded users."

"What did he say?" Jeff asks me. "I know it's not a haiku because I looked that shit up."

"I think he said we're screwed."

"This." Max holds up the backpack. "This is the future. Inside this are Araneae. They will aid our efforts in transforming our planet into a state-of-the-art resort for high-end, upscale vacationers from across the universe. The Araneae will allow me to assemble a high-performing, impactful security team."

"Why are you wasting your time telling us your plan?" I ask. "You're violating a basic rule of villainy."

"Because you two are about to become members of that elite squad." He holds the gun out to fire only to have it knocked from his hand by a blast from a stun gun. He drops his weapon and we turn to see Randi Williams standing at the janitor closet elevator and aiming her gun at Max.

"Let's not do this, Max," she tells him. "Put down the backpack."

"I'm going to have to pushback on that," he says.

"Where the hell did you come from?" Jeff says to Randi.

I seize an opportunity to act while Max is distracted. I jerk the Phobia Inducer from my pants pocket and fire at Max. A yellow bolt hits his chest and spreads out across his whole body. He stands stunned for a couple of seconds. His expression falls into blankness then morphs to abject terror as he trembles all over. Perspiration beads on his face as he looks at the three us.

"Oh, god," he whispers. "You're all looking at me. Why are you looking at me?"

"What's wrong with him?" Randi asks.

"I'm not sure yet," I say. "I shot him with the Phobia Inducer."

"What's he afraid of?" Jeff asks.

"I dunno."

Max swallows hard. "I hate being in situations like this. We're just standing around having to make small talk. I hate small talk. It's like you're judging me for every word I say."

"Aw, man," I sigh. "I gave him social anxiety disorder. I feel bad now."

"I'm judging you because of that backpack," Jeff says. "You look ridiculous."

"Oh, my god." Max starts shaking and gasping. "What do I do? What do I do?"

"Set it down gently," Randi advises, "and slowly back away."

The average effect from a behavioral weapon lasts anywhere from thirty seconds to several minutes based on the intelligence of the victim. It taps into that part of our psyche which is susceptible to suggestion. The greater the lack of intellect in the victim, the longer the effects. Max always struck me as smart and learned. We must act with urgency if this is going to work.

Max sets the backpack down as instructed and holds his hands out. He steps backward twice and his face morphs from that of a teenage boy whose parents walked in on him smoking pot to the Max Gentry who seconds ago nearly shot us with a sleep gun. A flash of recognition in Max's eyes tells us the Phobia Inducer has worn off and the jig is up. He lunges toward the backpack only to be greeted with several shots from Jeff's Passive Aggressive Agitator. He backs away with each blast, allowing me time to rush over and pick up the bag. I toss it to Randi and she catches it.

"Go! Go!" she barks.

"Oh, okay," Max calls out to us. "Well, I was going to use that backpack for my plan, but if you guys need it more, that's cool. No, really, take it. I'll find another backpack. There are so many backpacks. It won't quite be as cool as that one because it has the Corporate logo on it, but as long as you guys have what you need then it's all good. Don't worry about me."

"I wonder how long he'll be like that," I ask. We hear one more pout from Max as the janitor closet elevator doors slide shut.

"It's fine! Really!"

*

Randi, Jeff, and I stand poised for action as the janitor closet elevator of Rube Goldberg Protocol 47 rises.

Randi holds up a copper plated laser pistol as she speaks. "When that door opens, I'm going to open fire because I'm sure there will be agents waiting for us."

"What gun is that?" Jeff asks. "Never seen it before."

"An early prototype of one of Simon Tybalt's behavioral weapons," she replies. "The White Girl Waster. One shot of this and you are drunker than a sorority girl at a homecoming tailgate party."

"I gotta get me one of those," Jeff says.

"Max has already downloaded a shitload of Araneae into agents here," Randi tells us. Once we get through these first agents, we'll head to the lobby and out the front door. You use the JazzHands gun and any other weapon you have time to shoot on the next wave to distract them."

"Agreed." I nod. The doors to the elevator open and two agents stand before us wearing golf shirts and khakis, weapons aimed at us.

"Let me be P.A.C. with you both," says one of the them. He wears a salmon-colored golf shirt with thin white horizontal stripes across the front.

"P.A.C.?" I ask.

"Perfectly Absolutely Clear." This point man rattles off an impressive stream of Corporate speak without a shred of human emotion. "It is our understanding the three of you have obtained a vital piece of our business intelligence that directly impacts several Corporate workstreams. It is critical that Bob here and I work this problem immediately."

"Just to piggyback off of what Alan said," pipes in the other agent. "We'll need you to come with us so that we can debrief this situation and action plan some possible outcomes."

"Oh my god!" Randi unloads several blasts from her laser pistols. Agents Bob and Alan slam against the Plexiglas wall behind them, but the cubicle dwellers on the other side seem oblivious to the violence. Bob and Alan stagger to their feet and lean against the wall. Their eyelids are only half open and they struggle to remain upright. Bob sips from a beverage only he can see.

"Ugh! This vodka and cranberry juice is disgusting." He makes a gagging face and then holds up a hand to suggest he can't even with this anymore.

"Girl, we just got here!" Alan announces. "Let's do some shots! Woooooooo!"

"Wait!" Bob holds up his phone and leans into Alan. "Selfie!"

The pair strike a pose involving duck lips and snap several pics that will provoke many questions when they find them later.

"That's freakin' awesome," Jeff says. "Where'd you get that?"

"Old Simon Tybalt prototypes," Randi replies. "We gotta go!"

I follow Jeff's lead down the hall as Randi brings up the rear looking for agents coming behind us. As she predicted, about a dozen more agents are waiting for us, all dressed smartly in various forms of business attire and look as if they are headed to work at a well-respected firm of some kind, except they are pointing guns at us. At the front of this group is a black man with a shiny bald head.

"We have been tasked with bringing you to a town hall meeting with Max regarding the stolen nanotech," he says.

"Aw, man," I say. "I know what they are. That's a tiger team, a highly specialized group of experts tasked with solving complex problems." Saying that feels like an out-of-body experience.

"Fire on 'em!" Jeff shouts. "JazzHands! JazzHands!" I comply with his order and unleash a blast from the JazzHands 6375 at the tiger team. They immediately drop their weapons and launch into an impressive rendition of "You're The One That I Want," from *Grease*.

A third wave of agents shoots from behind us, but they fortunately have the aim of Imperial Stormtroopers. Randi and I return fire while Jeff leads through the hall. I drop the JazzHands gun and retrieve my Phobia Inducer and an object roughly the size of a golf ball from my left pocket. I've never used it before, but my nano is in overdrive right now, so it's as if I've used it my whole life.

"What is that thing?" Randi asks.

"It's called a Panic Ball." I hold it up while running backward down the hall. "Pretty much does what you think it's going to."

"Ha!" Jeff calls out. "That's using your balls!"

"Throw it!" Randi commands and I comply. It lands at the feet of the approaching tiger team and billows of yellow smoke emerge from it. The tiger team stops and coughs and waves away the smoke. The yellow cloud around them dissipates and their eyes are wide with fear.

"Raptors!" I yell and point behind them in the greatest show of terror I can muster. "Oh, my god! Raptors! Run for your lives!"

The tiger team members scream and begin stampeding toward us. A different wave of panic washes over me, Randi, and Jeff as we realize they might trample us running away from the imaginary raptors.

"Why didn't you tell them the raptors were coming from behind us?" Randi asks.

"I'm making this up as I go along!"

"It's freaking awesome!" Jeff shouts. "We own the night!"

We turn the corner and enter the atrium where two more teams await. Jeff fires on one team with the JazzHands while I hit the other with another Panic Ball. Team One launches into the opening number from *West Side Story.* Team Two loses their shit at the sight of it. They point, scream, and scatter in all directions.

"Oh my god, you guys!" yells a woman pointing at the dancers. "It's the Jets and the Sharks! Let's get outta here!"

The security guards Jerry and Dale appear, so I reach for the Gulliball, but realize I didn't bring it with me after using it on them earlier. I freeze, sure that the jig is up.

"We must've missed Scarlett Johansson?" asks Dale. "Did you get the plumbing job done?"

"Yep," I say as I step past them. Clearly the Gulliball is still working on these two. "We'll send you a bill."

"Sounds great!" says Jerry. "Hey! Dancing!"

*

We are in a full sprint toward the parking lot. A laser shot from behind us hits the pavement while another grazes my ear. I feel a slight burn from it and turn to see where it came from. I stumble and fall and another shot from an agent's laser hits the pavement beside my head. A tiny flame emerges from the landing spot and burns away. Max Gentry is shooting at us with a more dangerous weapon than any of us have. Randi pulls me to my feet and we start our run toward the Cosmic VW Bus only to be stopped by the sight of Jeff's 1976 Chevy Vega. His beloved *Miss America* – the one powered by the quintonium drive- is parked in the fire lane of the Corporate HQ parking lot. Clint Hudson's Truck of Overcompensation looms behind it. Clint and his two cronies, Dalton and Tyler, sit on the Vega's hood each wearing the kind of cocky sneer that begs to be slapped off with a tire iron. A few steps in front of them stand Grandor the Malevolent and Jackleigh the Curvaceous. The metallic orb once inhabited by Jackie hovers above them.

"We have an appointment with Max Gentry," Grandor announces. "Is he still available?

"He's shooting at us," I say and point toward the front door where Max stands.

"Take all their weapons," Jackleigh orders the three dumbasses and they do as they're told. They're breath smells of sulfur, stale coffee, and a low GPA.

"So help me," growls Jeff, JazzHands gun aimed. "If you've done anything to my car, I will kill you. I don't care what it is. Scratched a fender. Messed up the drive settings. Played bro country on my stereo. I will find you and I will kill you."

"They have the backpack with the Araneae," Max calls out as he walks toward us, weapon poised. "Give Grandor the backpack."

Randi surveys the situation around us, appearing to weigh any options we may have.

"Hand over the Araneae, please," Grandor says. "Slowly." And with that, the orb shoots a blob of bright pink energy at us. It envelops us like warm goo though it's not liquid. I'm aware of my movements slowing to a slightly faster rate than a frame-by-frame advancement of a movie. Reaching for weapon to fire is futile. Randi has no choice but to ease the backpack onto the pavement and slide it over to Grandor. He opens the pack and inspects its contents. His face is one of a child opening a disappointing birthday present.

"What's the problem?" Max asks. "Everything is there."

"You placed valuable nanotech in a backpack?" Grandor asks.

"Yes," Max says. "That is a very secure pack designed by our top-notch R&D team at Corporate."

"It seems so…basic."

"Enough of this." Jackleigh waves a hand at the orb. "Release them."

The slow-mo force field dissipates and we stand in helpless inactivity. Jeff makes a rush toward his car only to be greeted by a shot from one of our Neutralizers held by Jackleigh. The bolt sends Jeff spilling backwards clutching his chest.

"These are fun little toys," Jackleigh says, "but a girl likes something with a little more firepower."

CHAPTER EIGHTEEN

Jackleigh points a remote at the floating orb. An arm extends from it in the same manner as The Jackie Took Over Leigh Ann Shocker in Grandor's basement on planet Lloyd. Jackleigh turns around and raises her long raven hair to expose her neck. The arm attaches to her neck and Jackleigh spasms a couple of times while thin tentacles of electricity crackle around the extension. The spasms stop and the arm disconnects from the human form of Leigh Ann. She staggers disoriented.

"What the hell?" I look at Randi who can only shrug. Jeff runs to Leigh Ann and helps her to feet.

"Leigh Ann?" He coddles her as they walk. "Baby?"

"Where are we?" the doe-eyed girl asks. "What's going on? Is everyone going for waffles?"

The orb buzzes over to the Vega and enters through the open driver's side window. It hovers around the steering wheel and I can see the extension arm attach to something on the car's dashboard. *Miss America* rocks and shakes. Her headlights flash on and off and the horn honks in short blasts as if her alarm was going off.

"Tony!" Jeff shouts. "I'm about to say something misogynistic!"

"Don't do it," I shout back.

"All kinds of sexist comments are forming right now!"

"Fight the urge! It's not worth it!"

All is silent.

"This is not at all what I expected." Jackie's voice echoes from somewhere deep inside *Miss America.* "I like it, though."

"What the hell?" Jeff shouts.

"Simon Tybalt broke under our torture," the Jackie Vega says. "He told us that your car is the quintonium drive and what it is capable of."

"She possessed my car," Jeff mumbles in shock. "That bitch possessed my car."

"Gentlemen." Grandor walks to the Vega and holds the backpack aloft. "I have a new haiku for you:

"I have your Vega
And I have the Araneae.
You suck at your job."

"I'm going to invent new ways to hurt you," Jeff tells Grandor. He pulls out his phone and starts swiping. "I'm Googling new ways right now, you big-headed purple shit."

"For our next trick." Grandor pulls a remote from the backpack and holds it out. "We shall turn an entire civic celebration into an enslaved humanity."

"Clint, Tyler, and Dalton," Jackie the car says. "Take care of them."

The sound of a car's blowing horn and screeching tires interrupts the proceedings from across the parking lot. We all turn and see my parents' minivan speeding toward the scene. Marlene speeds alongside them on her motor scooter and flanked on their other side is another scooter ridden by someone I don't recognize. The riders fire lasers at the scene, hitting light posts, parking signs, and even the side panel of the Truck of Overcompensation. My mom leans out the passenger's side window firing a kind of laser rifle.

"Well, I be damned," I say. "They escaped."

Randi elbows Max in the face and wrestles his laser from his hand. She opens fire on Grandor and the Vega. Jeff takes

Leigh Ann by the hand and starts a dead sprint for the Cosmic VW Bus. After a couple of more shots, Randi follows them. I stand frozen, unsure of what my move should be.

"Randi!" I shout. "I need a gun."

She tosses me the White Girl Waster and I spin and unload on Clint, Tyler, and Dalton. The round fuchsia balls of energy hit their chests and they trip backward.

Miss America's engine fires up and Jackie throws her into reverse. The car spins in a doughnut and heads toward the parking lot exit. Jeff steers the Cosmic VW Bus after them with Leigh Ann sitting in the passenger seat. I step toward Clint, Tyler, and Dalton ready to shoot again if need be. I stop when I see the three of them stagger and fight to stand upright.

"Hey, all y'all!" yells Clint. "I am, like, sooooo drunk! I think I've had, like, seven shots of tequila."

"Riiiiight?" says Tyler, his voice nasally and whiny. "This is the best night ever!"

Dalton, on the other hand, breaks down into tears and drops to his knees.

"God, you guys," he sobs. "Everybody hates me. They hate me!"

This is enough for Marlene and the other rider to open fire on the three male drunk females with their Herpezoid dissolvers. The blasts land and Clint, Tyler, and Dalton melt into puddles of green goo on the pavement, a reminder of their true Herpezoid form.

"I don't hate you, Dalton," the puddle formerly known as Clint says. "I love you. I wanna be you."

"Oh my god, you guys!" shouts gooey Tyler. "This is my jam! This is my freaking jam! Wooooooo!"

The unknown rider removes her helmet and I see she is the caliente lederhosen-wearing babe from the Taco Haus drive thru and the Waffle Palace.

"This is Clara," Marlene tells me. "She's kind of a freelancer like me."

"What do you freelance in?" I ask.

"We find alien scum and end them," Clara's words frighten me, but her voice excites me. The two hottest girls I've ever known are standing in front of me. If it weren't for all of the nonsense about stopping a potential cataclysmic event, life would be pretty good right now.

"Tony!" Dad yells from the minivan. "We gotta go!"

"You coming with?" I ask the girls.

"The River Luau is loaded with Herpezoids posing as carnies," Marlene says.

"We must end the scum," Clara adds.

"So, you're coming with, then. Good." I climb in the minivan and we speed away.

*

Dad navigates the Pershing Minivan of Action through the streets of Poplar Bluff with little to no regard for traffic law. Marlene and Clara stay close behind on their motor scooters. I look at my mom who is recharging a laser pistol with the van's cigarette lighter. Both my parents have dirt, mud, and green Herpezoid blood on them. Kevin Raulston sits in the back seat dispersing weapons from a briefcase. I recognize them as a straightforward High Powered Fusion Dissolver, or a good old fashioned Herpezoid killer.

"These are all freshly charged," Kevin informs us. "Should last us for a few hours."

"A few hours?" Dad shakes his head. "I hope this won't take that long."

A few months ago, I thought I was the only person in this group with a big secret. Nothing in my life was what it seemed. I see now we all have secrets. Like the character of Kilroy in Jeff

Harper's favorite song, I am now a man whose circumstances are beyond his control. Suddenly, I crave an apricot.

"Where's Jeff's mom?" I ask.

"Sandra stayed behind to take out some Herpezoids," Mom says. "She also wanted to find Simon Tybalt. We tried to get her to come with us, but she insisted on staying behind to rescue him. Kept saying something about closure."

"Dad?" I lean forward after looking out the rear window. "I think the entire Poplar Bluff police force is following us."

*

The Pershing Minivan of Action barrels into the dirt parking lot of the River Luau. We exit the vehicle and rush out of it. Three cop cars followed us here and the officers inside them climb out and demand we stop.

"Officers," Dad calls out. "We really can't –"

His attempt to explain this all to Poplar Bluff's finest is interrupted by a brilliant white beam fired from behind us. The beam hits the cops, freezing them where they stand. We turn and look in the direction from which the shot came and see Simon Tybalt holding what looks like a grenade launcher.

"Single Shot Photon Freeze Ray Launcher." He looks at the weapon the way one regards on old friend. "Sometimes you gotta play the classics."

"Where did you get that?" I ask.

"It unfolds from a pocket knife I had stuffed in my sock."

"How long will they be like that?" Mom asks.

"Long enough," he says. "It also fiddles with short term memory. They'll know they were supposed to be here for something, but won't remember why."

"Where's Jackie and Grandor?" I ask. "They're going to release the Araneae on the crowd."

"Oh, no." Simon Tybalt starts running toward the main entrance. "This is very bad."

"How did you escape?" I ask

"A lovely Hispanic girl raided the camper they were holding me in and freed me."

People are jogging toward the exit with their funnel cakes and souvenir stuffed animals.

They wear concerned expressions and those tacky plastic leis because this is a luau, after all.

"Excuse me." Dad stops one of the exiting fairgoers, a middle-aged man with what I assume is his wife and two children. "Why is everyone leaving?"

"Some asshole drove their damn car right up to Mo-Mo the Monster and started making some speech about portals, global domination, and shrewd real estate investments. Now he's reading some proclamation by haiku. He's dressed like an alien, so I think he's one of those cosplay nerds. There's more and more of those moving to town."

"It's really a shame," the man's wife says. "Our family looks forward to the River Luau every year, especially tonight since it's pig roast night." The couple shoos their children past us and out the entrance.

Screams rise up from the midway and more people are running in a dead sprint toward us. We scatter to allow a path for fleeing fairgoers. I look ahead and see three Herpezoids with weapons chasing after people. They no longer wear the guise of carnies and instead display their full Herpezoid form. They snarl and use their weapons to corral people away from the exit.

Marlene and Clara buzz by us on their motor scooters aiming shiny Herpezoid dissolvers and open fire on the three aliens. The shots land and three puddles of green slime pool on the ground where they once stood. The duo speeds up the midway toward Mo-Mo the Monster. More screams from our right as more people try to make a break for the exits. From behind them the Cosmic VW Bus roars into view. Randi Williams sits atop it firing the weapon she swiped from Max at any Herpezoid she spies. The bus skids to a stop in front of us and Jeff leans out the window.

"They're up at Mo-Mo," he says. "They're about to unleash those antennae or whatever."

"Araneae," I say.

"Yeah. Those."

Snarling Herpezoids and screaming civilians are running everywhere. Laser blasts fly around from all directions.

"We need a distraction," Mom says. "Something to temporarily get control of this chaos so we can stop Grandor."

"How do we do that?" Dad asks.

I race to Jeff to talk about ideas. My hands press against the door of the bus and rush of energy from the nanotech kicks in. My brain transports itself to some realm where I see the schematics for the Cosmic VW Bus. I flip through its pages and understand its every component. I snap back to reality and share my revelation.

"The F Bomb," I say. "This is the 1969 Volkswagen Microbus fully loaded with a version 6.1 quintonium accelerator, portal navigation software, CD player, and F Bomb cannon. The control panel for it is in the glovebox."

"That's right," Simon Tybalt says. "The cannon extends from the front, like your Vega. Fire that baby up and shoot it into the crowd. Their behavioral changes should allow us enough time to stop Grandor."

Leigh Ann opens the glove compartment and Jeff flips every switch on the panel. The cannon emerges from the front of the bus and Jeff smashes the fire button for the cannon.

*

The Poplar Bluff River Luau is an orgy of altered behavioral mayhem. Men, women, children, and Herpezoids are doing the "Thriller" dance, crying uncontrollably as they ponder the insignificance of their lives, panicked at the sight of snakes only they can see, and telling the other fairgoers it's really no big deal the funnel cake stand is closed because they didn't need the calories, anyway. Really, it's fine.

I pass a girl who appears to be in her early twenties staggering toward me. She points at me and calls out to me.

"You!" She holds her hands up to steady herself. "I need to tell you a secret."

"I can't right now," I tell her. "I need to stop some aliens."

"Oh, I see," she slurs. "Whatever. I hate boys. Take a selfie with me."

I push her away and sprint toward Mo-Mo the Monster, which sits about one hundred yards ahead. I'm running point with Mom and Dad close behind. A few humans and Herpezoids have yet to be hit with F Bomb fire, so we have to pick off any Herpezoids trying to harm the humans. We step in gooey puddles of Herpezoid blood along the way and they are quick to let us know how much that hurts.

I reach *Miss America*. She's facing us, pointed at the scattering crowd.

"Maybe we were better off letting people try to escape," I say. "No one knows to leave since they're getting hit with the F Bomb."

"You have arrived at a most opportune moment, Tony," says Grandor, perched atop the Vega. "One last stanza before I unleash hell."

"Will you deploy the Araneae already?" Jackie booms from inside the car. "Enough haiku!"

"You have no flair for the dramatic, Jackie," pouts Grandor. "You never have."

I point my gun and fire a laser at the backpack. The first shot misses, but the second one lands directly and knocks the pack from Grandor's hand. My parents open fire on Grandor and a few shots land, knocking him from the top of the car. Jackie fires up the engine of *Miss America* and ignites the quintonium drive.

"This plan is a failure," Jackie says flatly. "As with all your endeavors, Grandor."

The back wheels of the Space Vega spin, spitting dirt on Grandor. The Jackie-possessed vehicle speeds away from the scene racing through the crowd toward the exit. Grandor shoots a blast from one of his bracelets and knocks Marlene from her motor scooter. He commandeers it, flips us off, and rides away after Jackie.

"They're headed toward the portal," Simon Tybalt announces. "Jackie is going to use it for her own plans. We have to stop them before they go through."

The VW Bus skids to a stop in front of us and Jeff hops out.

"Where's my mom?" he says. "Has anyone seen her?'

We all shake our heads and look around. Jeff's face is covered in worry. He spins around firing his gun at Herpezoids. They are coming at us fast and furious. A line of them rushes us, opening fire from their own weapons. Civilians run screaming from the scene toward the exits, the last lingering effects of the F Bomb wearing off.

A heavy weight drops onto my back and I spill to the ground. A Herpezoid straddles me, his leathery claws around my neck. He bears his sharp teeth and I can smell his rancid breath. He draws one of his significant fists back to land what I assume will be a crushing blow. The creature explodes in a green gooey mess all over me. I turn to my left to see Jeff

Harper still aiming the laser he fired at my assailant. He runs to me and helps me up.

"I want to make an inappropriate comment right now," he tells me, "but I'll save it for later."

"Domo arigato," I tell my friend. "Domo arigato, Mr. Roboto."

"You're welcome." A flash of intellectual connection sparks in his eyes. "Oh, my god. I get it now."

"Um, guys." Dad points ahead at a line of nearly twenty Herpezoids advancing on us. We're cornered.

"Jeff!" Leigh Ann yells from the VW Bus. "Help!"

"You guys start shooting," Marlene says. "We'll charge them."

"Eliminate the scum," growls Clara.

"Who are you girls?" Mom asks.

"They work for me," Simon Tybalt says. "They're consultants."

"We got this," Marlene says. "You start shooting. When we advance, take off."

"That's suicide," I say.

"Only if it doesn't work," Clara says.

I grab Marlene's face and lean in for a kiss because the moment is right and I should perform a heroic romantic gesture. My lips barely reach hers when she pushes me away.

"Now is not the time, Tony Pershing!"

"I don't get how this works at all," I say.

The Herpezoids let out a collective roar that sounds something like an entire marching band of untuned tubas and start their final advance on us. The very familiar sound of a truck booms from our right and we turn to see Clint Hudson's Truck of Overcompensation barreling toward the Herpezoids. It gains a full head of steam and plows into the aliens sending bodies flying. Herpezoids lie scattered around and under the truck and we stand mouths agape at the sight. The driver's side door opens and out steps Sandra Harper.

"I gotta get me one of these," she says.

"Mom!" Jeff runs to her and they embrace. "I thought they got you."

"Oh my god," says Simon Tybalt approaching them. "Infinity Jones? Is that you?"

"Simon?" she says back. "I thought you were dead."

"Watch out!" Dad says pointing toward what was once thought a dead Herpezoid. The creature holds out a weapon intending to fire on Sandra.

"No!" Simon shouts and stands between the laser blast and its intended target. The shot burns into his chest and he cries out in pain. Randi, Dad, and Mom open fire on the Herpezoid and he oozes to the ground in a puddle of green yuck. The entire group starts firing on all the Herpezoids to finish the job started by what I shall now call Sandra's Truck of Awesomeness.

Simon hits the ground gasping for breath. Sandra cradles him in her arms and Jeff kneels next to them.

"You two know each other?" Jeff asks. "Mom, you're Infinity Jones?"

"You told him about that?" She puts her shaking hand on Simon's wound.

"You were my favorite person," he tells her and drifts into lifelessness.

*

The Jeff's Mom Is Infinity Jones and Holy Shit Simon Tybalt Died Revelations are still fresh in our minds, but we all know we have to flee the scene to the portal. Jeff speeds down the road barely making each twist and turn. I sit in the passenger seat offering little more than obvious reminders about needing to hurry. Kevin stayed behind to handle Simon

Tybalt's death. Sandra and Leigh Ann sit in the middle seat offering little more than pensive looks. Mom, Dad, and Randi follow in the minivan. Clara and Marlene stayed behind to finish off any random Herpezoids.

"Mom?" Jeff asks. "Is Simon Tybalt my dad? Tell me. Is he my dad?"

"Now's not the time to discuss this," she says. "Let's stop that Vega and then we can talk."

"He's my dad, isn't he? I can't believe you never told me."

"Drive!" I yell in unison with Sandra and Leigh Ann.

"The portal is around this curve," Jeff says. "How are we going to stop them if they haven't already gone through?"

"Jackie will use the cannon to open the portal on her own and try to go through," I say. "The car is Jackie, so, if you're going to stop Jackie…" I can't finish the sentence.

"I have to stop the car." Jeff says. "Well, shit."

CHAPTER NINETEEN

Jeff Harper looks as if he could vomit all over the interior of the bus. His chin quivers and the vein in his neck protrudes and throbs. My friend is clearly distressed at this lose-lose situation. Does he let us beloved *Miss America* go through the portal in one piece controlled by a villainous artificial intelligence or does he destroy her so she won't be used for nefarious purposes? Perhaps he can find her again on the other side of the portal if he lets her go.

I see it all perfectly; there are two possible situations – one can either do this or that. My honest opinion and my friendly advice is this: do it or do not do it. You will regret both.

I honestly don't know what I would do in his position. These are the very difficult decisions in life I fear most.

"Jeff," I tell him. "My nano tells me this VW Bus is equipped with Self-Guided Supercharged Photon Missiles. They shoot from the headlights."

"Your point?"

"That may be your only option."

We plow through the security gate at the portal. Jackie has poised *Miss America* toward the river and, as suspected, is attempting to open the portal above it with the quintonium drive. We are about one hundred yards away. I lean out the passenger window and see no sign of Grandor or Marlene's scooter.

"Jeff," I say. "We're closing in fast."

"I know!"

"Jeff, the switch for the missiles is next to hazard lights button."

"I know!"

"We need to fire now!"

"Shut up!"

"Jeff!"

"I know!" Tears trickle down my friend's cheek at the enormity of this decision.

"Do you want me to do it?" I reach over to flick the switch, but he swats me away.

"No! *Miss America* is mine! I have to do this!"

"You gotta do it now!" I yell.

Sandra reaches forward and places a maternal hand on her son's shoulder. Jeff gives her a half look as he chokes back emotion. He looks straight ahead as his beloved Vega nearly has the portal open. He mashes the brake pedal and we skid to a stop.

"I can't!" he cries.

"Fine!" I reach over and flip the switch. A brilliant white ball of light flies from the bus's grill and slams into *Miss America.*

"Bye, babe," is all Jeff says.

*

The elapsed time for a Self-Guided Supercharged Photon Missile to hit its intended target is only matter of seconds. Over the short distance between our van and *Miss America*, the time is probably two seconds. For Jeff and me, it feels like a day and a half watching someone you love slowly pass away in your arms. The ball of fire of the resulting explosion is brilliant and orange and beautiful. The cannon's connection to the portal immediately shuts off as *Miss America* burns in the night.

The sound of an approaching motor scooter pulls my focus toward my sideview mirror. Marlene and Clara pull to a stop next to me. They look at the blaze ahead and then to me. We say nothing.

Jeff stares blankly at the scene ahead. The glow from the fire lights up the inside of our vehicle. He shuts off the engine and exits the bus. I look at Sandra and Leigh Ann. None of us knows what to say or do. I get out and walk to my friend as he stares at the burning wreck.

"What just happened?" He takes off his top hat and runs a hand through his hair. Tears spill from his eyes and he blows out an emotional sigh and then a groan of frustration. "What did you do?"

"The only thing I could do." I pat him on the shoulder in the only real show of support I can offer. "I'm sorry."

"You killed my car."

"Be of good cheer," I say because I'm really lame.

The rest of the group walks up to the scene and regards the remains of *Miss America.* The flames which once engulfed her now are only flickers. Leigh Ann slides her arm around Jeff's and rests her head on his shoulder. Sandra stands on his other side and rubs his back in a small circle.

"I'm so sorry, honey," she tells him. "I know how much she meant to you."

Dad and Mom stand next to me and we hug. Randi Williams, Marlene, and Clara all walk around the car, surveying the damage. All is silent for a moment except for the crackle of the fire.

Jeff holds his top hat to his heart and through a voice choked with emotion starts singing the opening lines of Styx's "Don't Let It End."

CHAPTER TWENTY

I awake with a start. I rise up in a panic and look around my room trying to get my bearings. Where am I? Why am I here? I allow myself a slight smile as the space around me comes into clear view. I'm in Poplar Bluff, Missouri, inside my house at 2300 Baugh Lane in my bedroom waking from a good night's sleep. This will be my last time here as a regular resident.

I'm leaving home today.

I reach over and open a playlist on my phone. The first selection is "Bubbly," but I skip over it in favor of "Into You," by Ariana Grande because it gets me moving.

Four weeks have passed since The Tragic Sacrificial Death of Both Simon Tybalt and *Miss America.* My hometown looks the same, I guess, and life has moved on for the most part. Normalcy appears to rule the day once more, though I know this world is anything but normal. Nothing going forward will be normal for me. I see things differently now.

*

I place the last of my boxes in the trunk of my car and face my parents. They stand on the sidewalk in front of our house. A freshly posted for sale sign sits in our yard. They're both giving me The Look. I feel closer to my parents than ever. Saving the world from a takeover by a megalomaniacal artificial intelligence and his rogue valet will do that. I told myself I wasn't going to cry when I said goodbye to them, but I have failed myself miserably. I'm wrecked.

"Aw, honey," Mom wraps her arms around me and it's all I can do to pull away. She wipes some tears away with her thumb in that way moms do. It's one last hurrah for The Reassurance. "We're so proud of you."

"You're off to bigger and better things," Dad says in that way dads do.

"Can it get any bigger than what happened a few weeks ago?" I laugh.

"Ok, then," he agrees. "Better things."

I reach to rub a healing incision at the base of my neck. A few stitches bind it together. Randi arranged for me to have the nanotech removed by some R&D scientists. They used the same contraption Marlene used that night on Life Coach Gilbert and the nameless old woman outside the convenience store.

"Is it bothering you?" Dad asks.

"Just itches," I say. "I'm glad it's out, though."

"I can't believe Jeff put one of those nano things in you," Mom says. "What was he thinking?"

"I never know what he's thinking." I look to the ground. I need to leave, but my feet don't seem to be all that interested in guiding me to my car.

"I don't know why this is so hard," I say. "Eastern Missouri State is only a couple of hours away. It's not like I'll never come home again."

"Of course you will," Mom says. "You're just starting out your life journey. You'll always have a home wherever we are."

"Still feeling good about quitting your job?" I ask Dad.

"Early retirement is a good call," Dad says. "I needed out of the rat race. Your mom and I are going to travel."

"Are you done with Kevin's book club?"

"I don't think we'll ever be done with that," Mom says. "Kevin has said there's an entire network of book clubs around the country. We're going to see if we can find them."

"Sounds like we're all starting journeys," I say.

"No matter where life takes you," Dad says, "never lose sight of where you came from."

"What?" I scoff at his attempt at deep quoting. "Where did you get that?"

"Some stupid motivational poster I saw hanging at work."

"I hate those damn things." We laugh together and it feels nice and warm and I never want it to end, but it must. We group hug one last time and conduct the requisite wiping of tears.

"I guess I better get going." I linger instead of walking to the driver's side door.

"Drive safe, honey," Mom says. "Let us know when you get there. Don't text and drive."

"Are you heading straight there?" Dad asks.

"No." I finally take the necessary steps to my car door. "I need to make a couple of stops first."

*

Randi Williams sits behind the desk in her new office at Corporate HQ. She forgoes the usual business casual attire and opts instead for a simple black t-shirt with the Corporate logo and pair of jeans. The nameplate on her desk reads:

RANDI WILLIAMS
CHIEF OPERATIONS OFFICER

She stands as I enter and greets me with a tight hug. She gestures for me to sit and she takes her seat behind the desk. Behind her is a window overlooking the parking lot, but not much else. Someone as awesome as Randi Williams deserves a better view.

"So," she says through a beaming smile. "You're off to college?"

"Yeah. It's time to go."

"You're gonna do great."

"Hope so." I point at her nameplate. "How do you like your new job?"

"Growing pains," she tells me. "I'm used to being in the field, but this is good. I've got a lot of ideas I want to implement."

"Have you heard from or seen Max at all?"

"Not since that night." She spins a bit in her chair and faces her mediocre office view. "I came in early the next morning and he had posted his letter of resignation on my office door. No clue where he's at."

"Grandor's still out there, too," I say.

"Not sure where he's at. Maybe he found a way through the portal. We'll find him somehow. We also believe there are unaccounted for Herpezoids and Araneae." She spins back around to me. "I'm acquiring new resources as we speak."

"What did you say to the police? How did this get handled?"

She shakes her head and laughs a bit. "That took some doing. I spent the whole next morning finding an emergency set of Rube Goldberg Protocols in case of civilian impact."

"What were they?" I ask.

"Apparently Corporate owns a pest control subsidiary here in town." She stands looks out her window at the parking lot. "We spent the rest of the day sending out mosquito spraying trucks. Except we sprayed the same substance that powered Simon's Single Shot Photon Freeze Ray."

"So, you took away short term memory?"

"It seems to have worked. People have weird memories of that night, but we were able to doctor some official health department reports to make it look like bad food from the River Luau. Laced with hallucinogens and all that."

"Wow."

"Yeah." She spins back to me. "I guess you could say we quickly re-engineered tactical meta services."

We share a laugh.

"How did Kevin handle Simon Tybalt's death?" I ask.

"That one's a mystery," Randi says. "Kevin says Simon had a Rube Goldberg Protocol in the event of his death and honored it."

"Did he really will the company to Jeff's mom? He really was Jeff's dad?"

"He did," she replies. "He was. And Sandra made Jeff chairman in title only. He, of course, thinks he's some all-powerful entity, but Sandra is the real boss. She's awesome."

"What do you have Jeff even doing?"

"He was pretty depressed after you blew up his car, as you well know. I put him in charge of our fleet operations center. We're using Simon Tybalt's quintonium drive technology to create vehicles like *Miss America.*" An impish grin spreads across her face. "I cut him a deal. I let him have the prototype of our first upgrade and he agrees to stay out of the way."

A knock at her office door pulls us away from our conversation. We turn to see Sandra Harper poking her head in the door. She wears what looks to me like the same sad smile as the late Simon Tybalt.

"Tony." She enters and I stand and accept her hug. "Good luck at college."

"Thank you."

"My son is going to miss you."

"I'm going to miss him," I say, choking back the welling lump in my throat.

"Randi," she says to Corporate's new COO, "I finished debriefing our two new hires. They'll be a nice fit for the new position we've created. Don't forget we have our appointment later with Dean Larson and the rest of his team in Employee Connections."

"Employee Connections?" I ask. "What's that?"

"The new title for HR," Randi says. "We're trying to shake up some things around here. I'll meet you at three, Sandra."

"Sounds good." Sandra squeezes my arm once more and offers me a final smile. "Have you said good-bye to Jeff yet?"

"Not yet."

"I assume you know where to find him?"

"Yeah," I smile. "I do."

She leaves and I turn back to Randi. She opens a desk drawer, produces a file folder, and tosses it onto her desk.

"What's that?" I ask.

"Tony," she sighs. "You're fired."

I smile back. She knows I resigned from Corporate the day after The Tragic and Sacrificial Deaths of Simon Tybalt and *Miss America,* but I assume we need to make it official.

"This is your exit package." She opens the folder and takes the top two sheets from the stack. "These are duplicate documents stating you're leaving on this date officially. You'll also see the nondisclosure agreement. You can't disclose what you did here at Corporate. As far as anyone knows, you were a simple mailroom intern. Sign here and here. One for us. One for you."

I sign the documents and slide them back to her. She hands me the file folder of information in exchange for the security badge I've pulled from my pocket. She looks at the badge and I see tears pooling in her eyes now. I avoid direct visual contact by thumbing through the exit packet.

"What's in this, anyway?"

"Some reminders about proprietary information. Your copy of the non-disclosure agreement. Date you can expect your last paycheck to be direct deposited. Also, if you look on the last page, you'll find reference to a special token of our esteem for all you've done."

"Is it another Thanks for Being Awesome gift bag?" I ask. "I still haven't used my gift card from the last one."

"Just read the last page."

I flip to the final document, a check stub for one hundred thousand dollars directed deposited into my savings account. I gasp and look at Randi.

"What the hell?"

"For school. Good luck." She waves at her face in an effort shoo away a flood of tears. "You're a good kid."

I try to speak, but can only swallow hard and nod. I turn to leave and she stops me one last time.

"If you ever need anything." She grabs something from her desk. "You look me up."

Randi Williams hands me her business card.

*

I walk through the lobby of Corporate one last time and wave to Jerry and Dale as I stride toward the door. My steps feel light with the weight of my secret job off my back. I exit into the parking lot and prepare myself emotionally for my next stop. A honk from a car pulling up startles me. I turn and see the Cosmic VW Bus rolling to a stop. Marlene Hunter leans out the passenger's side window.

"Hey, handsome," she calls out to me. "Need a lift?"

I smile and walk to her. Her hair is pulled back in that ever-present ponytail. Her eyes still sparkle. Her freckles still melt me. I look past her and see Clara sitting in the driver's seat. She, too, wears her dark hair in a ponytail. She doesn't smile and I've come to the conclusion she never does. It doesn't change how striking her beauty is.

"Hi, Marlene. Hi, Clara."

"Word on the street is you're leaving for college," Marlene says.

"Where did you hear that?"

"I stopped by your house to see you. Your parents told me."

"That makes sense." I feel like I should say something significant and special here. "Yeah."

"You're gonna do great, Tony Pershing." She reaches out, grabs my shirt collar, and pulls me to her. She kisses me. The strength in my legs disappears and my knees buckle. I place my hand on her face and the softness of her lips causes my pulse to quicken and my stomach to flutter. We've shared many kinds of kisses during our relationship. There was the Parting Is Such Sweet Sorrow Kiss after our dates. We also shared the Full Blown Sloppy Make-Out Session in my car. There was even more than a few Here, Have A Stolen Peck in the Hallway Before Class moments when we were in school. This kiss very much feels like a This Is the Last One You're Going to Get, Buddy, So Make It Count kind of encounter. She pulls away.

"I imagined us going to college together," I tell her. "It's what I wanted."

"Then you shouldn't have backed out on prom," she says with a wink and a sly smile.

"Touché."

"Besides." She holds up a white oversized envelope with the words NEW HIRE ORIENTATION PACKET printed on it under the Corporate logo. "Clara and I have new jobs."

"Let me guess," I say. "Hunting alien scum?"

"Something like that. I believe our official title is Dynamic Tactics Facilitator." She reaches out and takes my hand. Her fingers caress mine and she offers me a sweet smile. "You take care of yourself, Tony Pershing."

"You, too." I say. "Bye, Clara."

Clara says nothing, choosing instead to nod in my general direction. The Cosmic VW Bus pulls away and with it takes the piece of my heart belonging to Marlene Hunter.

*

I pull up to the front of Someone Else's Books and walk up to the front door. A sticker I've never seen before on the window reads "A Corporate Entity." I enter the store and find Kevin Raulston placing some books on a shelf and pricing them.

"Tone-Man!" He sets down the books and offers a broad smile. "You off to school?"

"Yep. Time to make my way in the world."

I glance behind Kevin's counter into his office area. The maps and news clippings and drawings of Herpezoids are still there. An urn rests on top of his filing cabinet. I've never seen it before so I ask what it is.

"That's Simon Tybalt." He walks to filing cabinet, pulls the urn down, and sets on the counter. "This is what he wanted."

"How did you know?"

"I've been in contact with him for years. I was an intern at Corporate just like you a long time ago. I knew about the portal because he taught it to me. This was before Corporate became what it is now."

"Why did you leave?"

He sets the urn back on the filing cabinet and returns to pricing and shelving the paperbacks. They're Western novels.

"Well," he says. "I graduated high school. My time as an intern ended just like yours. I had an arrangement with Simon to set up a secret group that would fight the Herpezoids infiltrating our planet."

"The book club," I say.

"The book club." He places the last of the Western paperbacks on the shelf and tapes a sign advertising them for a quarter apiece or ten for a dollar.

"What are you doing to do now?" I ask.

"Sell old books. Replace them with new old books. Sell those. Rinse and repeat."

"What about Herpezoids?"

"There will always be Herpezoids." He turns and faces me. "That's what I've been saying for years."

*

Before I left Corporate HQ, Randi Williams informed me of the new Rube Goldberg Protocol for entering the portal security gate at the river. She told me she had them reprogrammed just for me, just for today. I ease up to the intercom box and press the call button.

"Security credentials, please."

"I'm here to see my friend," I say.

"He's been expecting you."

The now repaired gate slides open and I enter. Up ahead is the familiar image of Jeff Harper sitting on the hood of his car. The unfamiliar part of this image is the car itself. In place of *Miss America* sits a station wagon, early 1970s vintage. I pull up next to him and see it's a 1972 Pontiac Catalina station wagon and, while it's not the same as *Miss America*, it's the kind of car that perfectly suits Jeff. It's olive green with simulated wood paneling. I get out and walk to him as he stares out at the river. Simon Tybalt's fishing hat sits next to him on the hood.

"Nice car," I say.

"It's alright," he says. "I'm getting used to it."

"Have you named it yet?"

"Not yet. Too soon."

We stand for a moment and say nothing. It's not an awkward silence or uncomfortable lull. It's merely the unspoken moment between lifelong friends that doesn't require conversation. We both look at out over the river.

"Have you listened to any of the music Simon downloaded for you?"

"Yeah," he tells me. "Some of it's pretty good. I really like that REO Speedwagon."

"What happens now?"

"You need to tell the world about us." His voice is urgent. He faces me, his eyes searching me. "Tell everyone. Write about us in one of those stories you're always coming up with."

I scrunch my face and shake my head a bit. "What? I don't write stories."

"You don't?"

"No. I never have. No desire to start, either."

My friend turns back to the river, a little deflated. "Did I know this about you?"

"Where are you going from here?" I ask him. He lights up one of his Mongalisonian cigarettes and takes a drag.

"First things, first. I need some smokes. Then, I'm gonna spend some time on Nitz. Maybe find myself or some shit."

"Are you taking Leigh Ann?"

"No," he says with some sadness. "I zapped her with a smaller version of Simon's Single Photon Freeze Ray."

"Did it impact her memories of what happened?"

"She just keeps saying she remembers having weird dreams. I dunno. I can't take her. It's not right."

"Did you break up?"

He takes a long drag off his cigarette and exhales. "No. But it's weird now. So, we agreed to give each other some space or some shit. I dunno. It sucks."

He offers me a cigarette.

"I don't need it anymore," I say. "I had the nano deprogrammed. It doesn't work anymore."

"I know," he says. "I had Corporate put it in me."

"Why?"

"Why not?"

I offer a light chuckle. "You're finally Mr. Roboto."

"Like it matters," he mumbles.

"Are you okay?" I put my hand on his shoulder. "You've been through a lot."

"You blew up my car."

"You injected me with a nanotech against my will."

"Call it even, then." He drops his smoke to the ground and stamps it out. "It's been a wild few weeks. But, hey, I got my own company out of the deal, so that's cool."

"That's right. You're Mr. Corporate now."

"Yep. That makes me the boss of you."

I laugh. "You are not the boss of me. I got fired today."

We reach an uncomfortable conversational lull. He looks at me with tears in his eyes.

"I guess this is it." He puts the fishing hat on his head. "Time for me to fly."

Like a reflex response, we perform our ritualistic handshake: High five, low five, side-to-side, fly away birdy, turn away from each other, turn back, point at each other.

"Take care of yourself," I say.

"Try not to suck at college."

Now I'm doing that thing where I laugh through my tears. It's a strange sensation, but I like it. Jeff Harper locks me in a bear hug and squeezes tight.

"I love you, man," he says.

"I love you, too."

He pulls away, wipes his face, and puts on his aviators. "Well, I said bye to mom. Said bye to Leigh Ann. I'm gonna head through the ol' portal and go own the night." He turns toward his car.

"Hey," I call to him. "Domo arigato, Mr. Roboto."

"Domo arigato," he says. "Mata au hi made."

Jeff Harper climbs in his nameless station wagon, starts the engine, and backs up several yards. I shield my eyes as he ignites the quintonium drive. A white beam hits the soft spot above the river and the car speeds toward the opening portal. He disappears into it and it closes behind him. I blow out an emotional sigh and climb into my car. I've said my good-byes. My work here is done. I once more regard the site of The Prom Night of Which We Shall Not Speak. Life really is about choices and I realize I shouldn't fear them. I suppose I could continue working for Corporate or even join Jeff out in space doing God knows what. Instead, I'm going to college. I'm going to leave this behind me and move on to something new.

I think I'm making the right choice.

THE END

ACKNOWLEDGEMENTS

I started writing *Kilroy Was Here* in 2011 when it was titled something else and, aside from the first chapter, was a completely different story. I didn't intentionally set up to write a novel. I just wanted to write a funny scene to cheer me up while I was depressed because I was unemployed. I kept writing. I realized I had the bones of a story, so I decided to go for it. Writing a novel had been a dream since I was a kid. I needed to do this for me. I loved it, but it was not without its frustrations, stresses, and moments of wanting to quit.

You can't do something like this without the support and love of family and friends who believe in you. I am surrounded by people who gave me more than I knew what to do with: My wife Sandy encouraged me every step of the way and was my constant cheerleader. My daughter Sarah was right there to lift me up. I bounced ideas off my son Caleb, who came up with the idea of the behavioral weapons. My brothers Joey and Chris South encouraged my storytelling and imagination from an early age.

My writer friends: Casie Emerson Bazay, Mary Miller, Shirley Hall, Bill Grasso, Janet Brook, Deniece Adsit, and Peter Biadasz. Your feedback was immeasurable.

I could fill the pages of another book with more names, so if yours isn't listed here, it doesn't mean it's not on my heart. I would be remiss if I didn't mention our pets. Our dogs Daisy and Lady and our cats Scooter and Khaleesi provided many hugs and comforting cuddles when I didn't think I could finish this.

I also wanted to acknowledge anyone who ever told me I was funny. This is all your fault.

AUTHOR BIOGRAPHY

Jeff South was born and raised in Poplar Bluff, Missouri, and started writing stories about a ghost hunting cat named Midnight when he was only eight years old. He wrote short stories all through school and then discovered the world of theater and acting. He obtained a Bachelor of Arts in Theater from Southeast Missouri State University in Cape Girardeau and then a Master of Arts in Theater from Central Missouri State in Warrensburg. He has taught theater, directed several plays, and acted in dozens of roles. As a writer, he maintains a blog, Upstream of Consciousness, where he writes about film, television, books, music, pop culture, and the occasional memory of growing up in southeast Missouri.

In addition to stage work, Jeff has acted in the 2014 short horror film *Innards* and in the 2017 feature length comedy *Drinksgiving*. He and his wife Sandy have three adult children, two dogs, and two cats. They currently live in Broken Arrow, Oklahoma.